A Deadly Discovery

A Thriller

Ed Day

Published by PELL Resources Publications

ISBN 10-978-0-9974555-1-9

DISCLAIMER

This book is dedicated to all the scientists and engineers who died under questionable or mysterious circumstances while pushing the frontiers of discovery.

*"I NEVER MADE ONE OF MY DISCOVERIES
THROUGH THE PROCESS OF RATIONAL
THINKING"—Albert Einstein*

*"DEATH IS THE SOLUTION TO ALL PROBLEMS.
NO MAN-NO PROBLEM"—Joseph Stalin*

PART ONE

UNINTENDED CONSEQUENCES

CHAPTER 1

CAMBRIDGE, MASSACHUSETTS—
OCTOBER 3RD

The failure to crystallize his thought would be the death of him.

Like a lost memory from a dream, the thought eluded him—it was just out of reach—as if he could touch it but couldn't quite grab hold of it. Dr. Phil McPherson, Chief Scientist at Entropy, LLC, rode the escalator up from the Kendall Square subway station platform trying to retrieve the thought, which he intuitively knew was profound and important but was hidden somewhere deep in the crevices of his frontal lobes. Whatever the camouflaged idea was, it kept him from celebrating the enormous life-changing—hell, world-changing—discovery he and his co-inventors, Tucker Cherokee and Dr. Maya Li, publicly announced last week. He knew that he should be elated about the financial windfall, fame, and professional accolades that would come to him from the full launch of the technology, but he couldn't shake the feeling that it was a little too good to be true.

He shook off the feeling that something dark loomed and told himself that the reason he couldn't uncover the thought just below the surface of his consciousness was the fact that he was headed home from another long workday to an empty and lonely condominium in a cold drizzle on a gloomy night. Phil wished he had someone in his life with whom he could share the fruits of his success—someone to travel the world with him while he gave speeches to admiring audiences of scientific peers.

He thought, "It's time to get a dog."

He was unaware of his surroundings and was totally focused on forcing the lost thought into the open as he approached the historic brownstone that housed his condo. Phil placed his briefcase on the brick entryway, closed and shook the rainwater from his umbrella, slid his key card through the security reader, and opened the front door. To his surprise a man was right behind him who reached over his shoulder to hold the door open and said, "Thank you."

Phil turned to say, "Your welcome" but instead looked directly into the barrel of an ugly-looking handgun with a silencer attached and into the cold eyes of an equally ugly, large Asian man whose name he would never learn.

Though he'd never been robbed, fear didn't grab Phil.

Not yet.

Phil looked around in search for help but saw none. There was no one in the building foyer, and there was no one just outside the entrance.

The armed thief got right into Phil's face with his huge nose almost touching Phil's, and said, "Please, let me carry your briefcase for you. It's an honor to accept your invitation to tea in your home."

If Phil yelled for help, he suspected that he would be shot right there on the spot. He decided that it was better to be robbed than killed, so he acquiesced as the dangerous-looking criminal pushed Phil in the direction of the building elevator bank, into a waiting elevator car, and up to the third floor where he was forced to open the door to his condominium.

At this point, McPherson suspected that there was more going on here than just a simple robbery but said, "I'm not sure I have anything of great value here. I have $140 in cash in my pocket and..."

"Shut up and make us some tea."

Phil processed the odd request from the thief as he wandered into the kitchen, pushed the "on" button of his Keurig coffeemaker, and opened the pantry. He brought out two coffee mugs and "Chai Latte K-cups" to brew.

Still under gunpoint, Phil contemplated his predicament, formulated an escape plan, and felt in control—that was until he looked back at his unwanted guest.

Phil began to shake uncontrollably with fear as he watched this big guy put on latex gloves. Phil was, after all, just a chemist—not a fighter, not an athlete, and he was unarmed. He was a forty-eight-year-old man, was five feet nine inches in height and 165 pounds in weight, wore titanium wire-rim trifocals, and appeared physically unthreatening. Though he intimidated other scientists with his brilliance, to a hard-boiled criminal, Phil was dead meat.

Phil contemplated the reasons why a man who was holding him at gunpoint would need to put on gloves and quickly formulated a mental list. The list grew in seconds, but he could think of no good reasons.

It was time for action.

McPherson looked toward the drawer that contained kitchen knives, but his "guest" stood in front of the drawer as if he knew in advance what his victim was thinking. Phil suddenly wished he had made the time out of his busy schedule to get self-defense training and gun-handling lessons.

He filled the two cups full of chai and wondered whether he should execute his now weak-sounding escape plan and throw hot tea into the criminal's face and run.

"Sit down," his unwanted Asian guest said. Phil chickened-out, obeyed the criminal, and sat on one of his kitchen bar stools.

"How does it work?"

Phil asked, "How does what work?"

"How does the invention you announced on YouTube work?"

It finally hit him—the fleeting thought, the suppressed memory, the item on the tip of his tongue, and the reason "it was too good to be true."

One's gain often becomes another's loss—not everyone in the world would be happy about the discovery, named Project MEG by Entropy. Moreover, there were those who would not accept the impact the technology would have on their livelihood. Phil finally remembered that he and his co-inventors were potential targets of companies—maybe even countries—that would do anything to learn how to replicate the discovery or erase it from existence to prevent a competitor or enemy from using it. If his thought had crystallized earlier, he might have been more alert, taken a taxi, or hired a bodyguard.

The criminal, Gang Chung, exploded, "I asked you a fucking question."

The thief's foul breath awoke Phil from his epiphany. He refocused and answered the intimidating man's question, "It is a combination of both physics and chemistry. We developed an algorithm that…"

Phil didn't finish the sentence. Knocked off the bar stool, Phil landed five feet from the bar, writhing in more pain than he had ever experienced in his life. To Phil, it felt like a brick hit him on the side of his face.

Gang Chung removed the brass knuckles and placed them back into his jacket pocket. He was impassive about the damage he inflicted on the side of Phil's face. He waited for Phil to regain his composure, dragged him off the floor, and instructed the dazed inventor to get back on the bar stool. The thug said, "Dr. McPherson, you will save yourself a lot of pain—pain which I will enjoy inflicting on you—if you just answer my questions. Now, how does it work?"

The soft flesh around Phil's left eye swelled, he was nauseated, and a jarred dental bridge made it difficult to speak. But he didn't hesitate—didn't miss a beat—and said, while his mind raced, "I'm not sure even I understand the physics of how it works. It just does. When we sprayed a combination of chemicals into a magnet field, we got an exothermic electrical reaction. There was no way the energy that resulted from the mixture should have occurred, but it did. It didn't make sense to us from a chemical or physics standpoint, but the reaction was repeatable. So, we performed additional tests to see if the reaction was also controllable—it was." Phil revealed the specific names of the chemicals required for the discovery to work, knowing full well this brute couldn't possibly remember the formal chemical names.

Gang Chung demanded, "I want a copy of your trade secrets, your patent preparation work, and operating procedures. I want to know what chemicals are required, at what rate, and absolutely anything else you consider proprietary. I assure you, my little friend, the quality of the rest of your life depends on it."

Phil asked the large Asian man for permission to retrieve his briefcase. He opened it under gunpoint, pulled out a thumb drive, and handed it to the Chinese thief of national and industrial trade secrets. Phil spoke as if he had a mouth full of marbles due to his injuries, "This is a portable memory stick. It contains all the information you need to know about the discovery, how to make it work, and a draft commercialization plan. It's the only known copy."

Gang Chung grabbed the thumb drive out of Phil's hand, smiled victoriously, but, surprisingly, bowed deferentially to him.

Phil said, "OK. I've given you everything that you asked for. Now, please, leave. I've got …"

He shot Phil in the forehead with his silenced weapon.

"As I promised, Dr. McPherson, you saved yourself a lot of pain." Gang Chung poured his untasted cup of chai onto Phil's dead body and said, "I asked for tea, not this swill."

From the Boston Red Sox jacket he wore, the killer pulled out kitchen utensils with fingerprints and DNA of another person. He placed them on the countertop as evidence that he hoped would point law enforcement in the wrong direction. He secured the thumb drive and picked up Phil's briefcase after he made sure that it contained his laptop. Chung recovered the spent casing, left the room, and closed the door behind him without looking back.

Moments later, a happy tune interrupted the cold dead silence in Phil's condominium. Phil's cell phone, still in his suit jacket pocket, sang.

CHAPTER 2

ALEXANDRIA, VIRGINIA—
OCTOBER 3^(RD)

Tucker Cherokee was surprised, disappointed, and maybe even a little angry that Phil didn't answer his cell phone. It was uncharacteristic of Phil not to notify Tucker if he was unable to make a prescheduled call, especially one of such critical importance as the call he just missed.

Tucker's adrenaline ran at Mach speed. His excitement as a co-inventor of the discovery produced a high that he doubted a recreational drug could offer. The accidental discovery of the technology, the invention, proved once again that *we don't know what we don't know.*

Tucker repeatedly called Phil's cell phone without success—without Phil touching the screen of his iPhone. The subject of the call was to discuss a commercialization strategy for their invention. They both wanted to move the discovery to market as soon as possible.

So, where the hell was Phil?

A knot formed in Tucker's stomach—a dark premonition clouded his mood. He began to worry about Phil and started to call around to check with coworkers. Tucker's failure to reach anyone who knew Phil's situation made his heart race.

Tucker received his first ever phone call from Stephen Sanders, the reclusive Chief Executive Officer of Entropy, two hours after the initial missed call with Phil McPherson.

In a very subdued tone, Sanders said, "Tucker, I have some dreadful news."

Sanders paused. Butterflies fluttered in Tucker's stomach.

"I'm sorry I'm the one that has to tell you this, but," Sanders paused and then said, "Phil McPherson is dead."

The Entropy CEO paused again to let the shocking news sink in.

Tucker didn't even try to stop his chin from quivering as his heart fell to his stomach. This news was much worse than his greatest fear. Melancholy overwhelmed him.

Sanders continued with a trembling voice, "Phil was home in his condominium. The Cambridge police said that he was shot in the forehead at close range. Reading between the lines, he was most likely murdered by a professional, even though there was no evidence of forced entry."

There was another long pause before Sanders said, "And his laptop is missing."

Because Tucker was in shock, he didn't immediately grasp the importance of the statement about the laptop. The news of Phil's death shook him to the core. Tucker thought, "How shallow of you, Mr. Sanders, to worry about a company laptop or even the information on it under such sad circumstances."

But seconds later, the significance of what the CEO had said hit him. Clearing his throat and speaking with a cracked voice, Tucker asked, "Sir, are you concerned that Phil's murder had something to do with the announcement about Project MEG and that someone stole his laptop for the secrets that make the discovery work?"

"Yes, the thought had crossed my mind," said Mr. Sanders. "Further, as just a precaution, I suggest that you disappear for a while and hide until the police have a clearer picture as to the motive for Phil's murder. Until proven otherwise, I think it is wise to assume the killer was an industrial technology thief after Entropy intellectual property.

"Listen to me, Tucker, whoever killed Phil may also come after you. Knowing Phil, my bet is that the killer didn't get everything he needed. So, get a move on but contact us frequently so that we know that you are safe. Use untraceable methods like a burn phone to reach us. And please, contact Dr. Li at Fermilab to let her know that she also may be in potential danger."

"OK," said Tucker, "I'll take your advice."

Stephen Sanders exploded, "It's not advice, Tucker, it's a damned order. Take some time off at the company's expense, and get the hell out of Dodge. Go somewhere where no one can find you. And don't even tell us where you are—just in case."

"In case of what?"

"Use your imagination, Tucker, for crying-out-loud. This is damned serious stuff." Sanders abruptly hung up.

Tucker understood that people react to stress and fear differently. Sanders's impatience with Tucker's apparent failure to grasp the seriousness of the situation was a case in study. Tucker, however, knew exactly how dangerous the situation was and found himself shutting his emotional side down while his logical fact-based decision-making side sharpened. As Phil used to say, *"Sometimes your greatest strength is also your greatest weakness."* Of that, Tucker was guilty. He would allow himself to grieve for his friend later.

But, now, it was time to move.

Though Tucker kept no information on his home computer that would be of value to someone trying to steal intellectual property or the patentable details of the discovery, he did have files he wouldn't want in the hands of criminals. He took ten precious minutes to delete files of concern and then emptied the deleted folder.

His laptop computer, however, was another story. Though he wanted to travel light, Tucker decided he had better protect the information on the laptop. He packed only enough clothing, shoes, and toiletries in his gym bag to allow space for the computer.

He grabbed his jacket, car keys, cell phone, mini-iPad, and a hot spot. Tucker took one last look around his home before he turned the lights off and locked his front door. It was almost 10:00 p.m.

Little did Tucker know that he would never again return to his apartment.

The uncomfortable experience of being on the run, and maybe even hunted, was new to Tucker. With nerves tightening every step of the way, he cautiously walked down to the parking garage, frequently looking over his shoulder.

Five minutes later, he drove toward the Inner Loop of the Washington Beltway in his late model Mustang with the car doors locked. As he negotiated through the surprisingly heavy traffic, Tucker contemplated the potential motives for his friend and co-inventor's murder. Who would want to hurt Phil? What could he have done to deserve his fate? After fifteen minutes in deep thought, Tucker could only come up with one reason for his friend's death: someone wanted to eliminate everyone who knew how to make the technology work.

Tucker wished that Phil, Maya Li, and he hadn't posted the technology in operation on YouTube. It was Tucker's big idea to promote the invention. It sounded like a good marketing plan at the time, but apparently, the three of them hadn't thought it through. In their euphoria, it hadn't crossed any of their minds that people would kill for the knowledge of how the discovery worked. At least the YouTube video didn't disclose the formula or other details. However, the video did list the contact information for all three of them.

Tucker had no idea where he would go to lie low—he had no preconceived clue of where he could hide. He had no family, no vacation home, no favorite spot, no nothing. If criminals were after him, they might research his childhood and discover that he was brought up in western North Carolina, so he decided that he would not head south from Alexandria.

The good news was that if he didn't know where he was going, no one else could know.

Unless someone followed him.

He headed west on I-66, used the car's Bluetooth feature for his phone, and, even though it was late in the evening, called to warn the most important person in his life about the threat.

11

Tucker pulled over and had a long and emotional call with Maya. Together, they grieved the loss of their friend and discussed their potential fate. Tucker made a compelling argument for Maya to escape to a secure location and assured Maya that he knew how to stay safe. They agreed to buy burn phones and remain in contact.

I-66, Virginia

Tucker was blessed with good health, loving parents, an interest and aptitude for science, a good sense of humor, and a love for reading. He was a mixed breed, and at a fit 185 pounds and six-feet one-inch height, was called "handsome" by his late mother and former lady friends. His green eyes—inherited from his mother's Irish side of the gene pool—on his decisively Native American-looking face made him appear a bit unique, if not a little intriguing. Though he enjoyed the company of ladies and had even considered proposing marriage to one, he just couldn't bring himself to make the plunge.

But unlike his late friend, Phil McPherson, Tucker knew with whom he wanted to share the joy of the discovery—the brilliant and lovely Dr. Maya Li. He thought he'd been in love before until he met Maya, who swept him off his feet like no other woman.

While cruising down the interstate, Tucker reminisced about how his relationship with Maya had evolved. Tucker had worked with Dr. Li long before he had a new idea for an invention that he wanted to recommend to the Entropy Board of Directors.

He had to suppress his strong physical attraction for her and focus on her intellectual and scientific attributes. Tucker needed Maya's knowledge and expertise to advance his idea. He thought about how to approach and convince Maya to help him, but in the end, had decided he would just fly to her office in Illinois and ask her out for dinner. The risk was that she would say "no," but he sensed that she found him interesting enough to accept his invitation.

She said, "Yes."

The rest is history, as they say. Together they would become both famous and infamous.

Route 55, West Virginia

Thirty minutes after Tucker left the interstate system and two and a half hours after he left Alexandria, he crossed the border of Virginia into West Virginia.

He couldn't keep his eyes open. Tucker turned his radio on to a hard rock station, kept the temperature in the Mustang just above freezing, and slapped his own face a couple of times. He still couldn't stay awake on the dangerous winding road and couldn't think straight. Every couple of miles Tucker passed small crosses adorned with artificial flowers on the side of the road, a reminder to him of just how dangerous it was to drive when sleep deprived.

He fell asleep within minutes of parking behind a closed Shell gas station. It was pitch black out—until a bright spotlight beamed into the front seat. A groggy Tucker couldn't immediately comprehend what was going on, and his eyes couldn't adjust quickly enough to know who was invading his sleep. A hard tap on the driver's-side window stimulated Tucker's memory—he was on the run and whomever this was could be one of the killers after him. He dug into his front pocket for his car keys thinking that, maybe, the Mustang could outrun the potential assassin.

Tucker looked through the driver's-side window directly into the double-barrel of a shotgun. So much for running.

"Roll the window down."

Tucker yelled through the closed window, "Power windows."

"Open the door."

Tucker couldn't decide whether it was good news that the guy outside the door hadn't shot the window out, or bad news that maybe the killer wanted to keep him alive to torture Tucker for the secrets of his discovery. Tucker still hadn't been able to see the man, the light damned near blinded him. He moved his hands slowly and deliberately to the power lock switch. Click. Tucker felt even more vulnerable.

"Slowly, open the door."

Tucker cracked the door and slowly pushed it farther until it swung fully open.

The killer backed off a few feet and said, "Get out, turn around, and put both hands on the roof of the car."

Relief swept over Tucker; he smiled and gladly followed the instructions given. This was a local cop, not an assassin.

Twenty minutes later as Tucker was cruising west, he made a sage decision—considering his new circumstances—to call the only person in the world he could trust with his life—Tank Alvarez.

Even back when he and Tank were seventeen-year-old boys in Boone, North Carolina, Tank was already a monster who towered over his friends at six feet four and a half inches tall and weighed 310 pounds. He was the only bright star on their high school football team as a defensive tackle. Tucker's childhood friend continued to grow not only physically, but also personally and intellectually. Tank evolved to become an entrepreneur who owned a personal security and private investigation firm called *White Knight Personal Security, LLC*.

Tucker decided that he probably needed protection and that Tank was the best, most reliable person to provide it.

He would need it.

CHAPTER 3

MOSCOW, RUSSIA—SEPTEMBER 28TH—OCTOBER 3RD

Very close to the pinnacle of Russian society were the champions of the nation's second-most-favorite pastime, chess. Chess masters were revered, honored, respected, and envied by millions of lesser players who lacked the gift to be able to plan ten or twelve moves ahead. Like all proud Russians, President Vladimir Petrov loved to play the game and thought that if he had dedicated more time and study to it, he could have become a master player himself. But he had a demanding day job, so he became the next best thing, a master geopolitical strategist whose next chess-like move was to block a check-mate—in the form of an American discovery—on Russia. His block or counter-move required him to contact someone he could trust to follow his instructions implicitly—his cousin, Alex Pashkov.

A Deadly Discovery

From an encrypted cell phone, Petrov called and said, "Alex, I have a new assignment for you. One, I think, you will enjoy."

Alex asked, "Who is the target, this time?"

"I really don't know with specificity. There are at least three possibilities. All three are Americans," said Petrov dryly, "but when you figure out who, eliminate him or them. There is a new technology, an invention, the secrets for which must not become known. It is paramount. As dramatic as that sounds, the long-term economic survival of Russia may depend on you. Time is of the essence, so as we speak I have already sent you a link to a YouTube video. After you view it, you will know what to do. Arrangements have been made. You know which brick to pull.

"After you land in America and assess the situation, let me know what you need. I'll make sure you have all of Russia's resources at your disposal to complete your mission. Good luck, my dear cousin." Petrov then hung up on Alex without further elaboration.

Alex Pashkov smiled broadly—he loved his job. He didn't think of himself as the psychopath he was; he thought of himself as a national hero protecting the motherland and an artist with maybe a few flaws, if sadistic tendencies were considered flaws in his profession.

He said aloud but to no one in particular, "Is it so wrong that I enjoy my work?" Alex knew he wasn't as smart or clever as his power-crazed billionaire cousin, the "hard one," but Alex knew he was just as ruthless. Vlad and Alex shared typical superhero-type comic book dreams as children. Except that Alex identified with the villains while Vlad dreamed of achieving power.

While watching the YouTube video, Alex observed three smart, happy, and proud people. He couldn't believe that their two of their names and contact information showed up at the end of the video—it just didn't get any easier than that. He was excited because he just received three possible assassination jobs for the price of one.

Alex drove thirty-five kilometers to the abandoned building where he and Vlad went to school as teenagers. Down in the basement, an old coal-fired boiler sat atop fire bricks. With his high-powered flashlight, he found the loose brick they selected for hiding secret messages and pulled it. He reached into the opening and pulled out the waterproof satchel that contained a fake passport, a printed note, nine thousand US dollars, and an airline ticket to Atlanta with a layover in Frankfurt, Germany. Also, included in the satchel was the name of a weapons supplier in Atlanta who would also provide him with a car registered to a fake corporation.

Alex read the note and groaned.

Don't come back without the secrets of how to make the discovery work.

I-85, Georgia

The act of assassination was a sport to Alex taken to an art form—it was all about the hunt. His ideological cousin once said to him, "Sometimes, we must sacrifice a few for the better good of the many." Alex didn't say it at the time but thought, "That doesn't work well for the sacrificed few."

For this assignment, the sacrificed few included Tucker Cherokee and anyone who got in Alex's way of assassinating him. Then he'd hunt down the other two people announced on the video.

One reason that Alex was a successful assassin was that he could blend in wherever he went and because his American English was perfect. Alex even looked like an American, as he was six feet tall and a little overweight, had a small nose by East European standards, and had an American-style haircut—hair longer than it should be. It was a good time of year to be in the United States—he could wear long shirts and a jacket with his collar up, which allowed him to cover up many of his scars.

His targets never saw him coming.

Though it was a long drive from Atlanta, Georgia, to Alexandria, Virginia, Pashkov took his time, stopped often, enjoyed the scenery, and spent the first night in Durham, North Carolina, where he enjoyed his favorite thing about America, Hollywood-produced special-effect 3-D movies in IMAX theaters.

He eventually reached Alexandria a little after 10:00 p.m. on October 3rd and quickly found the apartment where Tucker Cherokee lived. Old Town Alexandria was a comfortable place to wander around on foot. It was a tourist hot spot with hundreds of people still milling around late in the evening who looked no different as tourists than did Alex.

He blended with the crowd, kept moving, passed in front of Tucker's apartment, and performed surveillance multiple times to assure himself that no one was in Tucker's third-floor apartment on King Street and that it was safe for Alex to enter Tucker's apartment, await his arrival, and ambush him.

It was very easy for Alex to pick the locks of both the building and Tucker's apartment front door. "An amateur could have broken into this establishment," Alex mused. He searched the apartment to confirm that he would not surprise a potential roommate or lady friend. Alex then searched for weapons and found in Tucker's nightstand top drawer a loaded Smith & Wesson BodyGuard 380 with the safety on. Pashkov smiled as he jammed the gun between his waistband and the small of his back.

He knew how to kill, but he didn't know how to steal industrial secrets. He wandered into a second bedroom apparently used as a home office, looked around for a safe where Tucker might store confidential information about the invention but found none.

Pashkov turned Tucker's computer on but couldn't get past the password. Alex was no computer geek, so he decided he would take the PC and have a computer guy download all the data off it.

Alex waited six hours in Tucker's apartment for him to come home, but he never showed up. Alex concluded that Tucker must have a girlfriend somewhere and was not going to show up tonight, so Alex left with Tucker's computer and the handgun to contact a computer hacker. It just so happened that he knew where to find one.

This was not his first rodeo, as the Americans say.

CHAPTER 4

CHICAGO, ILLINOIS—OCTOBER 4ᵀᴴ

Maya looked at the rear-view mirror one more time and, again, wondered whether someone was following her. Her mother, a renowned psychiatrist, would probably diagnose her as paranoid, but after Tucker had informed her that their friend and co-inventor, Phil McPherson, was murdered, she felt like she had earned the right to be a little paranoid. Tucker further reinforced her anxiety when he strongly recommended to her that she follow his example and hide until the dust settled.

Maya took a leave of absence from her job at Fermilab and headed to her mother's penthouse located on the North Shore of Chicago, which Maya thought would make a good temporary safe house while she planned her next move.

On her drive to Chicago, she thought about the good that was supposed to result from their invention and wondered how others could twist it into a bad thing.

She lamented, "*No good deed goes unpunished. Poor Phil.*"

She didn't want to lead potential bad guys to her mother's home. With only five miles left to reach her destination, she decided that she had to find out with certainty whether someone was following her. So, she downshifted, revved the engine, let the clutch out, and empowered her electric sports car to accelerate—if only for a short distance—before she made a sharp right turn onto an unfamiliar side street.

It's not paranoia if it turns out to be true. Someone was following her.

Batavia, Illinois

Thirteen months ago, Maya met Tucker when he was on assignment to Fermilab to support basic research, a subject with which, at the time, Tucker was unfamiliar. The national lab allowed him on-site on the basis that all cost would be born by the contractor and in the hope that Entropy would write a favorable report that would be forwarded to the Congressional Budget Office. The report would be used by Fermilab to secure additional Congressional support for future lab activities. After all, taxpayer-funded basic science research was harder to sell to the voting public as the federal debt increased and the demand for ever-increasing entitlement programs surged. The government lab did not want to have to face the same fate as NASA where space exploration was forced to subcontract its mission to Petrov's Russia.

Dr. Li, who, at the time, was a recent graduate of the University of Chicago, was Tucker's point of contact at the lab. She was excited at the opportunity to work at a national lab and was happy to impress Tucker with her knowledge about the basic research conducted there.

She succeeded—he was, in fact, very impressed. She was not only well educated and extremely intelligent, but Maya Li was also breathtakingly beautiful. She did her best to conceal her beauty by wearing baggy clothing under her white lab coat, no makeup, no jewelry, no polished fingernails, and glasses that Tucker eventually would learn she did not need. Her hair was always up in some form or fashion; her work shoes were flat with extra cushion for people who stand on their feet all day; and the top button on her blouse was always fixed.

But all that did not disguise her beauty. The mixture of her father's Chinese heritage and her mother's Norwegian genes produced a glamorous and exotic offspring. At five feet nine inches tall with apparently low body fat, an athletic physique, and radiant almond-shaped dark brown eyes, it was hard for Tucker not to stare at her. Tucker fantasized about what their offspring would look like considering his native-American and Irish contribution.

She was accustomed to being stared at. She initially ignored his gawking when he first arrived. He never got used to being near her, and he frequently fought the feeling of arousal. She noticed that he had to excuse himself and limp away at times—though he always claimed his foot fell asleep.

But he was kind, unaggressive, soft spoken, humorous, respectful, honest, and damned good-looking, so she put up with his weakly disguised stares.

Little did she know that their lives would become intertwined, adventurous, dangerous, loving, and so damned important.

23

Chicago, Illinois

Maya drove at high speed down the trash-littered side street, which was more like a one-lane alleyway and was just barely wide enough for her car. The larger car following her was falling far behind and she was hopeful that she could lose them. Her hope was dashed, though, when Maya saw a dumpster up ahead in the alleyway. She mentally calculated whether there was room for her to pass. Maya thought not, but she had no choice—she accelerated in the hope that the car's momentum could force it past the obstruction.

The tortuous, high-pitched sound of screeching metal on metal lasted only seconds before the car came to an abrupt stop. Maya was unhurt but realized that she had managed to wedge the vehicle between the side wall of the adjacent building and the dumpster. She was unable to open either the driver's-side or passenger's-side doors. Maya put the car in reverse to see whether she could dislodge it. She had no success. Maya put the vehicle in first gear, but the severely wedged car didn't budge. She didn't panic. Instead, she calmly assessed her options.

Fifty-five seconds later, the slower, wider car that had followed her into the alleyway stopped about twenty-five yards behind her jammed and wedged sports car. Four men with automatic weapons exited their full-sized sedan and walked casually in the direction of Maya's crashed and immobile vehicle. The leader of the four men nodded, and the three other men opened fire and emptied their clips into Maya's sports car.

CHAPTER 5

GRANT COUNTY, WEST VIRGINIA— OCTOBER 4TH

Tucker felt confident that no one was tailing him and that no one was likely to find him just south of Nowhere and west of Bumfuck Hollow. He felt that he had ventured far enough into the unpopulated West Virginia countryside to stop for a few minutes at a fast-food restaurant to prevent his hunger pangs and bladder pressure from monopolizing all other senses. Tucker parked his Mustang at an Arby's in the small town of Petersburg, went inside the virtually empty restaurant, and ordered a roast beef sandwich with a to-go cup of unsweetened ice tea. The tea was ready before his sandwich, so he took a sip and placed it on a table. The restaurant's men's room called, so he took the opportunity to relieve pressure while the cook prepared his sandwich.

While Tucker was in the men's room, two men casually entered the restaurant. One, code-named Graf, occupied the order-taker while the second man, code-named Brock, slipped the contents from a vial into

Tucker's tea. While Brock and Graf spiked Tucker's tea, a third man, known as the Czech, attached a magnetic GPS tracker to the undercarriage of Tucker's car. The entire clandestine operation took only forty seconds. Brock and Graf had left the restaurant by the time Tucker finished washing his hands.

There were no other customers inside the establishment when Tucker had entered the fast-food restaurant, and there was no one in the restaurant when Tucker came out of the men's room. He went to the counter, grabbed the sandwich that was now ready and his tea off the table, and returned to his car.

Tucker had no particular destination and decided to drive as long as his adrenaline allowed. He continued to drive the Mustang through Grant County, eating his sandwich and drinking his tea when he observed a road sign that read "Route 42 - Mount Storm." Mount Storm sounded like an even smaller and better place for him to hide than in Petersburg. He impulsively followed the direction of the sign and turned right only to be surprised to see three other vehicles on an otherwise traffic-less road take the same route behind him. Though he knew he was a little paranoid and that it was highly unlikely anyone besides Tank knew where he was, Tucker couldn't shake the feeling that someone had followed him from Alexandria.

Tucker pulled out his cell phone, used the Bluetooth feature once again, and called Tank for the third time in less than two hours.

Tucker said, "It might be a good thing that I called you earlier and asked for your help. Tank, I think someone is following me."

Tank wasn't a conversationalist. He spoke in short sentences consistent with his laconic personality. Tank asked, "Where are you? Last we talked you were on Route 55 in West Virginia?"

"I'm still in West Virginia, but I just turned off 55 onto Route 42. It's not a very busy road, yet three vehicles followed me after I made the turn. It's reasonable and logical to suspect that at least one of the three cars might be tailing me."

Tank said, "OK. I think I'm about forty-five minutes behind you. Make a turn without putting your blinkers on and see if someone follows you. Keep this phone line open."

Brock and Graf were in an inconspicuous-looking Buick following their target, Tucker, in his Mustang. Brock said to Graf, "It's getting a little difficult on these back roads to covertly follow the target. He's eventually going to get suspicious. Now that we've introduced the cocktail into the target's drink and attached a GPS tracker to his car, we no longer need to follow him so closely. Pull over and stop at the next available opportunity. I need to call Aaron for instructions, anyway."

A white GMC van and an old Ford Ranger pickup truck continued to drive behind Tucker after the Buick pulled over. Without using his blinker, Tucker made a turn onto the next branch in the road. The white GMC van followed Tucker, but the pickup truck continued on Route 42.

"Tank, one of the three vehicles followed me onto Patterson Creek Road. Any suggestions?"

"Yes, increase your speed and keep the line open."

The Czech and two other mercenaries in the white GMC received a phone call from Brock, "Guys, hang back just in case the target has spotted us. Let him get out ahead of us now that we're able to follow him to his ultimate destination. We don't want to abduct him in

27

plain sight, and we hope he'll lead us to that scientist babe."

Tucker picked up his speed and watched the van fade behind him. A couple of miles later, Tucker made another sharp right at a crossroad, traveled a mile up a steep mountain road until he reached an industrial plant, and pulled into a parking lot. He said to Tank, "I think I've lost my tail."

"That's unlikely if they are professionals. Stay put. I'll be there in a half hour. Based on Google maps, I think I know exactly where you are."

Tucker felt a little nauseated and got out of his car to get some fresh air. He was amazed that he was at a rock quarry at the very crest of the mountain with a spectacular view of Appalachia, but the biting wind prevented him from enjoying the moment—Tucker wished he'd brought a heavier jacket.

He walked around the quarry briefly and observed large Volvo FM 480 trucks loaded with crushed rock navigating the winding roads. Not too long after Tucker reached the quarry, Tank showed up in his late-model Jeep Cherokee.

Tucker always thought it was nice that Jeep named a vehicle after him.

While Tank surveyed the area around the quarry, he said, "You don't look so good."

"Just a little nervous, I guess, and I think I ate something I shouldn't have."

Tank continued to look around and still hadn't made eye contact with Tucker or shaken his hand. "Leave your Mustang here in the employee parking lot and hop into the Jeep. I'll check your car for a tracking device. It's standard protocol in the security business."

Tank got out of the Jeep, crawled around Tucker's Mustang, and found the GPS tracker magnetically attached to the undercarriage.

Tank said, "This is not a good sign, my friend. Someone is, in fact, tracking you." Tank removed it and attached it to a large dump truck used to transport crushed rock from the quarry to a customer, which Tank suspected was probably a West Virginia road construction job.

Tucker grabbed his packed gym bag and iPod from his Mustang and opened the passenger's-side front door to Tank's Jeep.

Tucker froze, didn't move a muscle, didn't verbalize a thought, and pretended to be invisible. Tank's ninety-pound, two-year-old, military-trained K-9 occupied the front seat and gave no indication that he would move to make space for Tucker. The German shepherd made eye contact with Tucker and, to Tucker's relief, wagged his tail.

Tank said, "Ram, get in the back, and, Tucker, hand me your cell phone." Ram and Tucker followed the instructions, while Tank proceeded to throw Tucker's phone onto the quarry property.

Tucker said, "Hey, what the hell are you doing? I need that phone."

"Most likely one of the dump trucks will crush the phone. Tucker, your phone has a GPS microchip in it."

"What about your phone?" Tucker asked.

"No one is trying to track me." Tank said. "Yet."

As Tank, Tucker, and Ram rode back down the mountain in search of a place of temporary refuge, a white GMC Van, unnoticed by Tucker, drove past them going the opposite direction.

Grant County, West Virginia

Tucker looked south through the inside of a picture window on the second floor of someone's winterized log home. Tank had used a Google satellite app with Google maps to identify a couple of isolated houses in the area that were down lightly used dirt roads and that had the potential for use. He found this unoccupied log cabin and broke into it with the intent to use it temporarily as a safe place to hide.

At least, they both hoped the empty log home would be safe.

As Tucker peered outside and enjoyed the view of the setting sun shining on mountains east of the cabin, he thought he saw light reflecting off something metal in the nearby forest of hardwood trees and high grass. "Damn," he wondered, "How could they, whoever *they* are, have followed us here?"

Though Tucker was unsure *who* was trying to capture or kill him, he deducted *why*. Until the announcement of Project MEG, Tucker had no enemies. Nothing prepared Tucker for the inherent evil that was apparently linked to the discovery. Gone were the pride and exhilaration he once experienced after making the discovery. Even though the incredible discovery changed everything—if, and that's now a big "if," it sees the light of day—some people didn't want "everything" to change.

The invention apparently came with unintended life-threatening consequences for the inventors. He now believed he was a wanted man, maybe wanted dead by some, or maybe temporarily kept alive until they picked his brain, by others. Though it was nice to be wanted, it wasn't good to be wanted by assassins or kidnappers. He had to give Stephen Sanders credit for assessing the situation correctly.

He hoped Maya had taken his advice and was OK. She needed protection. Tucker was uncomfortable with the stirring inside him every time he thought about Maya.

He thought he saw more movement in the forest, only it was closer to the log home this time. Tucker suddenly wished he had more close combat and weapons training than what his father gave him. Tucker was more the cerebral type, yet, there he sat with a Louisville Slugger alloy baseball bat and a loaded semiautomatic Mossberg shotgun that belonged to the owners of this newly christened "safe house." He damned well use the weapons if he had to.

Tucker was very glad he had called in Tank Alvarez to watch his back. Tank and Ram were somewhere outside the log home surveying and scouting for would-be enemies to protect Tucker from whoever was apparently after him.

Tucker peered intently out of the log home's picture window at his surroundings. He was certain, this time, that he saw movement in the colorful forest. It could have been deer or a fox, or wind gusts that caused trees to wave their branches, but that was probably just wishful thinking. The fall colors of yellow, gold, red, and brown leaves over rich dark green grass provided the perfect background to camouflage movement. Tank and Ram were not the sources of the movement because they were both holed up on a hill on the north side of the log home where they could perform better surveillance.

Tucker was in constant communication with Tank as they used Brick House Invisible Headset earbuds.

"They know I'm here, Tank. How do they know? You swept our vehicles and removed the GPS tracker before we found this place. Do they have access to high technology methods for tracking me? Are they using prepositioned surveillance cameras with facial recognition software?"

Tucker realized his imagination began to run away from him. He removed stress from his thought process, took a couple of deep breaths, and calmly thought logically. The people after Tucker were most likely mercenaries hired by an entity threatened by Project MEG. The mercenaries, if caught by law enforcement authorities, probably could not be traced back to the hiring entity.

He wondered whether Copernicus felt this way, disappointed and disillusioned when his contemporaries hated him after he discovered that the earth was not the center of the universe. Or whether the scientists at Los Alamos felt this way when they saw the manifestations of their discovery in Trinity, New Mexico, when they tested the first atomic bomb.

Tucker knew it was time for him to utilize his God-given talent to think strategically. His ability to ignore stress, stay calm, and self-confidently select the right path forward needed to kick in. Tucker saw only one way forward. Tucker's approach, his idea as to how to reverse his situation, was convoluted and devious, and it had a low probability of success.

Grant County, West Virginia

Tank was at home in the forest, particularly with Ram by his side. Tank also spotted the movement in the woods around the violated log home in which Tucker currently resided. He pulled out his high-powered compact Vortex Viper tactical field glasses and viewed an area of about three acres around the spot of the movement to see whether whatever caused the movement had companions. He studied the field of view for a couple of minutes and concluded that at least three people moved clandestinely in the direction of the log home.

"Three what," Tank wondered, "Soldiers, state-sponsored hit men, mercenaries? How the hell did they find us? I can't just take out each one of the threats without knowing who each one was. Or could I? If the wrong people captured Tucker and tortured him to extract the knowledge he possessed, then, well, I couldn't live with myself.

"And what would happen if bad people stole the knowledge they were after?"

CHAPTER 6

WORCESTER, MASSACHUSETTS—
OCTOBER 4TH

Though they had completed missions together, Gang Chung had never seen his handler's face turn red.

After leaving the remains of Phil McPherson on the floor in Cambridge, Gang Chung hotwired a car and drove due west on back roads until he got to a Red Roof Inn in Worcester where he rendezvoused with his handler. She was an information technology prodigy that the People's Republic of China's Ministry of State Security assigned to work with Chung. The MSS gave mission assignments to Chung's handler, she planned the operation, Chung executed the theft, and the handler analyzed the value of the data stolen.

Gang Chung turned over the extorted thumb drive and stolen briefcase with Phil's laptop. His handler had opened the laptop and inserted a disk. He didn't understand the science behind the technology but whatever the disk did, it had allowed her to bypass the username and password functions. She searched

McPherson's laptop for a good thirty minutes for any information relevant to the discovery and surprisingly, found none. She then inserted into the laptop the thumb drive McPherson had given Gang Chung and reviewed that data.

That's when her face turned red.

The handler asked, "You already killed McPherson, right?"

"Yes, as you instructed. Now, China alone knows how to make the American discovery work."

"You killed him after he gave you this flash-drive with all the information we need to make it work, is that correct?"

"Yes."

"Did it occur to you that maybe you should have checked the contents of this thumb drive before you killed him?"

"No," Gang Chung said, "You were not there. McPherson was afraid that I would torture him. I am sure he was not lying."

"You are a fool. He lied to you. There is nothing on this thumb drive but music. Do you like ZZ-Top, Gang Chung?"

She continued, "Do you realize that you may have jeopardized our entire mission. McPherson was, allegedly, only one of three or four people with the knowledge that State Security ordered us to deliver. After you had texted me that you accomplished your assignment, I authorized the elimination of the woman scientist we'd been following."

Without changing his facial expression, Chung asked, "Did it occur to you that maybe you should have checked the contents of this thumb drive before you authorized that kill?"

She ignored his biting comment and said, "There are only one or two people left that might know the secrets we must secure. Break into the Entropy office and see if there is something of value there. Bring me McPherson's office computer hard drive. And see if his supervisor has access to the secrets."

"I don't think that's a very good idea. The police have probably already identified his body. They may be going through his Entropy office for evidence right now. Breaking into his office is too risky."

His handler said, "Beat the police to the punch. The sooner, the better."

"The other option is for us to track down Tucker Cherokee and see if he has the information needed. Did McPherson tell you anything before he died? Usually, you are more persuasive than you have been this time."

"He told me the names of the chemicals he used for the YouTube video experiment."

The handler said, "Ah, good work, write them down here for me."

Gang Chung said, "I cannot recall the chemical names; the names were too complicated. That is why I demanded the thumb drive."

She said, "He probably lied to you about the names of the chemicals anyway. I'll track down the location of the other two YouTube video participants. You get what you can out of McPherson's office."

The handler knew that failure of this mission would be catastrophic and career ending. She had to develop an alternative plan in case Gang Chung failed again. She knew her freedom and the freedom of her family probably depended on the success of this mission.

CHAPTER 7

FAIRFAX COUNTY, VIRGINIA— OCTOBER 4TH

There was no advance warning for seven-year-old Jenny Monahan that this day would be any different from any other day in her young life.

Mom woke her up in the morning, fed her breakfast, dressed her, brushed her long red hair, packed her backpack, put her in the SUV, and started their daily trek to school. The ride to school was normal, just like any other day, until, suddenly, the ride was rough and Mom said, "Uh oh, I think Mr. SUV has a flat tire, Jenny."

Mom, Dana Monahan, got out of the vehicle, still in her sweatpants and Washington Redskin sweatshirt, looked at her flat tire, and said words to herself that she wouldn't say in front of her daughter. Fortunately, they had AAA road service. She looked in the glove compartment and pulled out the AAA card with the phone number on it, but before she dialed, a man in a ten-year-old Lincoln Town Car stopped and said, "May I help you?"

Dana said, "No, thank you. We have road service to assist us in such situations as this, and it's about time we get our money's worth."

The man said with a thick Brooklyn accent, "Fine. I'll just stay here and watch over you until they get here."

"Thank you, but that's not necessary."

The man ignored her, pulled over, and got out of his car. Dana looked around nervously to see whether there was anybody else around in the event this guy was illegitimate. She was somewhat comforted that there was the usual traffic on the street, though it was an overcast and chilly day, such that almost all vehicles passed with their windows up.

She should not have been comforted. His smile was insincere, and his gait was confident. He looked her straight in her bright blue eyes with his narrow, cold, dark, frightening eyes as he approached the SUV, bent down to look at the tire, and said, "Look at the hole in this tire. Do you know what caused it?"

She said, "No, what?"

"This is a bullet hole. Your tire has been shot out by a marksman."

Dana said, "That can't be true. Who would do something like that?"

The man said, "I would. Now hand me your cell phone, get your daughter out of her booster seat, and get into the back seat of my car. If you scream, I'll kill your daughter before anyone can save you. Smile as if I'm helping you and get into the car. I will kill Jenny if you don't."

Dana immediately reacted to his comment with fear and trepidation and said, "How do you know my daughter's name?"

"Get in the fucking car and don't forget to smile."

Dana sensed that the hard-looking man with an ugly scar on his neck was evil and would follow through with his threat. She also knew that if she got in the car, he might kill them both anyway. The man read her thoughts—he'd been at this sort of thing a while—and displayed his nine-inch stiletto. "You scream, and I will kill you instantly with this and torture Jenny with it over a period of a couple of weeks."

Dana forced a smile, handed the man her cell phone, opened the SUV back door, unbuckled Jenny's seat belt, and picked her up. She wished she hadn't dressed Jenny in a dress. "Where are we going, Mom?" Jenny knew something was not right.

"To school, sweetheart. This man is going to give us a ride." Dana tried to think of a way to escape but couldn't come up with anything extemporaneously. An older concerned citizen pulled beside them and asked whether he could help, but Stiletto Man quickly answered and said, "Thanks, but I think we have it under control."

A third vehicle then pulled over to the curb, and two men got out and jumped into Stiletto Man's Lincoln Town Car: one in the driver's seat, the other in the front passenger's seat, while Stiletto Man got into the back seat with Jenny and Mom. He said, "Go."

The car accelerated, stayed within the speed limit, and drove off—in the opposite direction from the school. "Here is your cell phone back. Now, call your husband, Mrs. Monahan, and put it on speaker."

She asked, "Why?"

He said, "Because, if you don't, I'll use the chemicals in a syringe stored in my jacket pocket on your daughter. You won't like the effect it will have on her. That is if I guessed her weight accurately. If I misjudged her weight, it might kill her."

Dana pushed the speed dial number for her husband.

She rarely called her husband at work. His number was on speed dial for emergencies only.

"What's wrong, Babe? Is everything all right?" Art Monahan asked when he answered the phone. Stiletto Man interjected, "I am what's wrong, Agent Monahan. I have your wife and daughter, Art, and I'll leave it to your imagination as to what will happen to them if you don't do exactly as I say."

Dana yelled, "Honey, these are bad men! I'm so sorry I let this happen and put Jenny in harm's way!" at which time Jenny started to cry in reaction to her mother's palpable fear—just as Stiletto Man orchestrated.

"If you don't follow my instructions to the letter, the next proof-of-life call will be your wife's scream—after that, your daughter's scream."

"OK, OK," Art said. "I get it! What is it you want?"

"I want you to pick up a satellite phone with encryption capabilities so that we can speak at any time without your employer eavesdropping. Then I want you to send to the following email address, 3165rz@yahoo.com, the satellite contact number. Await contact from me on your sat-phone, exactly six hours from now. In the meantime, I'll enjoy the company of your family. If everything goes well, you'll get to do the same again sometime. I love how Jenny looks in her little dress."

Stiletto Man signed off and handed the phone to the man in the car's front passenger's seat. The car stopped, and the man got out of the car with the cell phone. The Town Car moved on and left the man behind with Dana's cell phone. Stiletto Man looked at Mrs. Monahan and said, "That should keep your husband's employer busy for a couple of hours."

Fort Belvoir, Virginia

Art Monahan sat in his bullpen chair and contemplated his response to the outrageous kidnapping of his wife and daughter. Art was a communication engineer in his early forties with an army intelligence background. He knew that he needed to think more calmly than he ever had. His family's lives depended on it. He'd been in life-threatening situations in the field in Bosnia where he'd had to make quick decisions. But, now, he couldn't think straight. Horrible images of torture of his wife and daughter crept into his mind.

The kidnappers had Dana's cell phone, so he should be able to track the GPS chip in the phone, easy stuff for a National Geospatial-Intelligence Agency analyst. Too easy. The kidnapper would probably ditch the phone. But at least Art thought that he could get the coordinates from where Dana had made the call. It took him only three minutes to determine that Dana had made the phone call from the 13200 block of Franconia Road in Springfield, Virginia—not too far from Jenny's school.

"It doesn't tell me anything," Art thought. "I should tell my boss that I think I am about to be blackmailed. I need to get my family back from this sick motherfucker." Then he thought about what he had just said and thought, "Damn, I hope that isn't what he is!"

Monahan concluded that he had to tell the FBI about the blackmail. His only fear was that there was someone on the inside of the government who was supporting Stiletto Man. How else could the kidnapper know to pick on Art's family? He could not think of a any other reason.

"Hell," he thought fearfully, "they're going to kill them no matter what I do." He decided to wait and not tell his superiors or the FBI until he knew what the asshole wanted.

Art proceeded to secure a satellite phone through an acquaintance of his who sold satellite phone bandwidth. He sent the contact number to the email address he was instructed to use and waited. He had three hours to wait. He wished the blackmailer would reach him sooner, but he didn't. Art paced and paced, wrung his hands, sat in his chair, jumped up, paced again, and looked at the clock on his desk every few seconds.

Seeds of hate that he didn't know he was capable of grew in Art's heart.

Fairfax County, Virginia

Stiletto Man made another call, this time to an operative of his in the field. "This is Aaron. Do you still have the target in your sights?"

Brock said, "Yes. He has consumed the cocktail you gave me, we attached a tracker to his car, and he is holed up in a log cabin. The three amigos are approaching the cabin, and to the best of my knowledge, the target has not spotted any of us."

Aaron asked, "Is anyone else following him?"

Brock said, "No one else is following him, but he now has someone with him."

Aaron said, "That complicates things, but take no prisoners. Call me immediately after you successfully capture the target or if he leads us to one of the other inventors. Out."

Aaron did not mind the wait; it was part of the job. He asked his driver to pull up his GPS locator and find an off-the-beaten-path, cheap motel— they were the best places to hide from law enforcement.

There was no doubt in his mind that what he planned was against the law.

CHAPTER 8

ARLINGTON, VIRGINIA—
OCTOBER 4TH

The Pentagon is known for many things, but one under-appreciated thing the military does extremely well is plan for all possible contingencies.

Are we prepared for an attack on Taiwan by the People's Republic of China?

Do we have enough naval platforms to be superior in the Pacific?

What is our plan to mitigate such a situation?

Are we prepared for the consequences of an Israeli attack on Iran's nuclear bomb-material-making centrifuges?

Are we prepared to defend South Korea and Japan from an aggressive and nuclear-armed North Korea if Dennis Rodman's and Jimmy Carter's peace initiatives fail?

The possible scenarios are infinite, and the Pentagon has a contingency plan for all of them. So, it was not a surprise when two-star Christopher Woodhead walked into Lt. Col. Ray LaSalle's windowless office in 'C' ring and said, "SecDef brought us a new assignment. He handed it to the Joint Chiefs this morning."

Ray, a twenty-year Air Force veteran, was obsessive-compulsive and took his duties seriously, too seriously. He was humorless and perpetually anxious. He hated to start a new task when he hadn't finished an old one. He practically had a nervous breakdown anytime he was asked to drop what he was doing and start something new. General Woodhead knew this, of course, and proceeded to pull LaSalle's chain, "This is now your priority. You get off on scenarios like this, so I know I've made your day."

As Woodhead was leaving, he dropped a large manila envelope onto LaSalle's desk and said, "Status report tomorrow 1700."

LaSalle wouldn't open the new file until he organized the scenario assessment he had been working on before the little dick, Woodhead, had walked in. He spent roughly ninety minutes to check each computer file he had opened, made notes to himself, prepared and color coded a list of action items, categorized the disposition of each unresolved issue, and copied the scenario assessment to a backup file.

It was time for Ray to go home. He had a brutal commute, and he looked forward to a walk with his dog in the evening. He locked the top-secret file in his office safe, put on his raincoat, locked the door, and started to walk down the corridor.

"Damn it," he thought. "Why can't I be a normal person and walk away from the new assignment until tomorrow morning?" He turned around, went back down the corridor, opened his door, took off his raincoat, hung it on the rack, opened the safe, took out the top-secret envelope and proceeded to read.

Fifteen minutes later, he called his dog sitter and asked if she wouldn't mind walking Sugar tonight.

CHAPTER 9

GRANT COUNTY, WEST VIRGINIA—
OCTOBER 4TH

Tucker watched chipmunks scurry for bird seed and hummingbirds compete for nectar. Under different circumstances, he might have enjoyed a vacation in this secluded log home.

"Tucker."

Tucker adjusted his ear bud.

"Earth to Tucker," repeated Tank.

"I'm here," Tucker said.

"Do you remember that frequency monitoring device Entropy patented? You know, the one you gave me for Christmas a couple of years back. Well, it has come in handy today to monitor the discussion between these three guys who are up to no good. I found their communications frequency quickly with this gadget, which was also programmed to identify the language they were speaking, and it translated the discussion directly to English. Cool, huh?"

Impatiently, Tucker asked, "Do you think you could share their discussion with me?"

"They plan to ambush you and take you alive. Ha! Like there's a chance Ram will let that happen. How the hell do you think they found you? I don't believe anyone followed you, and you no longer carry a cell phone or anything that could be used to transmit a signal. We were very careful."

"I don't know how they found us, but I assume these guys are hired guns." Tucker asked, "Do you know who they are since you've listened to their conversation?"

"No, but they are adult Caucasian males, and one of them has a thick Eastern European accent. Other than that, I haven't a clue."

"Is it time to call in reinforcements?"

"No, not yet. Ram and I can handle it."

Grant County, West Virginia

Tucker trusted Tank's judgment implicitly. They rode the same school bus every day as kids, and lots of unmentionable things happened on that bus. Tank became the de facto school bus enforcer. He had evolved over the last twenty-two years to be the epitome of a survivalist and the perfect personal protector for Tucker in this kind of situation.

Tucker had defensive skills of his own, but his skills paled in comparison to Tank's whose intimidating size and strength coupled with his quick reflexes and tactical mind made him a natural for the personal security business.

Tank had taken it upon himself to be Tucker's guardian angel and had taken a personal oath to protect Tucker at any cost, at any time.

Tank owed Tucker.

Tank's younger sister used to fish on a lake with Tank and Tucker when they were kids. The three of them would go out in a little eight-foot two-person Jon boat and fish for anything they could catch, mostly sunfish. One day Tank hooked an unusually large bass for the size of the lake and jerked quickly to pull the fish in. Because Tank was so large, the boat overturned in the lake and spilled all three of them into the water. Tank had never told Tucker until that moment that neither he nor his sister could swim. Tank panicked and held on tightly to the overturned boat.

Tank's sister went under.

Tucker dove under, saved Tank's little sister from drowning, and pulled her to the side of the lake. Then Tucker went back and pulled the boat with Tank on it to safety. Tank was permanently indebted to Tucker. If it were not for Tucker, Tank would have been responsible for his sister's death. After that incident, Tank compelled himself and his sister to become excellent swimmers.

Tank loved Tucker like a brother

After high school, Tank started his career as a bouncer for nightclubs and as a roadie for a country music band. He took martial arts classes, studied about weapons in books and from the Internet, took a few classes in law enforcement, and spent hours in the gym honing his physical skills and stamina. However, all of that work still did not provide him with the litany of skills necessary to excel in the personal protection security business, and because Tank did not have the honor to serve in the military—something he would always regret—he was not a candidate for hire for high-skilled security positions.

That became most evident one day fifteen years earlier when Tank was employed as a bodyguard for an eighteen-year-old rising female country music star at an outdoor theater in Asheville, North Carolina, where Tank was observed and videotaped in action. A lean and mean drunk in his mid-twenties had an urge to touch the beautiful, young, sexy, dressed-to-kill star. "Hell, who wouldn't want to touch her?" the redneck thought. Some urges, however, need to be controlled. But alcohol, in copious quantities, can impair one's judgment and ability to think rationally.

Tank scanned the audience for potential threats to the band's safety and, though the intoxicated young man was not noteworthy in appearance—he was just one of many lustful-looking fans—Tank's internal radar picked him out of the crowd.

The potential threat to the sexy country music star arrived in the form of an unsmiling, hard-looking young man who was with four other guys and two female companions. The man's six friends were smiling and singing along with the tune; bodies swaying in rhythm to the song. But the threatening-looking man was serious and did not act like his buddies. He didn't smile, didn't mime with the song, and didn't dance. Instead, he moved forward gradually toward the stage, fixated and in a trance.

Tank was at one end of the stage, and as the threat to the band members moved closer, Tank moved perpendicular toward the center of the stage and could now be seen by the audience and fans. Because of his height and breadth, Tank began to obstruct the view of the performance by fans on the far edges of the first couple of rows.

So, he held back.

By the time the band's performance reached the end of the last song, even before the perfunctory encore, the redneck reached the front row, within twenty feet of the country music star, as the standing crowd cheered. Tank was about thirty-five feet from center stage but had the tactical advantage of being on stage instead of in front of the stage and five feet below it.

The redneck tried to climb onto the stage, and though he was young, athletic, and determined, he was a little slow due to his state of inebriation. By the time the redneck stood up erect on the stage, Tank's huge outstretched right hand had him around the throat. He lifted the redneck vertically until both feet were off the stage floor and proceeded to carry him off stage to the roaring applause from the audience.

The knife caught Tank's right forearm.

The pain caused Tank to loosen his grip and drop the perpetrator, but with his left hand, Tank was able to grab the guy's knife-wielding hand at the wrist. Tank continued his momentum and proceeded to twist the arm at the wrist until something popped. The attacker screamed, flailed, and tried a couple of ineffective kicks and jabs, but Tank ultimately restrained him within fifteen seconds of the initial contact.

The redneck did not get to touch the country music star—he never even got close. Though she never thanked Tank for preventing the redneck from assaulting her, it was OK with him. He was just doing his job. Afterward, when the paramedics treated the attacker's dislocated elbow and stitched Tank's knife wounds, a rough and self-confident-looking guy waited to speak with him.

With a smile and an outstretched hand, the man said, "Boy, did you fuck that up!"

Incredulously, Tank said, "Who are you and what are you talking about?"

"My name is Powers, and I'm talking about you taking a knife. If you knew what you were doing, that would not have happened. You obviously have no formal defense training. I'm retired Special Forces, and I train men and women in the art of personal security, self-protection, as well as offensive measures. Here's my card. You need me if you're going to survive in this business."

The rest is history. Powers turned Tank into practically a one-man army.

Tank suffered through an unwanted fifteen minutes of fame after the country movie star incident. A video went viral of Tank carrying the stalker off the stage with just one arm while the redneck's feet were off the ground. A week later, the country music star's agent reached out to him and offered Tank an opportunity to be in an MTV video with the star.

Tank declined, but he never again had trouble finding work and eventually translated his fame into the start of his personal security firm, *White Knight Personal Security, LLC*. Powers, famous in his own right in the small circle of Special Forces, would later become a partner and the firm would become legendary.

Grant County, West Virginia

Tucker trusted Tank's judgment not only because of his training but because Tank was obsessed with the survivalist's doctrine. Tank had learned every trick in the book and invented a few of his own. Despite his size, he'd become an expert in disguise and camouflage. Tank could find food, water, and shelter in the wilderness, and it took a lot of food to keep Tank running on all cylinders.

Tank was also a master of stealth, and Ram was even better. They used their skills to stalk the three mercenaries who were after Tucker. The mercenaries had spread out; one approached from the east, one from the south, and one from the west. Tank was on the high ground on the north side of the log home in an area that was almost exclusively evergreens. It was slightly easier to walk on pine needles and remain stealthy than it was for the mercenaries who would have to walk on dry leaves under the hardwoods. As good as Ram was, he couldn't outrun a bullet. To protect him, Tank kept Ram behind him as they approached the bad guys. However, when it came down to close-contact combat, Ram was invaluable to Tank.

The wind gusted through the forest, which provided sounds that masked his movement. Dry fallen leaves whipped along the ground, branches creaked, and the wind whistled past colorful leaves still hanging on to their hardwood life-line. The light faded as dusk enveloped the valley. It seemed like the temperature dropped a degree every couple of minutes.

Tank, fully outfitted in tailored rugged camouflage, moved counterclockwise with Ram from the north to the west and then moved in behind the first mercenary.

The mercenary moved slowly and methodically toward the log home, one deliberate step at a time. He moved from tree to tree so that his target wouldn't see him from the log home. The mercenaries knew they had the maximum tactical advantage of surprise on Tucker. But, they were unsure whether Tucker was armed, so they remained cautious.

Each time the mercenary took a step, Tank and Ram took two or three larger steps. Eventually, they were less than five yards behind the first mercenary. Tank threw a fallen tree branch away from the mercenary, who looked in the direction of the noise that had distracted him. The mercenary looked just long enough for Tank to hit him in the back of the head with the butt of his sniper rifle. Tank disarmed, tied, and gagged him and then continued to move counterclockwise to the south and then east with the same success.

"All clear," Tucker heard in his earpiece.

"How did you manage to capture the mercenaries? And who are they?"

Tank ignored the question. "Do you want to do the interrogation? One of these bad guys may eventually be able to speak when he regains consciousness."

"No, please, that's not in my skill set."

"You need to broaden your talents and not be just an egg head."

"Unfortunately," said Tucker, "I think they call it on-the-job-training and baptism by fire."

Grant County, West Virginia

Ram was a great warrior. Powers had trained him and given him to Tank as a graduation gift after Tank had passed Powers' first unbelievably rigorous set of courses in hand-to-hand combat, offensive driving, weapons handling, and underwater combat.

Ram had no natural instincts or ability that allowed him to distinguish a good guy from a bad guy. Tank told him who was good and who was bad. Ram was fun and playful and could almost be described as gentle with good guys, as he was trained to protect them.

But Ram had an "on/off" switch. When he was "off," he was a teddy bear. When he was "on," he was his target's worst nightmare. If Tank told Ram that a person was "bad," Ram would bare his teeth and growl intimidatingly. If he told Ram that a person was "bad-bad," Ram would go for the throat. And he would back off in mid-air if told to "stop."

The interrogation went well until the leader of the three mercenaries, Mario, had stupidly spat in Tank's face after Tank asked him how they had followed Tucker to this log home—a home which even he did not know they would occupy. Tank just gave the fool an open-hand slap to the face. But an open-hand slap to the face from the big guy was not your typical slap.

When the mercenary awoke, Tank said, "It is time to demonstrate Ram's talents." He decided that since these guys had intended to torture Tucker, all bets were off. He'd show no mercy and use whatever means were necessary to persuade his guests to talk. Tank pointed at the mercenary that spit on him and said, "Bad."

Ram lifted himself off the ground, ran over to the mercenary, placed his snout less than an inch from the mercenary's nose, bared his teeth, and growled in such a frightening way that any sane person would know that the dog could rip his throat out. The mercenary must have gotten his brain a little scrambled from the interrogations by Tank earlier that day because the macho mercenary foolishly spat in Ram's face.

But Ram did not react. He awaited instructions. Tank said, "Bad-bad." A millisecond later blood splattered, and Tank said, "Stop." Ram stopped and moved over next to him and lay down. Tank timed his instructions to cause injury to the mercenary but not serious enough injury to be fatal.

But Tank must have gauged the timing of the "stop" instructions incorrectly. Ram did entirely too much damage to the guy's throat. Tank desperately tried to save the man's life, but he was unsuccessful. It was not pretty, and the noises the leader of the mercenaries made sounded inhuman. Nothing could stop the bleeding as the other two mercenaries watched as their leader, Mario, bled out.

After that, the two remaining mercenaries became even more cooperative.

Grant County, West Virginia

Ninety-five minutes later, Tank returned with Ram to sit down in front of Tucker and share the actionable intelligence unwillingly provided by the remaining two mercenaries during the interrogation.

During the enhanced interview, the mercenaries had admitted their plan to Tank that after they had captured Tucker, they had planned to torture him, if necessary, to learn all they needed to know about the discovery.

"Ram is a great tool to interview bad guys. Can you believe these tough guys are afraid of my little puppy, here?"

Frustrated with Tank's failure to get right to the point, Tucker asked, "What did you find out?"

"Houston, we have a problem."

Tucker said, "And you're just now discovering this?"

"When was the last time you ate before arriving here to your illegal safe house?

"This is no time to compare favorite restaurants."

Tank said, "When we met at the quarry, you told me you didn't feel good because you might have eaten something that didn't agree with you."

"I stopped at an Arby's before we rendezvoused. Why?"

"Someone slipped you a mickey. They followed you into the restaurant and found some way to get whatever it is into your drink. Anyway, it's a dye or something in your blood that some sort of high-tech special instrument can detect. You know I'm not the scientist in the group, and neither were these two mercenaries, but it's the best they could do to describe how they track you. Tucker, they intend to track you by satellite."

"That could mean my country is after me and that I'm a fugitive."

"Not necessarily. Lots of countries have satellites. It does mean, however, that whoever is after you is likely to be state sponsored, unless someone with unauthorized access to satellite imagery is covertly tracking you. Or, maybe it is an underpaid US Government civil servant doing a little moonlighting.

"You know, Tucker, when you called me and asked me to help you, I didn't take it as seriously as I do now. I thought you might have overreacted. You are truly in danger, my friend, so, it's time to call in reinforcements.

"I also learned that there is a ten million-dollar bounty on your head if you are captured alive."

"Whoa, I wish Maya felt I was worth that much."

"That's the good news."

Tucker's frustration with Tank peaked, "What the fuck is the bad news?"

"Your death is worth one million dollars."

Tucker was shocked. He'd always thought MEG was worth a lot. Though it had recently occurred to him that it was worth a lot to make the technology disappear, it jolted him to hear Tank say it.

"You're right Tank; that is bad news. I thought my demise would be worth more," he joked to hide the fear he felt. "Who are they? Who wants me dead?"

"As to the second question, how much time do we have to talk? Apparently, you are a popular guy. These guys are part of a well-known multinational group of mercenaries.

More than one potential customer contacted them. These guys say their mercenary competitors are also on our trail.

"What do you suggest is our next move, Tucker?"

"Seems to me that we need to engage the Feds somehow."

Tank thought for a moment and said, "I suggest that we hold off on engaging the Feds until we have more evidence to support our claim that you're being tracked down via satellite by alleged allies of the United States. I eventually will learn how these guys tracked us down—I do not buy this satellite BS, but I'll protect you as if it's true just in case I'm wrong. Hell, if it is not by satellite, how could they track us? Even we didn't know we would end up here. How could they know?"

Tucker ground his teeth, shook his head, pursed his lips, and clenched his jaw. "If you were anybody else, I'd try to beat some sense into you. Why hold back information?"

"What?"

Tucker asked in frustration, "Quote, 'tracked down via satellite by alleged allies,' unquote? You want to explain that?"

Tank shrugged his massive shoulders and said, "Oh, yeah. Though the mercenaries are American and Eastern European, these guys were employed by the First Consortium of Nations."

"Though I understand why they'd feel threatened by the discovery, I'm a little surprised that all the member countries could come to an agreement to assassinate an American citizen on American soil."

"We probably need to move before more mercenaries show up. I forced the two remaining mercenaries to dispose of their leader. I'll duct tape them to chairs inside the log home."

The log home had a basement where Tank "secured" the mercenaries under Ram's supervision. As he and Ram returned, Tank said, "It should take them a day to get free given their injuries.

"What do you say we jump into the Jeep and look for supplies and dog food before we go very far? It's usually not a good idea to let Ram get too hungry."

Tucker thought, "What injuries, disposed of how, what supplies?" but decided to ask those questions another time.

Tank said, "Let's go. Time to move."

As they were traversing down a dirt road toward a county-maintained road, Tucker asked, "Where are we going? How are we going to evade detection? What's our short-term survival plan, master of security?"

Tank said, "Hell, I'm going to turn you over to the bad guys and cash in a sweet ten million dollars for Ram and me."

Tucker thought about yelling "bad-bad" but thought better of it in case Ram didn't have a sense of humor.

CHAPTER 10

GREATER WASHINGTON, DC AREA—
OCTOBER 4ᵀᴴ

The head of the intelligence arm of the First Consortium of Nations picked up a satellite phone, contacted his agent in the United States, code-named Aaron, and said, "Tell me you have made progress on eliminating the most recent threat to the Consortium."

Aaron Zyttle immediately began to perspire. The Consortium leader always had that effect on him when they spoke. He responded, "We located the target, successfully got him to ingest the tracking cocktail you provided to us, and dispatched a team of professionals to secure him."

"And?"

"We're awaiting confirmation from the team."

The silence was deafening.

"What are you not telling me?" asked the leader.

"We should have heard something by now, but we've lost contact with them."

"The target is just a simple man with no known defense skills. What's the problem?"

The agent said, "We've launched a surveillance drone to get real-time visuals, which will allow us to assess our overall status."

"You apparently do not understand the consequence of failure."

Aaron started to reply until he realized there was no one on the other end of the satellite phone.

Fairfax County, Virginia

Aaron, also known as Stiletto Man, did not want to stay in the greater Washington, DC, metropolitan area. He thought it was too dangerous. So, he instructed his driver to take him northwest with the mother and daughter in tow. They traveled for hours and stopped only at rest areas for bathroom breaks for the little girl. The ladies' rooms had to be evacuated before Stiletto Man would allow them to go in—so he could go into the ladies' room with them. He gave them no privacy, and this way he ensured that Mrs. Monahan did not leave any messages behind to alert law enforcement.

The kidnappers finally stopped in Cumberland, Maryland, for food where the driver went into a fast food restaurant and brought out meals for all of them. Jenny complained that they didn't have any chicken nuggets, but Dana sternly stopped her from whining, fearful of the wrath of Stiletto Man. A tired and frightened Jenny cried.

Stiletto Man called Art Monahan on his satellite phone at exactly the prearranged time. Art picked up immediately, "Hello, are Dana and Jenny OK? Can I speak with them?"

"In due time," Stiletto Man said just to maintain control of the conversation. "There is an individual who I want you to track by satellite. Can you do that for me?"

Though he wasn't entirely sure he could, it depended on a lot of things, not the least of which was the demand for satellite time by other agencies, but Art volunteered, "Yes, sir, I'll do whatever you want."

"Good, that's the right attitude. I'll give you the target's coordinates and the parameter that needs to be used to track the target when I get them. The target, a man named Tucker Cherokee, consumed some iced tea contaminated with traceable amounts of Technicium-99 radioactive material. Now find him with all your high-tech equipment. Do your stuff. Or I'll do stuff to your wife. You can find him, right?"

"Right. Can I speak with my family now?"

Dana was allowed to speak, "Please, do whatever this man asks you to do. Jenny and I are unharmed, but I'm confident this man will harm us if you don't do as you're told. I love you."

"That's enough," instructed Stiletto Man. "That's proof of life. I'll call you again in six hours." He disconnected the contact.

Aaron Zyttle knew he had to kill his two kidnapped hostages—they had seen his face. His thought drifted to how much he'd enjoy playing with them before he killed them.

Dana also concluded that Stiletto Man would kill them both even if Art did what he was blackmailed to do. At twenty-eight years old, healthy, and fit, she thought she could somehow escape with Jenny. Dana was constantly alert and looked for that opportunity. At least she wore sweats and running shoes in the event that she discovered an opportunity to escape.

Cumberland, Maryland

Aaron Zyttle walked outside the motel room to light up a cigarette and call Art Monahan. Monahan answered on the second ring, "Yes, sir."

"Do you have anything for me?"

"The target is in Grant County in West Virginia. He is headed southwest. I'll catch him. Can I speak to my wife and daughter?"

"No." Aaron disconnected the satellite phone. He thought about Monahan's statement. "He is in Grant County." He had never told Monahan that the target, Tucker, was in Grant County. The only way Monahan could know is if the tracers were working—the chemicals put in Tucker's drink are now in his bloodstream and are emitting a signal. Monahan was doing his job—the plan was working. "I'll keep Mrs. Monahan and her daughter alive a little longer," he thought.

Back in Fort Belvoir, Monahan hoped his lie to Stiletto Man that he could track Tucker by satellite worked—at least long enough to give him a little more time to figure out a plan to get his family back. He hoped Stiletto Man had forgotten that he'd previously given him the coordinates that put the target in Grant County, West Virginia.

While Stiletto Man was outside on the satellite phone, Dana Monahan pretended to be asleep cuddled up against her daughter. Jenny was not handling the kidnapping well, as one would expect, so Dana comforted her as best she could. She felt like garbage—she had not even brushed her auburn hair this morning before she put Jenny in the SUV.

Stiletto Man's driver and guard also thought Dana and Jenny were asleep and had allowed himself some shuteye. The driver/guard had left his cell phone on the table in front of him. Dana had noticed him text on it earlier, so she moved slowly toward the phone, sweating profusely with shaky hands. She picked up the phone and texted her husband, gave him their location and vehicle tag number, and subsequently deleted the text. She crawled back into her cuddle position with Jenny just as Stiletto Man walked back into the cheap motel room to awaken the driver/guard.

Stiletto Man said, "I think it's time to move. Get the car ready. I think that we'll head southwest to the Deep Creek Lake area. I understand it is beautiful there."

Art Monahan received the text from his wife and with enormous relief made the decision to confess to his boss his predicament. With a heavy heart and with great trepidation, Art called his boss, Glenn Fisher, and said, "Sir, we have a security issue I need to discuss with you."

CHAPTER 11

CHICAGO, ILLINOIS—OCTOBER 5TH

Dr. Maya Li, Fermilab physicist, one of three people identified in the YouTube video that had announced the discovery, and lover of the on-the-run Tucker Cherokee, made it successfully to her mother's Chicago Penthouse. The beautiful view from the penthouse of the Great Lake Michigan offered no solace.

The wine her mother had given her didn't help Maya think straight, but it did calm her nerves and make her feel a bit more normal. Maya suspected that Tucker was right and that it was highly probable that Phil's murder had something to do with their discovery. The fact that men with automatic weapons had followed her and tried to kill her convinced her that she either was a target for murder to prevent her from revealing details of the technology, or, worse, she was a target for kidnapping and torture to disclose the secrets as to how to make the technology work.

Maya had crawled through the sunroof of her sports car stuck between a building and a dumpster in the alleyway and jogged the rest of the way to her mother's penthouse. She had heard the automatic gunfire when she was roughly 300 yards away from the jammed sports car and knew immediately that the bullets were meant for her. She thanked God that her car had a sunroof and that she could be far enough away to survive by the time the bad guys following her had caught up with her sports car in the alley.

The story Maya had conveyed to her mother piqued her protective instincts and conjured up Mother Li's impressive intellectual prowess. Maya's mother was a sophisticated and refined woman who almost always maintained her composure. Her calm under crisis helped reassure Maya that things were under control. Her mother's blond hair, blue eyes, and well-maintained figure—even for someone in her early fifties—commanded admiration and respect.

After several hours of planning, assessing options, and performing research on the Internet, they had a plan.

Then they called the Chicago Police.

CHAPTER 12

PITTSBURGH, PENNSYLVANIA— OCTOBER 5TH

"Ah, Sir," Chief Operating Officer Charles Washington heard over the intercom in his Charleston Energy Holdings, LLC, Pittsburgh, Pennsylvania, headquarters office.

"Yes, Connie, what's up?"

"Officer O'Day of the Pittsburgh Police Department and three other officers are here to speak with you."

Charles, a well-dressed, handsome, muscular, sophisticated-looking African American at an imposing six feet two inches tall and 235 pounds with salt and pepper hair, could not think of a single reason why the police would want to speak with him. "OK, send them in."

Connie, the office front desk receptionist, escorted Officer Ryan O'Day and his team into Charles Washington's office. The office had a small round table with three chairs for private company discussions and visitors. "Connie," said Charles, "would you ask someone to bring us an extra chair and coffee?"

"Not necessary, Mr. Washington. We will remain standing, as we will not be long. Where were you on the evening of October 3rd?"

"That was only two days ago. I was right here in Pittsburgh. Why are you asking?"

"Your prints were found on a drinking glass at a murder scene in Cambridge, Massachusetts. Do you own a gun, Mr. Washington?"

"Yes, I have a 9mm Beretta handgun in my bedroom."

"May we inspect your office and home for weapons? We can get a subpoena, if necessary."

"Yes, of course. I have nothing to hide. Who was the murder victim?"

Officer O'Day said, "Do you know a Dr. Phil McPherson?"

"Oh my God, yes! I had dinner with him at Legal Seafood in Boston on, let's see," Charles pulled out his smart phone and looked at his calendar, "September 24. We were trying to negotiate an agreement for our company to license a new discovery, a technology that Entropy developed."

"Please come down to the station with me, Mr. Washington. I have a warrant for your arrest issued by the Cambridge Police Department. It sounds like we will be able to clear this up, but, nonetheless, you'll have to come with us now."

As he was escorted out of the Charleston Energy Holdings Headquarters, Charles said to Connie, "Please ask Stanley to come down to the Pittsburgh Police Station."

Pittsburgh, Pennsylvania

Officer O'Day sat across the table from Charles Washington and his corporate attorney, Stanley Pritchard, in the interrogation room in the Pittsburgh Police Department headquarters.

Washington explained, "I watched a YouTube video published by Entropy that announced a new and intriguing discovery. After looking at the Entropy home web page 'news' tab, I uncovered the names of Tucker Cherokee and Phil McPherson, who were inventors disclosed in the video. I noted that Mr. Cherokee's office is in Alexandria, Virginia, while Mr. McPherson's office is … or rather was … in Boston. It was just as easy for me to get to Alexandria, Virginia, adjacent to Reagan National Airport, as it was to get to Boston's Logan Airport from my office in Pittsburgh, so, it didn't make any difference which person I reached first. I was unable to reach Mr. Cherokee, so I contacted Dr. McPherson to schedule an appointment.

"Upon arrival at Entropy's offices the next day, I was escorted into Phil's office. I told him that I knew he must be busy and his phone must be ringing off the hook.

"He said to me that he didn't make the connection until now, but he recognized me from my football-playing days at Mississippi State.

"He stated that if his memory served him right, I was an All-American linebacker drafted into the pros by the New Orleans Saints in the first round. He told me that he was sorry about my knees, which prevented me from playing even one game, other than that preseason game when an asshole from the Raiders hit me with an illegal block at the knees.

"I told Phil that the Raider never said he was sorry. In fact, he brags about it, wears it as a badge of honor. Fortunately, as justice serves us, he was cut and never played again in the NFL."

Officer O'Day said, "Mr. Washington, get to the point."

"I told him that Charleston Energy Holdings was excited about his recent discovery and that we'd like to discuss the feasibility of becoming the exclusive licensee of the technology for commercialization. I told him we believe we could offer an attractive package that will serve Entropy well, that we could demonstrate that our plan for commercialization would be rapid, aggressive, and worldwide—that Entropy could expect to make billions of dollars.

"With that introduction, I proposed that we would like to get on his calendar to make a formal presentation of our marketing strategy and business plan to his company's decision-makers.

"Phil had said, 'As you pointed out earlier, my phone and the phones of my colleagues have been ringing off the hook. We are inundated with requests to meet with companies like Charleston Energy Holdings. The international community is also swamping us with requests. We have a board of directors meeting tomorrow, after which, we will hopefully make an internal decision about our path forward, but I will bring your offer to the table.'

"I thanked him and told him that it was all I could ask for. I then stated that I had made reservations at Legal Seafood for 7:30 p.m. that night and asked if he would join me for dinner so we could further the discussion. He accepted.

A Deadly Discovery

"At dinner, we continued the business discussion and discussed the short- and long-term potential for the technology, its commercial application, and its value, as well as how the two companies could structure an agreement and other relevant business-related issues. We even had time to discuss the NFL and Phil's favorite football topic, the New England Patriots. We parted, and that was the last I heard from Dr. McPherson."

Boston, Massachusetts

What Charles Washington and Phil McPherson didn't know back on September 24th on the night they went to dinner was that a listening device had been placed under the table by a waiter to record their conversation—it was the easiest $500 the server had made all week.

Gang Chung took video and digital pictures of the two men he followed. The video, digital photos, and recording were uploaded and wirelessly forwarded to his contact in Mexico City. His contact then encrypted all the data and sent the information to Beijing.

CHAPTER 13

ARLINGTON, VIRGINIA—
OCTOBER 5TH

Ray LaSalle was never late. He was anal about being on time, yet it was two minutes past 1700.

General Woodhead awaited the arrival of Lt. Col. Ray LaSalle in a Pentagon 'C'- Ring Sensitive Compartmental Information Facility. The Secretary of Defense was expecting a report tomorrow from the Joint Chiefs of Staff. General Woodhead was a kiss-ass bureaucrat who never had an original thought. He was a small man at five feet eight inches tall weighed 170 pounds; and had a permanent chip on his shoulder. Though two-star generals are well paid, he thought all generals should be paid more than members of Congress or senators. Woodhead depended on Lt. Col. Ray LaSalle for strategic planning, and he knew his career success depended on Ray's situational assessments. Woodhead would hand deliver Ray's work product directly to the Chairman of the Joint Chiefs of Staff with self-serving edits.

The keypad outside the room announced that Ray had arrived. The door opened, and a disheveled LaSalle walked in. He was unshaven, his eyes were swollen and red, and his hair was uncombed. This behavior was most uncharacteristic, and so Woodhead was concerned.

"Well, LaSalle, you look awful. What happened?" General Woodhead asked.

"I have completed the scenario assessment you requested, sir. It took me roughly twenty hours. The postulated scenarios are not guaranteed to happen. However, their consequences are high if they do. The suggested potential options to mitigate the consequences are bold and will require aggressive action by the White House."

General Woodhead said, "Please, continue."

"First, my assumption is that the discovery of the technology as suggested in the YouTube video produced by Entropy is real. Based on that assumption, sir, I submit the following consequences:

"One, Russia will feel threatened for her economic survival and take whatever action is necessary to suffocate the technology's commercial application.

"Two, the First Consortium of Nations, better known by their popular name around here as the Consortium of Fascists, will feel equally threatened and will also take whatever action is necessary to suffocate the discovery's commercial application. As you probably know, sir, the United Nations had been deemed ineffective, if not incompetent, by the undemocratic nations ruled by dictators, fascists, families, tribes, kings, and militaries that comprise the Consortium. The First Consortium of Nations was formed as a shadow or alternative to the United Nations, and its membership includes such fine and upstanding nations as North Korea, Venezuela, Libya, Syria, Cuba, Somalia, and Yemen. Their goal is to become so powerful as to make the United Nations irrelevant.

"Three, Israel, the People's Republic of China, and Germany will do whatever it takes to secure the technology as their own.

"Four, news of the discovery will drive investors out of affected S&P 500 stocks, ETFs, MLPs, and mutual funds. The DOW will likely drop around twenty percent within two weeks.

"Five, Iran will take advantage of the chaos and support instability in other Middle East nations, and Hezbollah will attack Israel from Syria, Jordan, Palestine, and Egypt.

"Six, real unemployment in the United States will rise within two months.

"Seven, our neighbors, Canada and Mexico, will fall into a recession.

"On the positive side, some industries like aluminum, steel, chemical production, the auto industry, and agriculture will benefit from the discovery. Household bills will decrease, and the consumers will have more money to spend on other items, stimulating the economy."

General Woodhead asked, "From a military preparedness standpoint, what strategies do you recommend to the Pentagon to present to SecDef?"

"One, President Petrov will do something, sir. Count on it. NATO countries need to be on high alert. He's blackmailed Eastern Europe and the Ukraine for years. He won't like the impact this new technology will have on Mother Russia. I'd suggest that the State Department refuse any visas for Russians entering the

United States for the next several weeks to prevent GRU operatives from getting too close to the inventors.

"Two, provide protection for the inventors. My guess is that the lives of the inventors are at risk. Sir, I'd get the FBI or US Marshals to guard the inventors.

"Three, for reasons of national security, I'd suggest that the president issues a directive to stop the use of the technology until the Environmental Protection Agency completes an environmental assessment, which will allow the government to control the speed with which we integrate the technology into the economy."

General Woodhead said, "I'm still waiting for the military strategic plan you suggest."

"Yes, sir. Four, send a naval fleet to the eastern Mediterranean to support Israel. Arab nations will feel threatened and somehow blame Israel for their loss of Arab influence.

"Five, protect the Strait of Hormuz. Iran will use this crisis to stop shipments through the Strait.

"Six, maintain a robust Pacific fleet. China will take advantage of our preoccupation with the Middle East and Russia. We have a weak administration, and China, like Iran and Russia, will take advantage of it."

General Woodhead said, "Thank you for your usual good work and all your effort. I'll pass this on to the Chairman of the Joint Chiefs of Staff."

LaSalle added, "I don't think we have much time to save the inventors. Please pass on that it is urgent to protect them from the Russians, Chinese, and Consortium of Nations members."

CHAPTER 14

MOSCOW, RUSSIA—OCTOBER 5ᵀᴴ

"**Y**ou see, there is a God after all!"

Since the fall of the Soviet Union and the universal, though reluctant, acceptance of capitalism, Russia had leveraged, to the maximum extent possible, the concept of "supply and demand." Russia's President Vladimir Petrov frequently said to other members of his atheistic regime, "Russia will use capitalism against the western fathers of capitalism."

Petrov was old school. He remembered the pride of being Russian back in the heyday of the Soviet Empire, back when the Soviet Union was a feared superpower. His mandate, his fate, his legacy, his destiny was to return Russia to a dominant superpower.

One of Petrov's greatest achievements, as far as he was concerned, was the transition of one of the old KGB intelligence gathering units into the Intellectual Property Monitoring Ministry. The ministry's job was to steal from other nations technology and trade secrets that would benefit Mother Russia. The trade secrets that were stolen from other countries previously during his regime resulted in an enormous increase in Russia's oil and natural gas exports. Petrov repeatedly stated, "Screw international patent laws." He didn't rise to his position by playing fair. "Fairness is a foolish concept." He didn't rise to his position because of his charm or because he was handsome or because he was a compellingly eloquent speaker. He possessed none of those qualities. Petrov's attributes would have to be described as nefarious and Machiavellian, and he admitted to himself that he was likely a sociopath. "You can't implement a successful economic strategy if you care about whether people in Ukraine freeze to death because their government won't pay the Russian winter price for natural gas. Mother Russia is like a Camellia flower; it blooms in cold weather."

The devout fascist was not physically imposing at five feet seven inches in height, 160 pounds, and with a full head of hair of which he was proud (after all, he was sixty-four years old). But there was something about his eyes that would stop you cold. He even surprised himself when he looked in a mirror. They were intense, almost iridescent. Sometimes his eyes were green, sometimes they appeared greenish blue, and sometimes they appeared gray. They were captivating, hypnotizing and frightening.

Despite his undersized frame, he marketed himself to the Russian proletariat as a bare-chested, horseback-riding, macho man. Vladimir Petrov was referred to as the "Grey Cardinal" by his protection detail and both his friends and "Hardman" by most Russians.

Unlike Petrov, the General Minister of the Intellectual Property Monitoring Ministry, Dmitry Ranstropov, was large, round, and sloppy in his physical presentation. Petrov attributed his subordinate's pathetic appearance to Russia's number one pastime—vodka. Petrov himself never let the plague get to him, and distrusted anyone who let vodka take control of their soul. Vodka loosened the tongue.

Dmitry submitted the most recent report listing new technologies under development worldwide that were of interest to Russia. The report contained information gathered through whatever means was necessary—cyber theft, eavesdropping, threats, blackmail, bribery, or even more brutal means. The list was matrixed against the probability that the technology would be proven valuable, as determined by a Russian team of scientists and engineers, and the technology's economic impact on the success of Russia.

Petrov summoned Dmitry monthly, along with the Minister of Energy, Sergei Novak, to review the status of all items on the list to determining a path forward toward Russian glory. They usually spent hours discussing developments in technologies like hydraulic fracturing to establish what new information Russia must secure.

Not discussed because Petrov was "handling" it, was the American technology developed by Entropy.

Moscow, Russia

Dmitri Ranstropov sat with Serge Novak in the warmth of Ranstropov's office and watched the YouTube video for the third time while he enjoyed refreshments. Dmitri said, "I still don't believe it. You know, Serge, you can't believe anything you see on YouTube. People are talented with Photoshop and things like that. I saw a video with Hillary Clinton's head on a porn queen's body."

Serge enjoyed pushing Dmitri into a state of apoplexy. "True," said Serge, "but there's also an announcement made by a firm called Entropy that the discovery has been verified and validated."

"An elaborate con. Entropy is probably a CIA-funded capitalist organization trying to raise private funds for 'more research.' There's not one chance in a million this is true," said Dmitri.

"So, you are not going to bring this to the Hardman's attention?"

"No. The old bastard will overreact. The next thing you know there will be a tragic accident. The entire staff at Entropy will die in an airline crash."

President Vladimir Petrov sat in his office eavesdropping on the conversation with the new nano-bug manufactured by the Japanese that the Russians reverse engineered. He thought, "That sounds like a pretty good idea."

Leesburg, Virginia

Leesburg was a quaint little town about forty miles west of Washington, DC, in one of the wealthiest and fastest-growing counties in the nation. It's horse country with lots of old money. Leesburg was not the kind of place where you would expect to see Russian mobsters. A five-year-old, $850,000 residential brick house sat on 6.5 acres of land. It looked like many other homes in the same community—except for the basement. The basement looked like what you would expect to have seen in Cheyenne Mountain with many large flat screens, thirty monitors, four people scurrying around, and lots of apparent access control and security measures.

The relationship between the Russian Government and the Russian mob was simple: the government ignored the illegal activities of the mob if the mob helped the government with black operations. So, when Myron Kazinski received an encrypted message from Alex Pashkov, the first cousin of the president of Russia, Kazinski was eager to respond.

Alex showed up with the hard drive he had extracted from Tucker Cherokee's apartment in Alexandria and asked Kazinski to find out what was on it. Alex advised Kazinski to look for keywords like "McPherson and Li." Kazinski instructed one of his younger computer experts, one who looked like he was still in high school, and repeated the instructions.

Pashkov and Kazinski discussed common business issues for two hours and consumed copious quantities of Kalashnikov vodka. They discussed the drug trade, the escort business, gambling, and intelligence gathering. Kazinski offered Alex the use of one of his girls, which Alex eagerly accepted but suggested that he wait until after they completed their mutual business.

Myron Kazinski was frightened of Pashkov. Though he had never personally been threatened by him, he knew him by reputation. Alex was a well-connected assassin with sadistic tendencies. Uncomfortable, Myron checked on the status of his young computer hacker—the hacker was ready to discuss what he had uncovered.

After convening in Kazinski's office, the young Russian said, "It was easy to hack into the hard drive and get past the password. On his hard drive, there are many downloaded articles, papers, websites, and scanned documents on scientific research. But all the information is easily downloaded from the web, nothing particularly private. The emails between this Cherokee guy and the lady named Maya Li contained the only documents on the subject items of interest. Apparently, their relationship was more than just business. There were also emails between Cherokee and the guy named McPherson on the subject, but again, nothing special."

"Anything in the emails about where Cherokee might go in October," asked Alex?

"I didn't look, but I can go back and check that."

"OK, and when you come back, also see if you know where we can find this Li lady," instructed Alex.

"Maybe she knows where he is."

CHAPTER 15

GRANT COUNTY, WEST VIRGINIA— OCTOBER 5TH

"First, we need a new ride," Tank suggested, "just in case they've figured out who your protector is."

Tucker said, "You mean the Jeep is registered to Ram?"

"I used an encrypted satellite phone to contact the cavalry, our reinforcement, Powers. A Ford F-150 four-wheel-drive quad cab waits for us in Seneca Rock, about thirty minutes from here. We modified the truck in a way that may require you to drive instead of me. Hell, it's only fair that you get to chauffeur me around. We lined the roof with lead, and the windows are lead-impregnated and bulletproof. The head height is, therefore, lower and I won't be able to drive it as well as you can. You short six-feet one-inch guys have some advantages."

"Ah," said Tucker, "you mean you've never had sex in a Volkswagen. You don't know what you missed.

"The shielding is so they can't find me via satellite or drone by detecting whatever is in my bloodstream. Good thinking.

"No wonder they pay you the big bucks. What an analytical mind! After we stop and get Ram some food, we need to set up a secure forward operating base from where we can implement your duplicitous and nefarious plan to get all of us out of this fucking mess where we're hunted down like dogs by mercenaries."

Ram cocked his head.

"Sorry, Ram," said Tank. "Tucker, I'm sure you could use some food, too. To answer your other question, I'll respond to the question with a question. What is West Virginia famous for?"

"This is no time to share West Virginia jokes, Tank. Besides, I don't have a sister."

"Coal, coal mines, coal mines that are shut down and lightly guarded. You must admit, satellites and drones have minimal surveillance capabilities for detecting people hundreds of feet underground. Powers has identified a prime potential forward operating base in Davis, West Virginia."

The part of West Virginia around Davis is most known for its ski resorts in the Canaan Valley, Blackwater Falls State Park, the Monongahela National Forest, and Dolly Sods Wilderness. It was less known for its coal mines that feed the Mount Storm Power Station back in Grant County. The Davis Coal Mine provided bituminous coal to Mount Storm until it was finally mined out. Its closure five years earlier was conducted without fanfare. The 190 employees were transferred to another mine in the county to continue to support the power plant. However, the owner of the mine, Charleston Energy Holdings, LLC, determined that it was less expensive to guard the mine than to close it permanently. It was guarded to protect the intruders, not to protect anything in the mine. CEH submitted a permit to dig deeper into the mine to see whether there was more valuable coal another few hundred feet deeper.

CEH employed four guards, one per shift and one rotating shift guard. There was never more than one guard on-site at any time except for during shift change when they handed off the baton. The guards occupied a double-wide trailer that was used for office functions back when the mine was operational.

The most excitement Jimmy Jordan, (JJ), ever experienced was running off a couple of drunken kids who wanted to explore the mine shaft. He had never previously experienced a 9mm Beretta pressed onto the side of his head. JJ just about wet his britches.

"If you have any weapons in this trailer, you might want to show me where you keep them. Now." Tank encouraged JJ to stand up. He patted him down. He found no weapons on JJ, unless you consider his little pocket knife a weapon. Tank kept the Beretta up against JJ's head. "The weapons, son." JJ opened a coat cabinet and pulled out a Winchester pump action 12-gauge shotgun, loaded, and with the safety on.

"There's a 22 rifle in my pickup truck. I shoot varmints from time to time."

"You want to secure that?" Tank asked Tucker, "while I have a private discussion with our new friend here."

Tucker left the guard shack to open the unlocked Silverado and found JJ's Remington 597 long rifle in the back seat. He waited outside to give Tank and Ram time to persuade JJ to cooperate. He placed the rifle in the newly acquired Ford F-150 and swapped plates with JJ's truck just in case they were being tracked somehow by the bad guys.

After only a few minutes, the front door to the trailer opened. Tank said, "Come on in and meet our new associate. JJ here has graciously agreed to support us. He says there is another trailer in the mine from which we can work at the 200-foot level, so it is not too far down. A rail car runs down to that level and power to operate the rail cars and run the lights is active. He's volunteered to give us a little tour down there. His cooperation is remarkable, and his decision-making skills are admirable. However, it will cost us a few bucks to keep him on our payroll.

"He has agreed to run to Davis for food, water, supplies, and anything else we need, and I am confident he will keep his mouth shut. Our only problem here is that other guards work the two other shifts. We'll have to stay down in the mine during those shifts to make sure no one knows we are here. JJ confessed that there are no operating video cameras inside the mine."

Tucker asked, "Why are you so confident that JJ will keep his mouth shut?"

"What would you decide to do if you were given a choice of either an extra month's salary for a few days of silence or the opportunity to wrestle with Ram? I have his driver's license, so we know where he lives if he violates our agreement."

"JJ," Tank continued, "is there a Radio Shack in Davis and a place where you can buy some Purina dog chow?" JJ nodded his head up and down. "Good, here's what we need." Tank handed JJ a list and some cash.

JJ was a five-foot ten-inch, 140-pound redneck that you could tell before he lit up, smoked too much. He wore a light blue work shirt provided to him by Charleston Energy Holdings with a CEH logo on one side and his name on the other. He wore matching work pants to complete his uniform. With brown eyes and brown hair, JJ was nondescript.

Tucker asked Tank, "Where are you getting this money? How are we paying for all this?"

"I told you, I'm going to turn you in for the ten million dollars the Consortium is offering for you."

Tank realized that joke was no longer funny and said, "I pulled a lot of cash out when I got your call. As you know my firm has done well over the past five years. We will bill Entropy when this is all over. Powers is a subcontractor to *White Knight*. If we fail, then we won't submit an invoice for payment."

Tucker said, "You know Entropy does not have a contract with *White Knight* and that you're at risk without a signed contract."

Tank looked down at Tucker, rolled his eyes and said, "Do you think anybody would be stupid enough not to pay Powers, Ram, and me?"

Tucker said, "Good point."

Leesburg, Virginia.

"Is there anything else I can do for you, Alex?" asked Myron Kazinski.

"Yes, in fact, there is. I would like to secure a Rocket Propelled Grenade (RPG) launcher with three rounds."

Myron Kazinski's men were loading the RPG into Alex Pashkov's ubiquitous white van when Alex received a call.

"Cousin, how are you," said President Petrov. "Have you made progress?"

"Not fast enough, but the friends you put me onto are helpful and resourceful."

"I have other friends, some that monitor airwaves. I've learned some things. The person for whom you traveled so far to meet is in the wilderness town of Davis, West Virginia. He's at a coal mine called Davis Coal Mine. I think it's a four or five-hour drive from where you are."

"It's great to have friends," responded Alex.

"I think he may leave there soon, so if you want to meet him, you might want to leave now."

Davis, West Virginia

JJ returned from his trip to Radio Shack, the local grocery store, and Subway and gave Tank the requested supplies. Tank asked, "How soon before your replacement gets here?"

JJ looked at his Timex watch and said, "Ninety minutes."

"Well, we don't have enough time to set up the surveillance video equipment and intrusion detection system before he gets here. We should do that tomorrow. I'll pay you overtime, JJ if you stay discreetly out of sight in your truck and observe the surroundings for anything out of the ordinary."

"Except for you guys," JJ said, "there hasn't been anything out of the ordinary in months around here."

"I want you to stay awake through both shifts. Get some coffee. You can sleep during your shift tomorrow."

JJ asked, "If I do find something unusual, what am I supposed to do? You won't be able to receive a call down there in the mine."

"If a vehicle looks suspicious, take down their tag number. If they look like they have spotted you, hit the road. Call me because I will not be down in the mine with Tucker. I'll be close to the mine mouth and able to take calls. Disconnect your interior lights in the truck," Tank continued. "And stay awake."

"Can I have my varmint rifle back?"

"No," Tank said definitively.

Davis, West Virginia

Time alone at the top of the mine all night gave Tank too much time to think. When Tank had too much time, his mind wandered to Jolene. Tank missed her. Jolene had been Tank's "significant other" for going on ten years now. She was just about as tough as Tank. As a marine, Jolene Landrieu did two tours in Iraq. Like Tank, she also trained under Powers but not at the same time as Tank. Tank and Jolene met at a private firing range and hit it off quickly. Tank always had difficulty courting women because of his intimidating size and his misleading appearance. He didn't look like he would be very gentle.

Jolene did not like to fraternize with fellow marines, who were the only people who hit on her. She intimidated most other men with her military bearing, her six-foot one-inch height, and her hand-to-hand combat training. Jolene worked hard not to be very feminine in outward appearance to avoid sexually aggressive male marines. Her blond hair was short, she wore no makeup, and she always restrained her breasts in a sports bra. But that was the outward appearance. Behind closed doors in the privacy of their bed, she was quite feminine, and Tank was quite gentle.

She loved Tank to death. Through her eyes, she saw a Hispanic Howie Long. Tank even kept his hair styled in a 1950's-style flat top. She could joke with Tank without the risk of hurting his feelings. In fact, she found Tank's self-deprecating humor endearing. Tank loved Jolene's smile and infectious laugh. It put the world in perspective.

Jolene retired from the US Marine Corps and joined the *White Knights* as a personal security specialist. She was on assignment in Thailand for Tank, but he wished she wasn't.

Davis, West Virginia

JJ turned his guard duty shift over to his night shift replacement. Reggie Thigpen was older than JJ. He was a fifty-eight-year-old black man who looked like he'd been dragged through hell and back. He looked ill. He was maybe six feet tall and 160 pounds. The whites of his eyes were yellow, and his teeth were few and far between. JJ turned the keys over to Reggie and said on his way out, "See you tomorrow."

Reggie was asleep ten minutes into his shift.

JJ went into Davis, got a thermos of coffee, and returned to a place outside the mine. He found a spot about 200 yards from the mine entrance and parked his Silverado with the front facing the guard shack.

Absolutely nothing happened all night. JJ fought off sleep as best he could. County Road 9 was not a well-traveled road, so when the same car bearing Maryland plates passed by twice, JJ paid attention. The Dodge Durango slowed down each time it passed the entrance to the mine. JJ got the plate number and called Tank. "Sir, we might have a visitor," JJ explained his observation.

"OK, JJ. Good job. Now, go home and come back for your shift. I want you out of the way in case they spotted you." Tank proceeded to call Powers and said, "This mine is a great place to set up a forward operating base if no one knows we're here. It's a death trap if they know we're here. There's only one way out. One round from a shoulder-launched anti-tank weapon into the mine mouth and we're finished. It's the Alamo.

"We need the cavalry to make sure we're alone. Can you make that happen? We have reason to believe someone at least suspects we're here." Tank explained to Powers about JJ's observations.

Powers said, "As usual, I'm way ahead of you. That car with Maryland plates was me. Your flunky was evident. If I had been a bad guy, he would be dead by now. But your point is well taken. We need to move to a more strategic location as soon as we figure out how to keep Tucker from being tracked. I'll get a doctor friend of mine into the coal mine for you tomorrow. He'll take some blood samples from Tucker to see what's in the bloodstream. We'll get the blood analyzed, and we'll figure a plan from there."

Powers was a famous soldier emblematic of "*The Tip of America's Spear.*" The United States has the most capable special operations forces in the world, and Powers was known to be at the head of the class. As a Green Beret, he led a twelve-man A-team multiple times in black operations. He led a team in operations "Just

'Cause" that resulted in the capture of General Manuel Noriega. Powers later became famous within the Special Forces community by training candidates in hand-to-hand combat, close-quarters combat, martial arts, hand weapons, and tactical weapons.

Tucker felt very secure with Powers, Tank, and Ram as his personal security team.

Grant County, West Virginia

The two mercenaries in the basement of the log home were trying to escape, but they were still duct taped to chairs with their ankles tied together, their mouths duct taped, and their hands tied behind the back of the chairs. To add to their precarious predicament both were seriously injured from the interrogation by the large man and his dog.

The American mercenary had a broken trigger finger and a dislocated shoulder that hurt like hell. The Czech mercenary could not walk, as both of his ankles were broken. They'd been tied up for eighteen hours and had not made much progress in getting free. At least the big guy hadn't killed them—unless his intent was to starve them to death.

They both heard it.

Someone was upstairs in the log home. Whoever it was, they walked around upstairs, quietly. The owners would not try to be so quiet, so it had to be that either the big guy had come back for them or, it was someone else. They were silently praying for "someone else."

The door to the basement cracked opened.

Quietly, someone started down the basement stairs, five seconds between each footfall. At the bottom of the stairs, Graf said into his microphone, "I found them. They're alive." He looked around and said, "At least two of them are alive, but I don't see Mario." Graf searched and cleared the basement before he tore the duct tape off the American mercenary's mouth.

"Boy, are we glad to see you. We need some medical attention and some food and water. We're starving. Petr over there is in bad shape. He can't walk. We'll need additional manpower to get him to a hospital."

"Shut up!" yelled Graf. "What the hell happened here? How could some scientist nerd type get the better of you alleged professionals? And where the fuck is Mario?"

"Mario is dead. The big guy in the Jeep and his dog ambushed us, took us prisoner, tortured us, and left us here to die."

"Tortured you? So, he interrogated you? What did you tell him?"

"We didn't want to end up like Mario, so we answered whatever question he asked. He knows the Consortium is our client and that Tucker Cherokee has some sort of chemical tracer in his bloodstream that allows us to track him."

"What happened to Mario?"

"The big guy's German shepherd mauled Mario to death. We would have endured the same fate if we hadn't cooperated and answered his questions."

By this time, Brock made it into the basement and overheard the conversation. Brock called Aaron on the satellite phone and debriefed him on the status of the mission. Aaron said over the phone from his car, "Get all the information you can about the 'big guy and his dog' and when you are satisfied they have nothing else to contribute, kill the wisenheimers."

Dana Monahan overheard what Aaron, Stiletto Man, said over the phone and knew she and her daughter would not get out of this alive. She hugged Jenny hard.

Jenny asked, "What's the matter, Mom? Why are you crying? I wanna go home. Can we go home now?"

CHAPTER 16

WASHINGTON, DC—OCTOBER 6TH

At 0700 the President of the United States (POTUS), Jefferson King, presided over a meeting in the Situation Room of the White House. In attendance was the Chairman of the Joint Chiefs of Staff, the Secretary of Defense, the Secretary of State, the White House Chief of Staff, the National Security Advisor, the Secretary of the Treasury, the Director of the CIA, the Director of the NSA, and the Attorney General.

"Let's get started," the President said. "What developments occurred overnight?"

The National Security Advisor, Wendy Smith, somewhat of a hawk, spoke first and stated, "We understand that Russia has announced a thirty-five percent increase in the price of natural gas to Ukraine and other Eastern European nations, effective immediately. We see this as an aggressive move to secure control of these countries. Unless these countries acquiesce to Russian political positions, Russia will continue to raise the price of heating fuel. I think you can anticipate further instability in the region."

POTUS asked, "How is this our problem? What exactly are we expected to do to alter Russia's behavior?" He looked around the room with his challenging body language and raised chin for an answer but received no advice. "OK, let's move on to the next issue."

Oscar Becker, Director of the NSA, spoke and said, "The Consortium convened a special meeting last week. Since that meeting, there has been a lot of chatter about a new course of action against the United States. There are no specifics, Mr. President, but we intensified our monitoring of communications. As soon as we have something, I'll bring it to the Situation Room."

"If I may add, Mr. President," interrupted the Secretary of Defense, "the two previously mentioned issues that involve Russia and the Consortium may be connected. For contingency planning purposes, the Pentagon assessed the impact of a new American discovery, referred to in the Pentagon by Entropy's method of identification, Project MEG.

"The international entity most negatively affected by this development is the Consortium. We believe that they will do anything to keep the new technology from becoming exposed."

The Secretary of the Treasury added, "I heard about this discovery. There will be serious short-term negative impacts domestically as well if the merits of this technology are true. The discovery will seriously impact sectors of the economy, though, eventually, it could be a cure for many US systemic economic problems."

"Correct," added the Secretary of Defense. "One assessment is that the Dow Jones average and the dollar will take a significant hit in the near term and unemployment will rise. But maybe, more importantly, we can expect an escalating international crisis."

The Secretary of State, Walter Askeland, interrupted and stated, "Let me guess: you recommend an increase in NATO forces in the region. You guys will provoke another war. It's a self-fulfilling prophecy. The military takes actions that cause the very threat you tried to prevent. Same old story."

POTUS leaned back in his chair, used his left hand to remove his reading glasses, used the same hand to rub his furrowed brow with his knuckles, and looked around the room to make eye contact with each attendee.

He was pissed. No one spoke.

Finally, President King said, "Don't blindside me, again. Apparently, I'm the last person in this room to know what this discovery is, why it is so impactful, and what its international implications are. The DoD has already given it a code name, yet I'd never heard of it before this meeting."

A few of the meeting attendees wanted to speak up and admit they had never heard of it but knew to keep their mouths shut when POTUS was angry.

He looked over at his Chief of Staff and asked, "Do I have a hole in my schedule today? If not, cancel something and replace it with another meeting. I want a full briefing on this discovery.

"Back to the current issue, which involves the Consortium and Russia. Is there any news from the intelligence side of the house to add to this subject?"

CIA Director Watts responded, "Recently, a lot of bad guys have entered the United States. There seems to be a plethora of mercenaries from Eastern Europe and

Russia in the country. Even Vladimir Petrov's psychopath cousin is in the country. A surveillance camera with facial recognition capabilities picked him up in the Atlanta Hartsville Airport. Also, we recently learned that Gang Chung, a People's Republic of China industrial espionage agent, was identified in Boston through a surveillance camera. My British friends at MI6 and Israel's Mossad have advised us that they have picked up an unusual amount of chatter that implies that several assassins who are typically funded by Iran or Libya are in the country. We don't know why they are here. Now that we know about the discovery, we'll investigate the relationship between their presences in the country with that development."

The Secretary of Defense stated, "I'd like to add for the benefit of my colleagues here that one of the inventors of the subject discovery, Dr. Phil McPherson, Chief Scientist at Entropy, was murdered in Cambridge yesterday. I only bring this up because you spotted Gang Chung in the Boston area."

POTUS asked, "How many people know how to implement this new technology, what did you code name it, "MEG?"

SecDef answered, "Yes, sir. We're confident that an Entropy employee by the name of Tucker Cherokee; a national lab contractor, Dr. Maya Li; and the late Phil McPherson are the only people who know how to make the new technology work. We don't know how many others know—if it, in fact, does work and is not just another bad science-type announcement. Entropy, by the way, is a government contractor. We can exert some influence on their willingness to cooperate with us."

POTUS said, "Do we need to give the two remaining inventors of Project MEG protection? And based on the potential short-term downside of the technology to the US economy, should we control its commercialization?"

The Attorney General spoke for the first time, "We should give these two inventors the protections of the US Marshals and treat them like they are in the witness protection program, at least until we conclude whether they are the targets of the mercenaries and assassins in the country.

"As far as control of the commercialization of the invention, unless there is some danger to the public, I'm afraid we are constitutionally prohibited from interfering with free trade."

The Chairman of the Joint Chiefs of Staff spoke up and said, "Though this is not a military issue, our analyst who assessed the international threat 'suggested' and I emphasize the word 'suggested,' Mr. President, that possibly the EPA should review the invention and its environmental impact to users. That could delay commercialization by many months and give us time to comprehensively assess the consequences to world order."

"Mr. Attorney General, instruct the US Marshals to protect these two scientists. Instruct the FBI to give the US Marshals all the support they need. I'll have my Chief of Staff have the Director of the EPA report here tomorrow morning for the national security briefing.

"Director Becker and Director Watts, please provide the Department of Justice any intelligence you can to locate the assassins and mercenaries on our soil. Keep my Chief of Staff posted on any developments.

"All of you who have the honor of sitting at this table each morning better figure out pretty damn soon what the hell is going on.

"And do a better job of keeping the White House informed."

CHAPTER 17

FORT BELVOIR, VIRGINIA— OCTOBER 6TH

The satellite phone rang.

Art Monahan engaged the phone, took a deep breath, and said, "Hello."

Aaron said, "It's time for you to perform. I'm sure your wife would like for you to perform—finally." He chuckled and then paused.

"Of course," Art said. "May I speak to my wife?"

"Of course."

"Art, I want you to know that Jenny and I love you. Good luck, Sweetheart," Dana Monahan said with a heavy heart. Jenny was saying something in the background, but Art couldn't hear what she said because his brief contact with his loved ones was cut off by Stiletto Man much too quickly.

"That's enough. Now get going. I'll call you back in two hours."

Art did not admit to Stiletto Man that he could not do what Art said he could do. He didn't even admit it to himself. Stiletto Man obviously had no comprehension of satellite imaging and tracking limitations. His customer, The Consortium of Nations, must have falsely told Stiletto Man that a satellite could read the date on a nickel. So, Stiletto Man assumed you could find an individual anywhere in the world by satellite as if a satellite hovered over every part of the world continuously. Art knew that as soon as he admitted to Aaron that he couldn't find the target, his family would die. Art delayed the moment of reckoning as he hoped for an epiphany or a miracle of some sort.

The idea that a small amount of Technicium-99 radioisotope introduced into Tucker Cherokee's body via his tea would emit enough radiation to track him by satellite was ridiculous. But, nonetheless, that was what Stiletto Man believed.

Art's office phone rang—not the satellite phone this time. "Yes," he answered.

Art's boss said, "We have an emergency. The director instructed us to support an Attorney General lead mission to find a needle in a haystack—an individual. However, though the request to support a domestic target of interest is unusual, it comes from the very top."

"Of all times," Art thought. "I can't support the AG's mission and Jenny simultaneously. I'll fake it while I try to find Stiletto Man's target."

Art said, "Where do I start, who and what do I look for?"

"The license number of the target's car, a Mustang, is EMP-5454, Virginia. Track down its black box tracking device through the frequency emitted. That's a start. I'll be down in your office in a few minutes."

Since his boss was on his way down to join him, he started planning on how to track both targets simultaneously. Art entered the license plate number into the Virginia DMV database to find the model of vehicle, and, therefore, the black box frequency.

Art couldn't believe his good luck—a miracle happened—he might be able to save his family after all. The vehicle was registered to Tucker Cherokee.

Both the US Government and Stiletto Man were looking for the same target. "Why? What's going on here?" He typed in a few commands and located the vehicle in question. It was in a quarry on the border of Grant and Hardy counties in West Virginia. Art pulled up the satellite imagery of the vehicle and zoomed in for a closer look.

Art's boss walked in just about the time he printed out a copy of the photo. Art's boss said, "That was quick work." I'll contact the AG. Stand by.

"Sir," Art's boss said into the phone to the AG, "here are the coordinates of Mr. Cherokee's vehicle. It is stationary. He is not alive inside the vehicle, as there are no heat signatures displayed. Advise us what you would like for us to do next."

The Attorney General said, "We'll get local law enforcement on-site immediately. Send a helicopter with our FBI Critical Incident Response Group and determine a path forward. In the meantime, survey the area and let us know if anything looks unusual."

It was time for Art to shit or get off the pot. Art, desperately wanting to find something tangible to save his wife and daughter, began a grid-by-grid survey using various filters. First, he looked carefully in the quarry to see whether a body was evident—nothing. Then he widened his search until his boss's secure phone rang again.

The AG said, "West Virginia Highway Patrol responded to a call from a homeowner in the area, which resulted in the discovery of two bodies. The men were tied up in the basement of a log home not five miles from the quarry. Each shot in the forehead. It's not likely to be a coincidence. I'll send the coordinates of the log home to you. Move the satellite survey to that area."

Deep Creek Lake, Maryland

Stiletto Man and his driver selected an empty home on Deep Creek Lake to break into and occupy, and from which to operate. It was isolated, had no security system, and had a beautiful view of the lake. He estimated that he could operate from the new location for twenty-four hours or so without risk of being discovered. The kitchen had some canned food for the whiny little girl and her desirable-looking mother. Hopefully, they would stop complaining. Aaron sent his driver out for fresh food and other supplies—Stiletto Man was out of cigarettes.

While the driver was out, Stiletto Man called Art Monahan at the National Geospatial-Intelligence Agency to see whether Art had located the target, Tucker Cherokee. Aaron got impatient with Art who had picked up the phone on the first ring and demanded, "I want to speak with Dana before we do any business."

Stiletto Man laughed a hearty laugh and said, "You gotta lot of shit, Wichoo. You act like you're in charge here. I'm in fucking charge, and because of your insubordination and arrogance, I'll have my way with Dana after this call. And if you say another thing other than answer my questions, I'll have my way with your daughter. Are we clear?"

Art said, "Yes."

"OK, then. Where is he?"

Art had to play his part perfectly.

The Director of the National Geospatial-Intelligence Agency, the FBI Agent-in-Charge, and the Department of Defense strategist, General Woodhead, had told Art their plan.

"He's made it to Elkins, West Virginia," lied Art. "There's a Methodist Church in Elkins in which he has taken sanctuary. I have the church under surveillance. If he moves, I'll be able to track him."

"Good job. I'll call again in three hours. Until then, I'll enjoy my time with Dana."

Stiletto Man hung up and proceeded to go into the bedroom where, this time, Dana and Jenny were tied up and gagged—he grew tired of hearing them whine. He removed the gag from Dana and asked, "You or your daughter?"

Dana couldn't control herself from crying and begged him not to touch her daughter. He took his stiletto out of its sheath and teased Dana with the point of the knife near her daughter. Dana screamed even louder and said, "Please, please, take me." Stiletto Man moved the knife in the direction of Dana and started undressing her with his knife. First her blouse, then…his satellite phone rang.

He looked at the phone and saw that it was a call from his customer, the head of the intelligence arm of the First Consortium of Nations. "Yes sir, to what do I owe the honor of this call?"

"You know exactly what the honor of this call is about. What is taking you so long to eliminate the threat? He and his damn scientific experiment represent a significant threat to us. You have twenty-four hours, or I will replace you with a more productive, responsible, respectful, and results-oriented contractor. You are not the only option we have to accomplish our objective."

The customer repeated, "twenty-four hours" and hung up. At the same time, the driver returned with the food, cigarettes, and other supplies.

Aaron said to the driver, "As much as I would enjoy staying here a little longer, we're going to have to move. Figure out the shortest way between here and Elkins, West Virginia. I'll call Brock and Graf and tell them to meet us there." He looked over to Dana and said, "Put your blouse back on. We'll finish our fun later."

CHAPTER 18

WASHINGTON, DC—OCTOBER 7ᵀᴴ

"**Y**ou are empowered to do whatever it takes to protect these scientists and bring them to me. Oversee this personally. Don't delegate it."

The Attorney General of the United States couldn't believe he had heard those words from POTUS. But the President explained to him that during a briefing about the discovery from his advisors, the cabinet, and other trusted members of his administration, the President learned that Entropy's Project MEG was a bigger deal than he had realized. So, the AG cranked up the entire US Justice Department, including the FBI and the US Marshals Service.

Given the violent deaths of three professional mercenaries who had stalked Tucker, the AG advised the FBI to treat Tucker as a violent fugitive. Though Tucker was not a fugitive in the classic sense, the US Marshals' Fugitive Task Force and the FBI's Critical Incident Response Group were instructed to treat him like one but not to use lethal force—he must be captured alive.

Further, Tucker Cherokee was not expected to resist arrest by federal agents once convinced that the alleged capturers were friendlies.

Four Blackhawk helicopters were deployed from Quantico, Virginia, to circle the area in Grant County around the quarry and around the site of the mercenary murders. While in the air, the FBI contacted local police in Grant County and adjacent communities to see whether there was anything out of the ordinary to report. One of the helicopters landed at the quarry identified by the National Geospatial-Intelligence Agency as the location of Tucker Cherokee's abandoned vehicle. The FBI agents, in their intimidating full gear, interviewed people who worked at the quarry.

The FBI caught a break. A woman who sat in the weigh scale trailer had seen a man who fit Tucker's description who got out of the car and walked around the quarry parking lot until another guy picked him up in a Jeep Cherokee. The guy in the Jeep Cherokee was large; he looked like he was bigger than most NFL linemen.

The FBI Agent-in-Charge re-contacted the county police in a five-county area to see whether anything unusual that involved a Jeep Cherokee had occurred. It turned out that an abandoned Jeep Cherokee without plates sat in the parking lot of a restaurant in Seneca Rock, West Virginia. The FBI Agent-in-Charge said over his satellite phone to the Critical Incident Response Group, "Tucker Cherokee was not alone. He had at least two other people with him. One that drove him to Seneca Rock, the other that gave them a new ride to wherever they went. Check the VIN on the Jeep and find out who owns it. Get a hold of the National Geospatial-Intelligence Agency technician on this mission and see when the next time is that we can secure satellite access over the region."

Answers came quickly. "Sir," said an agent in Quantico, "the Jeep in question belongs to *White Knight Personal Security, LLC,* of Warrenton, Virginia. *White Knight* is owned by Jorge Alvarez, and the company is in the personal protection business. You know, sir, *White Knight* is well known for protecting famous people, actors, musicians, dignitaries, and others. In fact, sir, I see here that the FBI has contracted with *White Knight* in the past."

"Yes," said the Agent-in-Charge, "and they also provided support in Iraq to the Secret Service and the State Department. Well, now we know how Tucker Cherokee managed to dispose of three professional mercenaries. Can you uncover who in *White Knight* fits the physical description given to us by the woman at the quarry?"

"Sir," another voice was heard over the communications network, "this is Agent Stevenson speaking. The owner of *White Knight* is also the President and CEO of *White Knight* and fits the physical description given by the quarry lady. Few people fit that description. His nickname is 'Tank.' I don't think anybody calls him Jorge. One other thing: according to folklore, Powers trained Tank and Tank hired Powers as a *White Knight* subcontractor. You've heard of Powers, right?"

"Shit," said the Agent-in-Charge. "This is not going to be easy."

"Sir," said Agent Stevenson, "it might be very easy. Let's leave messages on Tank's and Powers' phones, emails, and websites and text them. Tell them the cavalry is here and we good guys want to team up with them. They'll get the message faster that way than us trying to track down a couple of real pros."

"Excellent idea, Agent Stevenson. On a related subject," asked the Agent-in-Charge, "were you able to identify the owner of the vehicle in Cumberland, Maryland, who allegedly kidnapped and holds hostage the family of one of the NGA agents? They're blackmailing the poor guy into using satellite imagery to track Tucker Cherokee by holding his family hostage."

"The plates belonged to a stolen car. However, the description of the car, an older Lincoln Town Car, texted to us by one of the hostages has been distributed to law enforcement in Cumberland and the surrounding area. Someone will call it in."

Grant County, West Virginia

Brock and Graf listened continuously to the police band for what seemed like forever to them. There was a lot of chatter about the murder of the mercenaries found in the basement of a homeowner's vacation log home. There was conversation about a Jeep Cherokee in Seneca Rock, West Virginia, and now and then there was a reference to the FBI. The two would-be kidnappers of Tucker Cherokee saw Blackhawks wander in an otherwise unused sky.

Brock called Aaron—Stiletto Man. "I think the Feds are involved, they're flying surveillance and have energized the county and state police. They are all looking for something, probably us."

"I don't imagine they have very many professional-style murders around here. Most of the killings around here are probably alcohol related. It's no surprise that the local police called the Feds in to investigate the demise of our contracted mercenaries. This is probably the most fun local law enforcement has had in some time."

Brock said, "I think maybe it would be a good idea if we left the area until your contact with the satellite data provides us with an exact location of Tucker Cherokee."

"What's the matter, Brock, are you starting to get a little frightened when the going gets tough?"

"No sir, but we do stick out like sore thumbs around here. I was trying to protect our mission."

"Bullshit. But I do think you two should wander in the direction of Seneca Rock. Call for instruction when you get there." Aaron Zytlle hung up.

Quantico, Virginia

The FBI Agent-in-Charge said, "OK, let's set these Blackhawks down over at the Grant County Airport in Petersburg for a couple of hours, refuel, and see if we hear anything from the *White Knight* contingent."

Thirty minutes later, a Garrett County police cruiser spotted an early model Lincoln Town Car in Oakland, Maryland. He checked the tags against the FBI all-points-bulletin. They matched. Instructions were explicit: "Do not approach." The officer called it in to the Maryland Highway Patrol and the FBI and followed at a careful distance for about five miles. He called another police cruiser down the road and asked him to watch for the Lincoln Town Car.

Boston, Massachusetts

3:30 a.m. is the best time of the day to break and enter.

Entropy occupied the fifth floor of a twelve-story building in downtown Boston. The building had two sets of double doors in series. The first round of doors allowed anyone out of the weather. The locked second set of doors prevented access to unauthorized users. Occupants gained access into the building by either swiping a card or punching numbers on a keypad. A security guard in the lobby kept the riffraff out. Gang Chung was a patient man and waited outside and out of sight for ninety minutes before the first person, a middle-aged woman carrying a briefcase, swiped her card to enter the building. As she swiped the card, Gang Chung entered right behind her.

She looked back at Gang Chung and said, "Who are you? Richard," she said to the security guard, "please check this man out, I don't recognize him."

Gang Chung reached into his jacket pocket as if he was going to pull out his credentials but, instead, pulled his Type 64 silenced handgun and shot the woman in the forehead. He pointed the gun at the security guard and said, "Hands up so I can see them, don't push the silent alarm button, and put your weapon on the floor—carefully."

Richard followed Chung's instructions. He knew the entire event was being video recorded. "Now, Richard, escort me to the fifth floor and open the door to Entropy's office."

Richard said, "I'll need to reach into my desk drawer and pull out the master key card."

Gang Chung walked around the back of the security guard's desk and said, "Keep your hands away from the desk drawer. Is this the drawer it's in?"

Richard nodded his head, and Gang Chung opened the drawer. In the drawer were a set of blank key cards and a silent alarm button. Gang Chung said, "Will one of these key cards get us into the Entropy's offices."

Richard nodded.

"Good. Now, before you escort me onto the fifth floor, move the lady behind your desk." Though Richard was perfectly able to move the woman, he thought it senseless since the next person to enter the building would identify the blood on the floor and find the dead body. But he did what he was instructed to do.

Entropy's offices were like many other corporate offices. The doors were glass so you can see into the lobby from the elevator corridor. Richard swiped the key card, the door clicked, and Richard pulled it open.

Phil McPherson's former office was easy to find; it had yellow tape across the door. Gang Chung pulled the yellow tape off and asked Richard to open the door. Richard said, "I don't have master keys for everyone's personal office in the building."

Chung had no more use for Richard and shot him through his ear.

He picked the lock and entered McPherson's former office where he was surprised to find no computer, no safe, and no files. The place had been sanitized.

He wandered around the office floor until he found the Chief Executive Officer's office. He broke in and found it fully functional, including a safe he couldn't break into. He took the hard drive out of the CEO's personal computer and removed papers from his desk that he thought contained some information that might locate where the CEO lived.

He looked at his watch as he left the building. He wished he had kept the guard alive longer so he could have removed the surveillance camera video.

Chung thought, "I need to get out of the country soon."

Chicago, Illinois

Maya argued with her mother, "Staying here is probably not the safest place for me to be. If I am a target, it will not be difficult for the bad guys to track me down here and put you in danger."

As if on cue, someone knocked on the penthouse's front door. Maya's mother said, "Security on the ground floor should not have let someone knock on our door without notifying us in advance. Don't answer the door."

Outside the door, a raised voice asked, "Dr. Li?" Of course, both mother and daughter were titled Dr. Li and responded simultaneously with "Yes."

"We are US Marshals here to protect Dr. Maya Li. I am Marshal Jeff Black. My partner here is Marshal Chuck Little."

Maya's mother spoke first and said, "Let me see your badges through the peephole."

Mother and daughter viewed the badges but neither could identify a real badge from a fake badge. Maya's mother angrily called down to building security and asked the desk whether they had viewed the badges of the people outside their penthouse door. Security said they had verified the shields and apologized for not calling up to let them know they were coming.

Though still apprehensive, Maya opened the door to two large hard-looking young men with their badges extended but who remained where they were until someone invited them into the penthouse. Maya moved her arm in a gesture to enter their domain and asked, "Who and why does someone think I need federal protection?"

The US Marshals were armed; they did not try to hide their shoulder holsters. "The US Attorney General is concerned that your life may be in danger, Dr. Li. After the murder of Entropy's Dr. Phil McPherson and the apparent attempt by mercenary assassins on the life of Tucker Cherokee, the Attorney General believed it wise to also protect you."

"What do you mean the apparent attempt on Tucker's life? Is he OK? What's going on? Why is the federal government involved? Who is after us?"

"Slow down," said Marshal Little. "We do not know for sure, yet, who is responsible, but we have reasons to believe it is a foreign state who sponsored the mission to stop the technology you announced on YouTube."

"How did he escape the attempt on his life?"

"We believe he is OK, but we're having trouble locating him ourselves. He was last identified in a log home in Grant County, West Virginia, where two professional mercenaries were found dead in the basement of the home and another buried on the property. Do you know Mr. Cherokee well? Can you provide any insight to law enforcement as to where he would go and how he would be able to get the better of two or three professional killers?"

Maya said, "I thought I knew Tucker pretty well. I'm not so sure now. And no, I have no idea where he might go."

Maya then related the story of her escape from the men following her into the alley, her dash to safety, and the subsequent sound from the discharge of automatic weapons.

The unsmiling US Marshal, Chuck Little, said, "Law enforcement already submitted a report on the evidence they gathered in the alley. Their report reinforced the fact that you need protection. We'll be inside this building until the situation stabilizes and we will try not to get in your way or be visible. Here is a medical alert button; wear it like a necklace. Push the button if you think you are in any danger."

"Dr. Li," said Marshal Little, "the US Attorney General does not usually take an active role to protect citizens. He must have good reasons to believe this is serious. Stay vigilant."

CHAPTER 19

CHARLOTTESVILLE, VIRGINIA—
OCTOBER 7TH

Powers called him, and that changed everything.

Dr. David Garfunkel owed Powers big time. A few years ago, back when the good doctor worked for the Agency, Powers saved him and his family from the wrath of a Colombian drug lord. Dr. Garfunkel—his new identity—and his family lived in Charlottesville, Virginia, where his medical practice was robust. The government had also arranged for him to teach a class or two on international medicine at the University of Virginia. Life was good.

Powers had never asked Garfunkel for anything, so when Powers called, Garfunkel jumped at the opportunity to repay him. Garfunkel rescheduled his patients, left his office immediately, and told his nursing assistant that he had a medical emergency and would be back whenever he got back. The assistant always suspected that Garfunkel's history included a little intrigue. She asked no questions.

The drive from Charlottesville to Davis, West Virginia, was too long for the good doc, so Powers agreed to meet up with him in Harrisonburg, Virginia, and from there, they rode together to Davis.

Dr. Garfunkel said, "Hello, soldier. Good to see that you're still above ground. You know, you need to change professions if you expect to stay that way. What the hell have you managed to get your sorry ass into this time?"

"Thanks for your career advice, Doc," Powers said, "but what I need is for you to check out someone in a jam that is even more complicated than the jam you were in."

"Sorry to hear that. Let's hope getting he or she out of the jam is not as dangerous as the jam I was in. What, specifically, do you need?"

"My current customer ingested something that was slipped into his drink. Allegedly, it is a chemical that emits something that they—whoever they are—can track by satellite. He is currently sheltering in place in an abandoned coal mine to prevent satellites from picking up the signal. We need for you to try to analyze his blood and figure out what the chemical is that is in his system and then, maybe, help us figure out what to do about it."

"As you know, when I worked with the Army's Defense Advanced Research Projects Agency I participated in a lot of esoteric top-secret research. It wouldn't surprise me if DARPA came up with a chemical which emitted a trackable signal. But then, I suspect that's why you reached out to me. You know, Powers, I'll need access to an analytical medical laboratory. Do you know where the nearest lab is to Davis, West Virginia?"

"West Virginia University in Morgantown has a medical laboratory and is, to the best of my knowledge, the closest lab to Davis. It's about three hours from here," answered Powers.

"Nothing closer?"

"Nope."

Changing the subject, the doc asked, "How are you, personally, my friend? I mean psychologically? No one goes through the loss you endured without some impact on their psyche. Have you discussed your trauma with anyone else besides me over the last decade?"

"No."

"That's not good."

"Will I have to listen to this all the way to Davis, or will you change the subject?"

Harrisonburg, Virginia

Powers had fallen in love only once in his life. She was perfect for him—she put up with the impact his profession had on their life with grace. She didn't ask him questions about his missions, which put him in danger and away for weeks or months at a time on short notice. She thought of him as the epitome of what a man was supposed to be. He was tough as nails but gentle with her; he was loyal to a fault; he was ruggedly handsome; and he treated her like a queen. They trusted each other implicitly and doted on each other when they were together.

He returned from a mission that put him out of the country and out of communication for ninety days. No one had told him that the love of his life had died of an aggressive form of brain cancer. It was quick—too fucking quick.

He hadn't often smiled since, and he refused to fall in love again.

Davis, West Virginia

Before Dr. David Garfunkel was escorted into the dark and dirty coal mine by Powers, he had to pass Ram's sniff test. Tank was expecting both Powers and the doc, so Tank had already explained to Ram that the doctor was "good." Ram stared down Garfunkel but ultimately allowed him to pass.

Doc walked into the trailer down at the 200-foot level and introduced himself to Tucker by asking, "From which arm do you prefer I take your blood?"

Tucker said, "Left arm. I have good veins, so you shouldn't have any trouble drawing my blood. By the way, I'm O-negative." Doc swabbed his arm with alcohol, stuck a needle into Tucker's left arm and took four vials of blood. Tucker said, sarcastically, "That was fun."

Doc said, "We'll run to Morgantown to perform some bloodwork. Expect the completion of the analysis and a work plan hopefully within the next five hours. Powers will call Tank with the assessment. Wish us luck." And with that short interface, Doc started to leave.

Tucker stopped the Doc and said, "Do you have any preconceived ideas as to what chemical was introduced into my tea?"

Garfunkel said, "No. But whatever it was, it's probably not good for you."

Morgantown, West Virginia

Since Dr. David Garfunkel had no legal or insurance-protected rights to use West Virginia University's medical laboratories, he made a few calls on the drive to Morgantown from Davis. Garfunkel discovered just how small the world was when he uncovered that a student and protégé of his from the University of Virginia worked in the West Virginia University Medical Center. The protégé opened the university's analytical laboratory to his mentor, gave Garfunkel "carte blanche," and even assisted him in the execution of his lab work. After about forty-five minutes of blood testing, Garfunkel said to Powers, "It's time to speak with Tank and Tucker."

Powers called Tank and said, "We're on speaker phone here in a private room. Ask Tucker to come up and join you."

Tank knew that meant that Tucker was not at risk of being tracked by satellite, so he went down to the 200-foot level and brought Tucker to the mine mouth where they had cell coverage. "OK, Tucker is here with me."

"Tucker," said Garfunkel, "the good news is that there are no chemicals in your bloodstream that could be used to track you by satellite."

"Great! I'm relieved. What's the bad news? I sense that the other shoe is about to drop."

"Technitium-99, a radioisotope, has been ingested into your system. Though it is only a Beta emitter, it has a 211,000-year half-life. Tc-99 is used in medical therapy to scan brain, bone, liver, kidney, and thyroids and for blood flow studies. Tc-99 is the radioisotope most widely used as a tracer for medical diagnosis. It concentrates in the thyroid gland and the gastrointestinal tract. The body, fortunately, constantly excretes Tc-99 once ingested. As with any other radioactive material, there is an increased chance that cancer or other adverse health effects can result from exposure to radiation. The amount in your system is on the threshold for long-term risk as a cancer victim."

Dr. Garfunkel continued, "I'll do a little research to see if there is a decorporation agent for Tc-99—that is something to aid in removing the radioisotope from your internal organs. I don't know what the people that wanted you to ingest this were thinking because there is no way they can track you by adding this to your blood unless I'm entirely in the dark and missing something revolutionary."

Tucker made light of the bad news and said, "Doc, I'm worried about living a couple more days. I'm not too concerned about cancer thirty years from now, but, sir, is there anything I can do to mitigate the impact of this stuff."

"Yes, drink a lot of beer; it will help flush it out. The body excretes half the ingested Tc-99 within five days. About one-quarter of the Tc-99 should remain in your body for ten days. The beer just helps it along."

Tucker said, "This has to be a first—a doctor telling someone to drink beer. So, you think it is safe to move out of this mine? It doesn't take long to get depressed down here in the dark."

Dr. Garfunkel said, "I can't say it's safe from the standpoint of your enemies—that's Powers' and Tank's expertise, but I can say that they can't track you through your contaminated blood with any technology I know of."

"Powers," said Tank, "we'll stay here at the mine until you get back after you take the doc to his car, but I suspect we need to move soon. Think about where we should go next."

Powers said, "Will do!"

Tank and Tucker said in unison, "Thanks, Doc."

Garfunkel had one more piece of advice, "Tucker, if they wanted you dead, they would have poisoned you with something lethal. One must conclude they want you alive. That, of course, is a double-edged sword."

CHAPTER 20

DAVIS, WEST VIRGINIA—
OCTOBER 7TH

The irritating sound that announced that he'd received another text message was getting on his nerves. He assumed it was from his office manager. It would be the fifth time in two days that she had asked him when he would return to the office.

Sometimes it was a pain in the ass to be the boss.

But when he looked down at his phone screen he was surprised to learn that the text message was from an FBI agent named Stevenson. "Well, well," said Tank, "it seems the Feds are now involved. Tucker, they want to know where you are so that they can protect you."

"Can we trust that the contact is really from the Feds and not someone pretending to be a Fed," asked Tucker?

"Hmmm," Tank continued, "whoever sent this text has figured out that I protect you. How would the bad guys know that? Wouldn't the enemy also know that it's too easy for us to check out if the contact was from the

FBI? Besides, this is not the style of a typical mercenary team. It's more likely to be legit than not."

"You know Tank, I get false calls from people who claim to be the IRS all the time. You never know."

Tank's phone rang, "Powers, here. I just received a text from an FBI agent named Stephenson. I've never heard of him, but he claims he wants to collaborate and help protect Tucker. What the hell gives here? How do they know we're protecting Tucker? This thing just took a quantum leap—pun intended. Ask Tucker who else knows, outside the federal government, about his problem."

Tank said, "I don't know the answer to all your questions, but I do know who else knows about the problem. Only law enforcement, Tucker's co-conspirator, Dr. Maya Li, and maybe the Entropy Board of Directors know about the problem—the problem being that Phil McPherson was murdered for information that only Tucker, the Board, and maybe Maya Li now possess. I'll reach out to my FBI contacts and determine if this text is genuine. You should do the same. Call me back when you reach a conclusion."

Tank and Powers made several calls and collaborated on the phone. Tank, Tucker, and Powers concluded that the text was genuine. Tank texted the FBI Special Agent Stephenson the coordinates of the coal mine where the *White Knights* were protecting Tucker Cherokee.

In less than twenty minutes, two Blackhawk helicopters hovered over the mine entrance. Fortunately, plenty of space was available in the old mine parking lot for both helicopters to land. After touching down, four heavily armed and intimidating FBI Critical Incident Response Group agents poured out of each Blackhawk.

Twenty-nine-year-old Special Agent Stephenson double-timed toward the guard shack to address a petrified JJ and asked where on the mine premises Tucker Cherokee, Tank Alvarez, and Powers resided. Before JJ could respond, Tank spoke over a loud speaker, "We'll be right up."

Tank was the first one out of the mine followed closely by Ram. He introduced himself to the handsome green-eyed Special Agent Stephenson who had his badge prominently displayed and said, "They weren't kidding when they told me you were a big guy. Where's Tucker Cherokee?"

"He's in a protected zone and unavailable to you until I verify your credentials. I must understand the driver behind your presence here. People have tried to kidnap or kill Mr. Cherokee, poison was added to his meal, his partner was murdered, and suddenly the Feds are interested in his well-being. Mr. Cherokee hired *White Knight* to protect him. I intend to do just that. Excuse us for being a little skeptical, but we have to understand how and why you Feds are here."

"The White House is aware of Mr. Cherokee's situation. A situation which has now been elevated to an international incident. The highest levels of the government directed this incident response. That's all I'm at liberty to say."

"What situation? What incident?"

"As I have said," repeated Special Agent Stephenson, "that is all I am at liberty to say."

"Geez," Tank said to the agent, "what the hell has Tucker gotten himself into? OK, follow me."

Ram stood his ground. Before Tank could escort the FBI contingent into the mine to meet Tucker, Tank had to let Ram know the visitors were "good."

Davis, West Virginia

Russian assassin Alex Pashkov used his high-powered Nikon Trailblazer compact binoculars to observe activity around the Davis Coal Mine. He was quite surprised to see two Sikorsky UH-60 Blackhawk helicopters land in front of the mine. He was equally surprised to see so many FBI logos on jackets around the Blackhawks. Alex surmised that the Feds were going to airlift his target to safety.

He couldn't let that happen.

Though he had hoped he could interview Tucker Cherokee to learn, as instructed, how the technology worked, he couldn't figure out how he could make that happen. Alex decided he was going to have to extract that information from one of the other scientists. He also concluded that he was going to have to shoot a fucking Blackhawk down.

"Damn. The US Government will hunt me down for the rest of my days." He wondered, "Did my cousin know this when he sent me here?"

Alex sat back and thought about how he would accomplish his mission without being captured or killed. He was afraid he didn't have long before he had to decide on a course of action. The RPG was hidden in a van a half a kilometer away through the woods. He thought, "I better go back, get the van, and put it in firing position."

An unusual amount of traffic, mostly locals, jammed the entrance in front of Davis Coal Mine. People from all around Grant and Tucker counties drove to see where the Blackhawk helicopters had landed and to investigate why they were there. The increased traffic made it easier for Alex to drive around without drawing attention to his white van, which contained his sniper rifle, RPG, and rockets. He brought out his digital camera and binoculars as if he were just another local gawker. Occasionally, he referenced the photo of Tucker Cherokee to make sure he assassinated the right man.

Alex worried that if he assassinated the target and left the Blackhawks unencumbered, they'd go airborne, hunt him down, and rip him to shreds with their .50 caliber cannons.

Alex wondered, "Will I be able to take both Blackhawks out before the FBI retaliates?"

He had one reloadable RPG-7 launcher and three high-explosive warhead rounds. He backed the van up into the ready position and prepared for the first launch.

Davis, West Virginia

The Agent-in-Charge instructed Special Agent Stevenson to direct one of the Blackhawks to head toward Elkins, West Virginia, to intercept a hostage taker. "Take the Hostage Rescue Team and your Critical Incident Response team with you," said the Agent-in-Charge. "We will continue to monitor the Lincoln Town Car's progress via drone, so keep your tablet on at all times to view his visual status.

"Use the other Blackhawk to bring Tucker Cherokee to Quantico."

Stephenson said, "What should I do with Alvarez, and for that matter, Powers, if or when he emerges?"

"Our mission is to protect Mr. Cherokee. Tell Alvarez that we are weight limited and to come to Quantico by vehicle."

Stephenson said into the microphone, "Ready Blackhawk Bravo three seven for deployment for hostage rescue. Ready Blackhawk Charlie eight nine for deployment home with the package."

Blackhawk Bravo Three Seven's blades started to rotate, its powerful T700-GE-701D twin engines exhibited its potential lifting capacity.

Through the binoculars, Alex could see the FBI team, fully dressed in combat-ready uniforms, enter the helicopter but, he did not see his target. However, with helmets and glasses on all the team members boarding the helicopter, he could not be sure Tucker Cherokee wasn't one of the occupants of the first Blackhawk.

Alex needed to shoot the first Blackhawk down while it was taking off and the other while it was still on the ground. The first helicopter was about to lift when he was pretty sure he saw Tucker Cherokee come out of the mine. Tucker was not in the first helicopter after all, so he must be boarding the second Blackhawk.

FBI agents were still boarding when the four blades of Blackhawk Charlie eight nine started to rotate. Alex couldn't see the door to the chopper, as it was on the far side facing the mine entrance. Happily, Alex did see his target walk around to board the second Blackhawk.

"You are a dead man walking, my friend."

The first Blackhawk loaded with the Hostage Rescue and Critical Incident Response teams and extra ordnance lifted vertically at a faster rate of acceleration than Alex had anticipated, so he was forced to react impulsively. He kicked the doors open in the back of the van, aimed the rocket-propelled launcher through the sight glass, and engaged its first round.

PART TWO

WINNERS AND LOSERS

CHAPTER 21

DAVIS, WEST VIRGINIA—
OCTOBER 7TH

The force from the explosion surprised even Alex. The first Blackhawk reached a height of sixty feet off the mine parking lot when the RPG struck the underbelly of the fuselage.

Even from 200 yards away, the intense heat, brilliant light, and deafening sound made it difficult for Alex to continue executing his mission. The second Blackhawk was severely damaged from the blast shock wave and was an unflyable sitting duck, and it contained his primary mission target, Tucker Cherokee. Alex, temporarily deaf, couldn't hear the screams and wailing sounds coming from the once-curious crowd of onlookers. He ignored the carnage he had created, focused his attention on his task at hand, and prepared the second rocket for launch.

He placed the fifteen-pound launcher over his shoulder, focused his aim through the telescopic sight and fired. Blackhawk Charlie eight nine, the second helicopter, exploded.

Alex threw the RPG onto the van bed, slammed the rear doors shut, dove into the driver's seat, quickly started the van, and peeled out through dark, putrid smoke toward the main street of Davis, West Virginia.

A couple of cars followed him—one was a local guy in a pickup truck trying to do his civic duty: follow and report the whereabouts of the white van he had seen as the source of the attack to his local police buddies.

A local person did not drive the other car.

Quantico, Virginia

Instruments on the first Blackhawk relayed signals immediately back to a control panel in the mission operations center.

"Activate our backup Critical Incident Response Group and another Hostage Rescue Team. Get the other two Blackhawks refueled at Petersburg in the air. Relocate one of the drones in the area to Davis and position a satellite to feed our monitors over the Davis Coal Mine," said the Agent-in-Charge.

"Damage assessment, Special Agent Stephenson?" No answer.

"Special Agent Stephenson, come in." No answer.

"Second-in-Command, Agent Murphy, please come in." No answer.

The Agent-in-Charge's voice cracked, "Anyone on the scene, please come in." After about ten seconds a voice came in over the live feed, "Loss of life is significant; no survivors in either Blackhawk. Special Agent Stephenson, Tucker Cherokee, and four FBI agents were in the second Blackhawk on the ground. The Hostage Rescue and Critical Incident Response Teams in the first Blackhawk were terminated. I repeat, no survivors in either helicopter."

"Who is speaking," asked the Agent-in-Charge.

"This is Tank Alvarez. I had just reentered the mine when the first explosion occurred. Even inside the mine, I felt the overpressure. Then I heard an incoming RPG round within thirty seconds of the first explosion.

"Please, send emergency medics. The scene here is nauseating and heart wrenching. Some civilian victims in the immediate area were severely burned or wounded from the explosion.

"Thanks to Agent Stephenson, I was prohibited from riding in either helicopter. I was contracted to provide protection for my friend, Tucker Cherokee. I've covered Tucker's ass for decades. Apparently," Tank began to choke up, "apparently, I failed this time. Fortunately for me, I was back inside the mine when the attack occurred."

Tank, still wearing an ear bud, furrowed his brow, and concentrated on the incoming message.

"Sir," continued Tank, "I just received a message from my associate, Powers, who informed me that he is following the terrorist who he witnessed from his car launch two RPG rockets. The terrorist is in a white van headed east on Route 93 toward Mount Storm. I strongly suggest you send an armed Blackhawk in that direction. I'm headed in my vehicle toward the Mount Storm Power Station myself to assist Powers. Out."

Agent-in-Charge said, "No, you stay put. Let the FBI handle this."

Tank thought, "Like hell."

"Good acting job, Tank. You sounded believable," said Tucker.

Tank turned to Tucker and said, "Stay here, go down to the 200-foot level in the mine. We want whoever paid for this act of terrorism to think you're dead, at least for a while. No one has seen you since the attack, and it will take FBI forensics weeks to determine that there is no DNA sample of you from the wreckage.

"The reason I pulled you into the privacy of the mine before you took off with the FBI was to advise you to trust no one. This situation involving the Feds and the deployment of a Critical Incident Response Team in Blackhawks escalated too fast. My antennae are up. I distrust the sequence of events. Something is wrong.

"There has to be a mole somewhere, Tucker. How else could the people that are after you know we were here, much less be waiting for us, armed to the teeth with RPG rockets? Someone in the government is feeding information to the people who are trying to kill you. The nasty bastards after you are willing to kill innocent people just to get to you.

"Here's my 9mm Beretta in case you need it." Tank looked down at Ram. He was grateful that Ram followed Tank back into the mine before the attack. He reached down, patted the top of his head, and said, "You obey Tucker's orders while I am gone."

Ram laid down next to Tucker in acknowledgment of his instructions. As Tank started to leave, Tucker grabbed his jacket sleeve to get his attention and said, "Thanks."

Tank exited the mine mouth to the smell of burning fuel, rubber, plastic, and flesh. He jogged a quarter of a mile through the smoldering debris and slid into the shielded Ford F-150, which fortunately was parked outside the blast impact zone.

Tank was mission focused—he damned well was going to capture the criminals who were trying to kill his best friend. With his adrenaline pumping and his anger peaked, he drove in an uncomfortable stooped-over position in the direction of the Mount Storm Power Plant.

Tucker wandered back deeper into the coal mine— at least for the time being.

Davis, West Virginia

While Tank and Powers were out there contributing something to capture killers, Tucker was embarrassingly holed up in the mine, hiding. He felt like a coward. By his count, around twenty-five people had died in the last few days—all because of him. Tucker felt worthless and responsible for the Davis Coal Mine carnage. He felt mostly responsible for the loss of life because of a scientific discovery he had announced to the world through a YouTube video. The video only showed the world what the technology could do, but not how it worked. Apparently, people were willing to kill to find out the "how." The situation made him and the surviving co-inventor, Maya Li, incredibly vulnerable.

He had overheard conversations between agents that they would use the heavily outfitted first Blackhawk to conduct their mission to rescue hostages located at a United Methodist Center in Elkins, West Virginia. Tucker understood that the hostage-takers kidnapped an innocent mother and child because of him—and his unwise decision to disclose the discovery on YouTube. He had to do something to redeem himself. Tucker thought, "Maybe I can help rescue the hostages—or die trying."

He knew it was a stupid idea, but he was going to do it anyway. He looked over at Ram and said, "You want to go for a walk?"

His thought wandered to Maya. He sure hoped Maya was safe. He had to get out of the mine and get somewhere where he could call her and assure himself that she was OK. His plan was to find his way to the Elkins United Methodist Center after he contacted Maya and see whether he could help in some way.

Quantico, Virginia

The Agent-in-Charge asked for the phone number of the Mount Storm Power Plant Manager and called. "This is the FBI calling. We need your help in apprehending a fugitive. He is driving a white van headed east on Route 93 from Davis in your direction. Please, block the road with either coal rail cars or a couple of your heavy coal trucks. We will be there within twenty minutes with an armed Blackhawk helicopter. After you block the road, get out of the way. The criminals in the white van are armed and dangerous. I don't know how many people are in the van. Stay out of the way."

The plant manager said, "If you need any additional help, we have armed guards ourselves. They might be able to support you."

"No, please, stay out of the way."

Mount Storm, West Virginia

Ten drop-bottom railcars, fully loaded with coal, were pushed across Route 93 by a Dominion-owned locomotive. Alex's van approached the rail cars at roughly seventy miles per hour when he concluded that he could neither cross the road nor drive off the road to get around the railcars. Forest on either side of the road prevented his escape, so Alex brought the van to a screeching halt. Pashkov thought for a second about whether his final RPG round could somehow create a space large enough between the rail cars to drive through, but he decided it was a bad idea—the rail cars were immovable.

He knew that he couldn't turn around and retreat without getting captured. He grabbed his rifle, his pistol, his knife, his phone, and a grenade; jumped out of the van; climbed over the couplings, through the space between rail cars; emerged on the other side of the rail spur; and ran in the direction of the Mount Storm power plant.

Idling on the road on the east side of the rail cars was a late model BMW occupied by a forty-year-old couple headed west on Route 93 waiting for the rail cars to move. The impatient and angry driver was on his cell phone trying to determine how long he was going to be trapped at his current location. The passenger was asleep while wearing her Bose sound-reducing headphones. Alex pointed his pistol at the driver's head and said, "Both of you, get out!"

Alex turned the BMW around to continue driving east on Route 93 leaving the vehicle owners standing on the side of the road, mouths agape.

Powers was not far behind the alleged terrorist and managed to crawl over the rail car coupling just in time to see Alex drive away. Powers had lugged his heavy sniper rifle with him for reasons just like this. He quickly set up, calmly took aim, and discharged two shots. Both rear tires of the BMW were blown out. Pashkov maintained control of the BMW and continued on the road, running on rims, for another half mile until the rear axle failed.

Alex jumped out of the BMW and searched for another means of transportation. He saw a fuel tanker truck headed in the wrong direction but hoped to find a better escape vehicle. But there was nothing else. Alex wondered, "Could the truck be turned around in time? Was there room to turn it around? Do I have a choice?"

Alex sprinted to the stationary Peterbilt cab, climbed onto the driver-side running board, and pointed his pistol through the open window at the truck driver.

Alex stared back at the barrel of a .45 caliber Colt Double Eagle. Alex was too fast for the truck driver and deflected the barrel of the Colt just as the driver pulled the trigger. The round landed harmlessly into the ground, but the 160-decibel sound painfully deafened Alex's left ear. Alex smoothly twisted the Colt from the driver's right hand and turned it against him. As Alex climbed into the sleeper cab behind the driver he ordered the driver to turn the truck around.

Alex kept his head down. He knew that someone was out there with a sniper rifle. He yelled at the driver to be faster at turning the truck around. The truck driver said, "These eighteen-wheelers are not easy to turn around on narrow two-lane roads, especially with a full load."

Alex said, "I don't want to hear any shit excuses. I will kill you before I let them capture me, so move it."

Powers thought about blowing out the tires of the truck, but he was apprehensive about shooting in the direction of a potentially loaded fuel truck.

The truck was on its fifth reverse move when Powers heard Tank behind him ask, "Where's the killer?"

"He's commandeered that truck, and he has a hostage. What took you so long to get here?"

Tank answered, "I had to restrain a civilian in a pickup truck who wanted to join you in this fun chase."

Tank pulled his communications device out to contact the Agent-in-Charge and said, "Tank Alvarez here. The terrorist is in a fuel truck, and he has a hostage. He does not have the RPG with him, I repeat, he does not have the RPG, so you are safe to approach."

The Blackhawk, loaded to the gills with ordnance, tilted at a thirty-degree angle with its cannons facing the cab of the truck. Over a loudspeaker, the pilot of the Blackhawk said, "This is the FBI, drop your weapons, and come out with your hands over your head." After about thirty seconds of silence, the truck driver opened his door, jumped out of the cab, and ran for his life.

Alex quickly slid out of the truck cab and crawled under the tanker frame to ensure that he was out of the line-of-sight of the Blackhawk. He crab-crawled the length of the fuel truck and out the back end, which was also out of the direct view of Tank and Powers.

Tank said to Powers, "You set up and get into your sniper position. Don't hesitate to take a shot. We'd like to get this guy alive but dead is better than for him to escape. I'm going to try to come up behind him. Try not to shoot me."

Alex surveyed his situation, identified an escape route, and ran out from under the truck for about ten yards before he took his hand grenade, pulled the pin, and threw it back under the tanker truck. He ran like hell away from the truck and threw himself over an embankment hoping the fall was not too far.

The Blackhawk pilot saw the assassin's intention before the grenade was thrown. She put the helicopter in an accelerated lift. The grenade exploded and ignited the fuel in the tank truck. The shockwaves from the explosion of the fully loaded-with-fuel tanker truck rocked the Blackhawk. The pilot lost control as it rapidly lost altitude, but the copilot managed a desperate last-second save. The helicopter landed hard, leaned to the side, and damaged the rotor blades, but it landed without loss of life to the crew.

Powers and Tank were far enough away to be unaffected, and after the blast had spent itself, Powers ran toward the fallen helicopter to see whether he could administer first aid. Fortunately, the helicopter crew sustained only a few injuries.

Tank ran to the point where Alex had jumped off, cautiously peeked over the embankment, and observed a fifteen-degree drop-off populated with scruffy pine trees, rocks, brush, kudzu, and movement. Bushes rustled about sixty feet away and below. Tank pulled his backup 9mm Beretta and repeatedly fired at the movement until he heard the killer yell in pain. Shot in the back of his right thigh, Alex fell, rolled in the underbrush, pulled his gun, and fired back wildly at Tank while trying to escape. Tank zig-zagged on his way down the embankment and continued to shoot. Alex took a bullet in the right shoulder forcing him to switch his gun to his left hand. For a big guy, Tank was deceptively fast. He was on Alex before Alex got off another round.

Alex used his left foot to strike Tank in the throat, stopping Tank cold for a fraction of a second. Alex pulled a knife out of his boot with his left hand.

Tank anticipated the move and said under his breath, "I refuse to take a knife again." Tank grabbed Alex's left forearm with his powerful right hand, ultimately rendering Alex's knife-wielding attempt useless.

Tank was dazed for several seconds after he was struck savagely in the head with a rusted piece of reinforcing rod. Blood ran down into his eyes.

Alex rolled farther down the embankment, knife still in his left hand. He spotted a culvert and crawled in its direction. Tank regained his bearing and started down the embankment after Alex.

Alex's chest exploded before Tank heard the familiar sound of Powers' sniper rifle.

Tank thought, "Damn, you scumbag. I wanted to interrogate you to find out who sent you to kill my friend."

It took some time before the fuel burned out, but the fire that the explosion caused was put out by the Mount Storm Volunteer Fire Department. The FBI forensic team took DNA samples of the killer, as it was important to all to learn his identity. The FBI and local law enforcement interviewed Tank and Powers for three hours before they were released on their own recognizance.

Tank said to Powers, "One assassin down. We had better get back to Tucker. God knows how many more people are after him."

139

CHAPTER 22

CHICAGO, ILLINOIS—OCTOBER 7TH

"**W**hy am I so worried about him?" Maya knew she was overly concerned about the safety of Tucker Cherokee and recognized with fear that she was in love with him. She called his cell phone many times, but he never answered, which further elevated her anxiety. "I can't think about anything else. I'm sitting here, for crying out loud, safely guarded by the US Marshals while he's out there, maybe, running for his life."

She felt compelled to get out and do something. "What can I do while stuck here in my mother's Chicago penthouse?"

Maya was pacing back and forth on the thick carpet in the spacious great room in front of the picture window with its beautiful view overlooking Lake Michigan while listening to cable news when a "Fox News Alert" was announced. On the wide-screen, the smoldering wreckage of two Blackhawk helicopters destroyed in Davis, West Virginia, was displayed. Interviewed witnesses said terrorists fired missiles that destroyed the two helicopters. The perpetrators were still at large. Local police and emergency response personnel reported that, so far, body parts were recovered from approximately seventeen victims.

"Mom," Maya said, "Didn't the US marshals say that Tucker was last seen in West Virginia? Oh, my God, Tucker might have been in one of those helicopters. Only the Feds and the military have helicopters like that, right?"

"Calm down, Maya," said Mother Li. "You're jumping to conclusions that this has anything to do with your friend." A concerned Mother Li showed fear on her face and said, "Having said that, if both Tucker and Phil McPherson were murdered, then it is safe to assume the US marshals were right and that you are in grave danger.

"Maybe this is the wrong place for you to be after all. What if the government is using you as bait to grab the bad guys who the government hopes **are** coming after you? We need a plan to get you out of here."

Chicago, Illinois

The lobby guards—the first line of defense—confirmed with Mother Li that she was expecting a delivery of Chinese take-out. As the elevator doors opened on the penthouse level, the US Marshals searched the young Chinese girl, instructed her to remove the scarf from around her neck, and patted her down carefully for weapons. Before the US Marshals allowed the delivery girl to pass, they inspected the food with chopsticks for things that didn't belong there.

The gracious and sophisticated penthouse matron told the marshals that she had ordered enough to share with them. The delivery girl left about seven minutes later thanking the Lis' for their tip. She waited for the elevator with her scarf back around her face, made eye contact with one of the US Marshals, and smiled while Mother Li distracted the man with a hot plate of sesame chicken.

Later, back inside the penthouse, Maya Li's mother said, "You may have just saved your big sister's life, Suzanne. It's a good thing you two are about the same size."

CHAPTER 23

WASHINGTON, DC—OCTOBER 7TH

No one had ever seen the big man more agitated or angrier. At 1830 in the Situation Room of the White House, POTUS Jefferson King presided over a meeting with the Director of the FBI, Secretary of Defense, White House Chief of Staff, National Security Advisor, Director of the CIA, Director of NSA, Director of the NGA, Secretary of State, Attorney General, and White House Press Secretary.

"To state the obvious, we have a major crisis, here," said President King in a loud baritone voice that demanded attention. "At least seventeen American lives have been lost through this cowardly act of terrorism.

"Or maybe, Director Watts, war has been waged on the United States, and we don't know it yet. Was this attack by ISIS? Has anyone claimed responsibility? I want to know, now, if we are under attack.

"Or is this is an act of domestic terrorism, Mike?" POTUS was staring at Michael Vincent, Director of the FBI.

Though appointed by President King, there was no love lost between POTUS and Michael Vincent. On multiple occasions, the Director, at his peril, had stood his ground and disagreed with the President on actions that the President recommended. The room was thick in anticipation of another coming conflict because Vincent knocked heads with the president in the presence of many of the people currently in the Situation Room.

Director Vincent, however, was uncharacteristically humble this time and said, "Mr. President, as you stated, we are in the middle of a severe crisis. I wish we could have apprehended the attacker so we could have questioned his motives and interrogated him, but unfortunately, the perpetrator is dead."

POTUS interrupted, "Are you saying this was the result of one individual? One guy brought down three Blackhawks on US soil?"

Undaunted, Director Vincent said, "The FBI forensic pathologists on the scene are performing tests as we speak, but the initial data collected at the site implies that a single foreign-sponsored assassin committed this act of terrorism."

The attendees in the room gasped. They understood the potential ramifications of this statement. Before Director Vincent could continue, President King asked, "Which foreign entity?"

"Russia."

The room broke out with many objections to the conclusion reached by the FBI Director. The loudest, as expected, was the Secretary of State, Walter Askeland. Secretary Askeland's face turned bright red as he said, "Wait a second, here, Michael, you damned well better have a solid basis for making such an inflammatory claim. Our relations with Russia are tentative at best as it is without making false accusations against them!"

The job of the Secretary of State is one of the most demanding jobs in the cabinet and had taken a toll on Askeland. His lack of sleep and tendency to overeat and overdrink without exercise made him a stroke candidate. Others in the room were unsure whether this was going to be the moment of his physical collapse. Everyone turned their heads almost in unison and returned their gaze back to Director Vincent to await his response to Askeland's outburst.

"We were able to lift prints off the white van used by the assassin. There were many partial prints, but several prints were a perfect match to a Russian mobster named Myron Kazinski."

"Again," stated Secretary Askeland, "that does not prove the attack was state sponsored with Russia's approval."

Vincent continued unabated, "Another set of prints, including prints on the RPG-7 in the back of the van, belong to Alex Pashkov, a well-known Russian assassin rumored to have blood ties to Russian President, Vladimir Petrov."

Secretary Askeland could be heard saying under his breath, "Shit!"

FBI Director Vincent continued, "As I said, our forensic labs are busy collecting more data. That data may change our initial conclusions, but I recommend we develop a strategy to deal with the potential implications of a subversive Russian threat to the homeland."

The President looked toward the CIA Director and asked, "Do you have anything to add?"

Director Watts cleared his throat and said, "Yes, Mr. President, we knew Pashkov was illegally in the country. We also knew that Myron Kazinski was illegally in the country and has been for months. Both Russians entered under false names and forged passports. We have not been able to tag them because we've been unable to track their whereabouts with any specificity."

"Is that all you have to add?" asked the President. President King knew the Director well enough to know that he had to pressure the CIA Director to extract information out of him—he's a "close-to-the-vest" kind of guy.

"There's a big shakeup going on in the Russian hierarchy," added Director Watts. "President Petrov removed Dmitri Ranstropov, who was Director of the Intellectual Property Monitoring Ministry, from his position. We're told by our agents that he had been fired, allegedly, for his failure to know about the new US discovery in advance. Apparently, Russia feels very threatened by it. I'd have brought this up sooner, but we wanted more corroboration before bringing it to your attention."

POTUS asked, "Is there additional 'uncorroborated' information you'd like to bring to my attention that is relevant to this crisis?"

Watts ignored POTUS's sarcasm and mild rebuke and said, "Yes, Mr. President, there is, but I think it would be better if the Director of the National Security Agency presented the information."

NSA Director Oscar Becker was a slight man in his mid-fifties. He wore thick trifocals and a dirty bow tie— rumor has it that he slept in it. He worked twelve hours a day every day. Work was his life. He constantly reviewed assessments from his legion of eavesdroppers. There was not going to be an attack on the homeland because the NSA missed something. Director Becker said, "Thank you, Director Watts. Mr. President, we intercepted a conversation between the Saudi Foreign

Minister and an unknown person here in the United States. We have recorded two such conversations. The first was a conversation where the recipient of the call was in Cumberland, Maryland. In the second conversation, the recipient of the call was in Deep Creek Lake, Maryland."

"Jesus," said the NGA Director, John Bowman, in unison with Michael Vincent. "Sorry for the outburst, Mr. President, but a subset of this crisis is a hostage situation that involves an NGA technician who is being blackmailed for satellite imagery information. The hostage takers were in both Cumberland and Deep Creek Lake recently. Our intelligence is that they are on their way to Elkins, West Virginia, with the NGA employee's family as hostages. We were trying to set up a trap. In fact, the Blackhawk's mission—the one that was shot down first at the Davis Coal Mine by the Russian assassin—was to rescue the hostages in Elkins. The implication of Director Becker's revelation is that the Saudis are behind the hostage taking of American civilians!"

POTUS asked, "And why would the Saudis risk such a subversive mission?"

"The Saudi mission, I suspect," interjected CIA Director Watts, "is to track and eliminate Tucker Cherokee, the remaining Entropy inventor of the discovery. The Saudis are members of the Consortium and probably even more threatened than the Russians by the discovery."

"This is pure conjecture," stammered an apoplectic Secretary of State.

"Compose yourself, Walter," admonished the President.

"Mr. President," spoke Director Vincent, "I hate to throw more fuel onto the fire of this discussion, but another disturbing fact has emerged that may be relevant to the crisis at hand."

Almost everyone around the table hung their heads awaiting the additional bad news.

Director Vincent continued, "Someone broke into the Entropy headquarters in Boston this morning and murdered the security guard and an innocent civilian. The surveillance camera caught a full-face view of the perpetrator. We suspect the perpetrator is also responsible for the murder of Dr. Phil McPherson, co-inventor of the subject discovery. The perpetrator has ties to the People's Republic of China."

"Oh my Gott," slurred the red-faced Secretary of State, "Ish this some short of a joke you all are purring on me? Tell me this shis a joke!"

"Wally, you're slurring your speech," said the President, "I'm calling in the White House doctor to take a good look at you. I think you're having a stroke or heart attack." The President made eye contact with and nodded to the lead Secret Service agent, who promptly and gently escorted the Secretary of State out of the Situation Room.

POTUS asked, "Now that Secretary Askeland is out of earshot, I'll ask the questions I suspect we are all wondering. Is there any possibility that the Russians, the Saudis, and the Chinese are in cahoots, actually working together to get the details on this discovery?"

Attendees moved nervously. Not a single head in the room nodded in the affirmative.

"OK," continued the President. "Is there anything else I need to know before we assemble a path forward strategy?"

The FBI Director said, "Yes, Mr. President. Both the Entropy inventors are now dead. It looks like our enemies have succeeded in their mission."

"Who else knows how to make this technology, this discovery work?" asked POTUS.

The Attorney General spoke for the first time and said, "Companies like Entropy protect their 'intellectual property' or trade secrets better than we protect top secret information. After all these years, the Coca-Cola formula is still secret. My guess is that the discovery 'formula' as it were, is under lock and key somewhere. They stole both Tucker Cherokee's and Phil McPherson's laptop and computer hard drives. If there was anything on their laptops, it is now in the hands of the enemy. We'll contact the Entropy CEO to see where they stored the data so that no one else gets murdered over it.

"Also, there is a possibility that the third person on the YouTube video that announced the discovery has the knowledge to replicate the discovery. Dr. Maya Li is currently under the protection of the US Marshals."

"You mean like the deceased Tucker Cherokee was under the protection of the FBI?" retorted the president. This was a great admonishment of Director Vincent.

"One other thing, Mr. President," said CIA Director Watts. "How could the Russian assassin know to find Tucker Cherokee at the coal mine in West Virginia? Until this morning, we didn't know ourselves where Mr. Cherokee was hiding. How could they have gotten an RPG in position shortly after we arrived with the Blackhawks?"

The president didn't like where this was going.

"We have a mole, sir."

The Situation Room, The White House

"I'm not going ask if there's anything else I need to know," stated the president. "We're done with that. I'm in an information overload state now. Let's discuss action items."

The White House Press Secretary, Tom Baer, said, "We need to get out in front and say something about the attack on the FBI Blackhawks in West Virginia. The media, especially Fox News, is going to ask very penetrating questions like 'What was the FBI doing at the coal mine?' and 'Was this a terrorist attack?' and 'Who is responsible for the attack?'"

The White House Chief of Staff spoke up and said, "We have to handle this better than the government handled Benghazi or Mogadishu. I strongly urge we fully disclose what we know and take it on the chin rather than fabricate another story."

The president stated, "However, I don't want the press release to be something that further provokes Russia, Saudi Arabia, or the People's Republic of China. The people of the United States elected me partly because of my anti-war position. I have a mandate from the people to keep us out of war."

"I think it is too late for that, Mr. President," said the National Security Advisor, Wendy Smith. "If what we discussed here is true, then the provocation has been by the three aforementioned nations. To not respond is to show weakness, which will encourage our enemies to further aggression and exacerbate the situation. I'm not proposing war, but I do suggest that you carry a big stick into this next news conference. This aggression may well be because the three nations feel we are weak and we will not act. We have been too weak in the past, and we are now paying for our weakness."

"Is there any chance," asked the Attorney General, "that the Russians are not responsible for the attack? Are we 100 percent certain? I'd say it's a high probability but not certain. Therefore, at this time, Tom, we should tell the truth. We don't know yet who the perpetrators are. We don't know for certain, yet, if it's foreign or domestic. In fact, because the attack occurred at a coal mine, we could fabricate the story that an environmental extremist group committed the crime. We don't know. Maybe we could claim that the FBI was there because we caught wind of an attack on the coal mine. Rather than attacking the coal mine itself, they took the opportunity and attacked the helicopters."

"That story won't hold water," said the president, "but it might be foundational. One thing I'll throw out on the table for consideration is that we announce that to the best of our knowledge, all the inventors of the discovered technology are now dead and that with them died the discovery. This could stop the short-term killings and remove the perceived threat to Russia, China, and Saudi Arabia, not to mention the Consortium of Nations. We don't know how many assassins have been hired to eliminate the threat of this discovery. Let's put an end to it."

CHAPTER 24

DAVIS, WEST VIRGINIA—
OCTOBER 7TH

The local emergency response teams dealing with the carnage at the mine were much too preoccupied to notice Tucker exiting the mine mouth to walk Ram. Tucker wanted to help the understaffed medics, but he had no first aid training or experience. He was concerned that he would do more damage than good if he administered medical help to a blast victim.

Tucker silently prayed for JJ as he approached what was left of the guard trailer—it had apparently taken a fireball. He checked through the mostly collapsed shed and could see that the emergency response team had already been there. Tucker hoped JJ had not been in it and that he was OK.

JJ's pickup truck was parked behind the trailer and seemed to have survived the blast. Tucker opened the driver's-side front door, and Ram jumped into the front seat of the pickup truck. Fortunately for Tucker, JJ had left the keys beneath the floor mat. He had to laugh when Tucker notices a new varmint rifle on the back seat.

Tucker said to Ram, "I guess you want to go for a ride."

Lights, seemingly everywhere, flashed yellow, blue, red, and white as Tucker slowly weaved the Silverado around the firetrucks, ambulances, police cruisers, and coroner's trucks. Media vans with their ubiquitous satellite dishes fought each other for position to spread news of the tragedy. Tucker was surprised that there were no police blockades looking for the perpetrators of this nightmare. He drove north, away from Davis, in the direction of the small town of Thomas.

He had no idea where he was going, so he pulled over at the first open mom-and-pop store he could find. He stopped the truck in one of the five parking spots and looked in the glove compartment for a Garmin but settled for a map of West Virginia. Tucker didn't know where Elkins was relative to Davis or how far away it was from his current position. To his surprise, he also found a loaded handgun in the glove compartment.

"Shame on you, JJ," Tucker mused.

He found the town of Elkins on a road map and determined that he soon had to make a left on Route 219. He went into the store to buy a cup of coffee and dog food. After placing the two items on the counter, he asked the old man at the cash register where he could buy a disposable cell phone.

Eyeing Tucker with suspicion, the old guy said, "Right here." He looked down at his key collection dangling from his belt and selected one. As he opened a drawer under the counter, he asked Tucker, "How many minutes do you want on the phone?"

"Forty dollars' worth." Pop rang it up. It depleted almost all of Tucker's cash, but he didn't want to use a credit card. After all, he was supposed to be dead.

Tucker climbed back into the Silverado, fed Ram some treats, initiated his disposable cell phone, and called Maya.

It went directly to voice mail.

"Damn it." He included the phone number with his message to Maya. The burn phone didn't have text capabilities, so he started up the truck and headed north until he got to Route 219 and then headed west. About five minutes into the drive his phone rang. "Hello," he said.

"Tucker?! Oh my God, is that you? Are you all right? They told me you were dead. What's going on?"

"Maya, hold on until I find a place to pull over; this is a very winding road." It took him another minute before he pulled over.

Tucker said, "I am so relieved that you are safe. I worried about you when you didn't answer the phone. Listen, only Tank and now you know I'm alive. Let's keep it that way." Ram cocked his head. "Oh, and Ram. He's my new protector. Listen, I think you're in real danger. Dump your phone. They, whoever 'they' are, can track you through a chip in your phone. Get a disposable phone like I have. Of course, you already have my number.

"And, Sweetheart, where are you? You need to hide somewhere no one can find you."

Maya said, "I'm at a Motel 6 in Clinton, Illinois, hiding. I'm driving my Honda since I wrecked the Tesla. It would have been too conspicuous to drive anyway."

Tucker asked, "You wrecked the Tesla? Are you hurt? Why aren't you at your mother's?"

"You were right about one thing: someone is trying to kill me, too! It's a long story. I'll tell you about it when we get together. And I'm OK, unhurt."

Tucker said, "This is unbelievable. I'm on my way to Elkins, West Virginia, to try to help a hostage rescue team save a guy's kidnapped family—probably kidnapped because of us. I overheard the now-deceased FBI agents mention a United Methodist Center somewhere there. I should be there in an hour or less."

"Tucker, you're going to get yourself killed. Let the police or a hostage rescue team, who are trained for this, do their job. It's stupid for you to try to get involved."

"I'm already dead, remember? Besides, I've got Ram with me. By the way, who told you I was dead?"

"The White House Press Secretary announced that the attack in Davis, West Virginia, resulted in seventeen casualties, including you. They also said that with you dead, and in conjunction with the murder of Phil McPherson, the US lost a new technology for all time. No one else knows how to re-create the process.

"I guess they are trying to protect me. They also said that it is possible that the attack could be a result of domestic terrorism by environmental extremists."

"What bullshit," responded Tucker. "That's why people don't believe a word that comes out of the government or the press. Benghazi proved that. Anyway, we need to rendezvous somewhere."

Maya said, "I'm going to head south and east. I'd say the midpoint between Elkins and where I am is somewhere around Lexington, Kentucky. If I don't hear from you for some reason that is out of either of our control, I'll meet you in front of Rupp Arena, say twenty-four hours from now."

Tucker said, "Sounds like a plan to me. I'm looking forward to seeing you. One other thing: in the event I don't make it to Lexington, I want you to know that I love you. Call me when you get your disposable phone." He hung up quickly—he was afraid she wouldn't say she loved him, too.

After Maya stopped the tears from flowing, she took her Garmin out and entered "Rupp Arena, Lexington, Kentucky." It was going to take her a little over five and a half hours to get there. "Hmm," she thought, "I could make it to Elkins in ten hours."

Tucker County, West Virginia

On the drive from Thomas to Elkins, Tucker contemplated about what went wrong and how his great new energy discovery became so damned deadly. The discovery was an accident; it wasn't even what they were initially looking to discover.

Tucker was a simple man with simple pleasures, unpretentious, and trusted other souls until proven otherwise. He was not the paranoid type nor did he ever see a conspiracy behind every action. He did not see people in terms of race, gender, or physical attributes, with the minor exception of his attraction to the physical characteristics of ladies. Tucker respected all hard-working people with good intentions.

However, Tucker was not so naïve that he didn't understand that there were criminals and bad people in the world. He just hadn't had the misfortune to run into many of them personally, until recently.

Tucker thought, "Electricity for lights, computers, or TVs is always there when I need it." But if Tucker was Jay Leno or Jesse Watters and asked the random "Jaywalk" candidate "Where does electricity come from?" they may say "from the plug!" But power to the electrical grid for hundreds of millions of consumers required an enormous infrastructure.

Tucker believed that if the world didn't need that entire infrastructure—if we could make electricity right where it was needed without fuel—wouldn't that be a great thing? People could have power in remote regions of the world, and poor people in Ethiopia, Indonesia, or on remote Philippine islands could have and afford electricity. He thought, "We would no longer need carbon-based fuels or those ugly transmission towers, and it would cost less to heat homes, cook, and run the air conditioner."

The discovery would change many things, especially for people in poorer nations. He remembered seeing the NASA satellite photographs where at night the wealthy nations were lit up brightly, and the poorer countries remained in the dark. The contrast was especially stark where the free people of South Korea shined while the suppressed people of North Korea were in the dark. Tucker was excited about the possibility of improving the lives of many millions of people and all the good that would result from their discovery.

The discovery could make the United States and the European Union energy independent and energy secure— electricity without consuming oil or natural gas, and electricity without burning coal or generating global warming greenhouse gasses. On top of that, the discovery could produce electrical energy at a small fraction of today's cost—something he initially thought was good for everyone.

The enemies who were previously outside the log home and the fact that he'd been on the run for three days from numerous people who wanted to capture or kill him for his knowledge of the discovery proved that not to be true.

What a great discovery!...Unless you're an oil or natural gas-rich nation like Saudi Arabia or Russia and your country's survival depends on the sale of fuel to energy-consuming countries. Unless you're an electric utility, a coal mining company, or a natural gas pipeline operator.

Tucker had a short-lived vision of being a billionaire philanthropist. He envisioned himself receiving honors worldwide for a discovery that had the potential to affect every person on the planet in a positive way. He looked forward to establishing a scientific institution for entrepreneurs with his newfound wealth.

It was his now-deceased co-inventor Dr. Phil McPherson who first brought to Tucker's attention at the time of the discovery that not everybody was going to be happy about it. Phil had asked, "Have you thought about the unintended consequences that may arise because of our discovery?"

Tucker responded, "No. I've been too caught up in euphoria to get my head out of the clouds. But offhand, I can quickly identify a few groups that would not initially benefit from the discovery."

"A few?" Phil had said incredulously. "We're going to have more people upset with us than a bear in a hornet's nest. This discovery isn't like the invention of the automobile where only the buggy whip industry suffered, or the invention of the refrigerator, which killed the ice delivery business. This is much bigger than that.

"The impact to the US is small in comparison to the impact to oil and natural gas exporting countries like Russia, the member countries of the First Consortium of Nations, and OPEC countries."

"True," Tucker responded, "but there are enormous upsides. Where there are losers, there are usually winners. Cheap electricity that does not require fuel for production will ultimately make every product manufactured anywhere less expensive, without the production of pollutants; preserve land and natural resources; and make the US completely energy independent."

"Good point."

He thought about one of Einstein's quotes, "*I never made one of my discoveries through the process of rational thinking.*"

Tucker reflected on how things had evolved from unabashed euphoria to a life of fear and desperation.

Western North Carolina

Twenty-two years earlier, when Tucker Cherokee and Jorge Alvarez had attended Tuscola High School near Lake Junaluska, times were simpler. Their biggest problem was trying to decide whether to go fishing or to sneak off and drive Jorge's old man's beat up panel truck through Tucker's family's apple orchard.

Tuscola means "Digging in Many Places" in Cherokee and Junaluska was a leader of the Eastern Band of Cherokee Indians who resided in and around western North Carolina.

Tucker's grandfather was a member of the Cherokee Nation and a direct descendant of Wilma Mankiller. Tucker's dad had left the reservation to marry Tucker's pure-of-heart mother. Tucker's mom was of Irish descent and named Tucker from the Anglicized form of the Irish surname O'Tuachair. She was a gifted mathematician who chose to teach high school math and to be a mother over pursuing loftier professions. Living with the family name, "Mankiller," added burden to life, so his father changed their last name to "Cherokee."

Tucker's dad was a Cherokee Nation Marshal and taught Tucker defensive skills, hand-to-hand combat, marksman skills, and archery. But Tucker gravitated toward science rather than law enforcement and his loving parents had supported him unequivocally. His parents had married late, and Tucker was born when his parents were in their forties. His mother died at the age of seventy-eight of congestive heart failure, and his father died a year later of a broken heart.

Tucker's dad had taught Tucker to be proud of his American Indian heritage and encouraged him to achieve success using his God-given talents.

Tucker achieved the highest SAT scores in all of North Carolina the year he graduated and received a grant and an academic scholarship to Massachusetts Institute of Technology where he excelled in mechanical engineering.

Upon graduation, Entropy, LLC, known publicly as a low-profile but well-funded private "think tank" organization recruited Tucker. His job as a junior investigator required him to cross-pollinate and integrate lessons learned from diverse industries. Through that process, the "think tank" leveraged, or force-multiplied new ideas into dynamic inventions or discoveries. Those discoveries, in turn, were perfected, patented, and either spun off, sold, or licensed to manufacturers or end users.

Tucker's personality, natural inquisitiveness, charm, and pleasant disposition were perfect character traits for interfacing with laconic scientists, anal engineers, and unfriendly researchers who were protective of their projects. His quick wit and disarming smile seemed to be useful in breaking down contentious barriers. Even in his youth, he could extricate himself from potential conflicts by improvising solutions peppered with a little humor. When that didn't work, his long legs, cross country championship skills, and natural endurance kicked in—after all, he was no dummy.

During an assignment at Fermilab a year before the discovery, he had learned from Maya that every second over one trillion neutrinos pass through every square foot of earth directly exposed to the sun. She stated at the time, "Fortunately, they are so small that almost all of them never make contact with anything on earth—they just pass right through and continue their trip through the universe."

She continued, "A neutrino is a subatomic particle estimated to be one billionth the size of an electron and thought by some physicists to have mass and charge, which would make them subject to electromagnetic forces."

Tucker wondered how humanity could benefit from knowing about neutrinos. He couldn't get the thought out of his head.

That is, when Maya's beauty and charm did not captivate his thoughts.

CHAPTER 25

JACKSON HOLE, WYOMING— MARCH 3RD

The winding West Virginia road required Tucker's total concentration, but he couldn't keep his mind from wandering back to the genesis of the discovery.

Entropy had sequestered a team of its staff scientists and investigators in a "thinking-out-of-the-box" session. The annual Jackson Hole, Wyoming, brainstorming retreat was where the company came up with some of its best ideas. It was Tucker's first exposure to an Entropy brainstorming session, so he stayed respectful of the attendees whose IQs and professional credentials were amazing.

Though Tucker was the junior member at the retreat, Dr. Phil McPherson recognized Tucker's potential to make a meaningful contribution to the session at hand. Phil was the only guy in the room with whom Tucker connected.

As Chair and Chief Scientist, Phil called the meeting to order. "OK, you all, let's get started. As is our practice, we swept this room for listening devices, and, as you know, this windowless room is damped so that no one can pick up and convert vibrations into audible sound. We inspected all ductwork to make sure there are no fiber optics present. And no one knows we're here except people who have a need to know. Our competitors would love to hear what goes on in here."

Phil connected the projector to his laptop and opened a PowerPoint presentation outlining the day's agenda. For the next three hours, the seven overly caffeinated people in the newly painted room talked about things too esoteric for Tucker to make a meaningful contribution. The scientists discussed new noninvasive surgical procedures using, heretofore, unused radioisotopes, new methods for improving the cost of manufacturing drones, legal surveillance methods to prevent Medicare fraud, and an approach for guaranteeing timely detection of Improvised Explosive Devices (IEDs).

Before lunch was brought in, the projector was turned off, the attendees covered all reference material and books, and all participants vigilantly watched the catering service people to make sure they did not pick up a document in the room.

After the catering service people had left, Phil started the next discussion item: "How to extend the usefulness of Ground Penetrating Radar?" After about thirty minutes of discussion and group interaction, Tucker finally got the courage to say something, "Since this is a 'thinking-out-of-the-box' brainstorming session, has anyone considered using neutrinos to perform the function of deeper earth penetration?"

This was the first time all day anyone had laughed. The Entropy Chief Technology Officer asked, "So how are we going to get them to detect anything? Billions of dollars have been spent worldwide by the US, European Union, and Japan just to try to measure a few hitting something."

Tucker said, "I have no idea," he paused. "Yet."

The team ignored Tucker and continued the discussion on what they had learned about Ground Penetrating Radar advances that could replace current methodologies for identifying minerals at greater depths.

"Imagine," Phil said, "if you could just hover over the ground with a helicopter or drone and get a read-out of mineral content at various depths up to a thousand feet deep."

Tucker leaned over and whispered to Phil, "We wouldn't want to sell that technology. We'd want to keep it for ourselves and find trillions of dollars' worth of new deposits of gold, silver, and platinum in the world."

Phil leaned back toward Tucker and stated, "Next week, let's meet privately in my office back in Boston."

Boston, Massachusetts

Tucker had walked into Phil McPherson's office the following week as instructed. He wasn't sure whether he was going to be reprimanded for suggesting such a dumb idea during the brainstorming session or Phil wanted to continue the discussion about the concept of using neutrinos to locate subsurface minerals.

Phil had said, "Your neutrino idea is way too premature to bring to the Entropy risk review committee. Though I have no idea what it would take to advance your idea, we have negotiated an opportunity to set up a test laboratory in Cape Canaveral, Florida. We can use

NASA abandoned facilities under the condition that Entropy employs a few laid-off NASA scientists. I need a feasibility plan and budget from you ten days from now if we're going to move this idea forward."

Tucker was pleasantly surprised that Phil thought there was enough merit to his brainstorming idea of using neutrinos to find deep geologic minerals that Phil would allocate funds for its investigation. Smiling, Tucker said, "Yes, sir."

Tucker immediately got on the phone and called Dr. Maya Li. To his disappointment, the call went to voice mail. He thought that the phenomenon belonged to one of Murphy's Laws: "The only calls people answer right away are calls that you didn't want to make in the first place." That's right up there with "The only flights that take off on time are the ones you're late for."

CHAPTER 26

BATAVIA, ILLINOIS—MARCH 10ᵀᴴ

Tucker had made a bold decision to catch a commercial flight to Chicago on the chance that Maya would agree to meet with him. From a center seat in coach on the trip between Logan and O'Hare, Tucker silently practiced his pitch to convince Maya to have dinner with him. After three unsuccessful attempts to reach her by phone, Tucker wondered whether she was avoiding him. But he persevered until Maya finally answered the phone. To his relief, she cheerfully agreed to meet him for dinner.

He was more excited about this business dinner than any previous "date" in his life. Tucker was not a clothes horse and did not pay much attention to men's dress style. He believed that "what you see is what you get." That had all changed for this date. He went to Brooks Brothers, bought a tailored suit, new shoes, stylish cufflinks, and a handkerchief for his sports coat breast pocket. He got a haircut at the airport and though his shoes were new, a shoe shine. He observed himself in the mirror and was reminded of his mixed American Indian heritage. Tucker had made dinner reservations at a four-star restaurant, grabbed a rental car, and headed for Batavia, Illinois.

Dr. Maya Li, daughter of a respected psychiatrist in Chicago, tried to restrain herself from analyzing her feelings. She intentionally did not date anyone at work. God knows she's had enough offers even over the short time she'd worked at Fermilab, and she worked long hours. So, she didn't get much of a chance to meet people except at the gym during runs. She belonged to a group of young women who ran in groups for their protection. She didn't like running with the guys because they would always slow their pace down, get behind her, and run at her pace.

So, a date with Tucker sounded like fun. It would get her out of her routine and give her a chance to dress up for a change. She elected to meet Tucker at the restaurant so he would not learn where she lived—she wasn't ready for that.

Tucker stood just inside the restaurant when the valet opened the driver's-side door of her Tesla Roadster to let her out. Tucker felt paralyzed. He hyperventilated and breathed through his mouth. As the maître d' opened the restaurant door for her, Tucker was the first person she saw. She smiled brightly and leaned forward and offered her cheek to him. He was totally unprepared and clumsy. He managed to give her a peck and regained some composure, offered her his arm, and proceeded to the reserved table.

It was a good two minutes before Tucker could speak in full sentences. Finally, Tucker said, "You look stunning." She wore a full-length dark green dress that was made of a material that tightly clung to her body,

167

revealing her athletic physique. The dress was cut low and revealed a little cleavage. She wore a pearl necklace with a shawl that matched the color of the pearls, high heels that made her even taller and sleeker, and she wore her hair down almost to her waist.

She was exotic—not your stereotypical PhD physicist.

Maya was in a state that was the antithesis of Tucker's. She was relaxed, confident, self-assured, and genuinely happy. She said, "You dress up nicely yourself." The waiter saved Tucker from further clumsiness and offered the two of them a wine list. After making a couple of suggestions to which she agreed, he ordered the wine.

Before he got down to business, Tucker thought it wise to conduct some small talk to get to know each other. Though they worked together some, they never delved into each other's personal lives. Besides, he had never told her there was any business to get down to. As far as she knew, it was just a date.

"How do you like the Tesla Roadster?" Tucker asked to break the ice.

"It drives like a dream. It has fantastic pickup, zero to sixty miles per hour in 3.7 seconds, and is very comfortable inside," Maya said.

Tucker wondered how she could afford a $120,000 car on a starting physicist's paycheck. The answer to that question intrigued him, made Maya a little more mysterious, but it made him a little uncomfortable. He suddenly feared that she was in class outside his reach.

She continued, "For an electric car, it has great range. Though I don't have to charge it every night, it is easy enough to do."

Maya and Tucker talked comfortably with each other through dinner. They learned that they both enjoyed many of the same things, including running, tennis, camping, and reading mystery thrillers and adventure novels on their Kindles. They tiptoed into politics and discovered they shared common positions. Tucker was fascinated to learn that Maya was a member of the National Rifle Association and kept a semiautomatic Mossberg shotgun in her bedroom. She said, "I'll call 9-1-1 first, but just in case they don't arrive in time, I know how to defend myself."

They sat at the restaurant table for three hours. Maya thought about inviting him to her condominium. Tucker thought about inviting her to his hotel for a nightcap. Instead, he asked her whether he could see her again tomorrow, and this time mix in a little business.

She said, "How about lunch at your hotel?"

He could not have thought of a better idea.

Batavia, Illinois

She came the next day to Tucker's hotel to meet him for lunch. Unlike the evening before, Maya did not drive her conspicuous Tesla Roadster. Instead, she drove a late model Honda CRV. She was dressed for work, and, therefore, Maya only looked beautiful instead of breathtakingly stunning. She said, "I enjoyed last night. I don't get out much, and I rarely enjoy myself like I did with you at the restaurant." She said this without the slightest bit of hesitation.

"I share those sentiments and hope we are embarking on a journey together," he said. His face reddened, and he thought to himself, "Where the hell did that come from? It's not like me to wear my emotions on my sleeve like this. I'm going to scare her away. She's way out of my league." And then she touched him, ever so gently, her hand on his forearm.

Talk about electricity. He reacted impulsively and kissed her lightly on the lips.

And it was on.

They never made it to the hotel restaurant. They practically had each other undressed in the hallway before Tucker could slide the key to his room.

Later, when they regained some equilibrium, they talked shop. Maya asked, "So what was the business you wanted to speak to me about today?"

He said, "Whatever it was, it seems unimportant to me now."

She said, "No, seriously, I want to know."

Tucker asked, "Would you be willing to 'brainstorm' with me from time to time?"

She smiled, "I think I prefer 'body storming' with you more."

"Body storming! I like that concept. Want to do some additional body storming research?"

Her smile was broad, and her eyes were bright with anticipation. "Please, Tucker, what was it about?"

"Neutrinos. What good are they? Do you envision any usefulness for them? Any way humanity can harness them and benefit from their existence? I understand the need to know about them from a quantum building block standpoint, but I was wondering if anyone was thinking about what we can do with the information researchers are dedicating their collective lives to gather about neutrinos."

Tucker thought for a moment that she was going to laugh at him like the brainstorming team did in Jackson Hole, Wyoming.

She looked kindly at him, smiled a knowing smile, and kissed him again. She said, "It took you long enough. I did a little background check on you and your employer. I knew from the day you arrived as an Entropy investigator months ago that there had to be a logical reason why your company would invest in sending you here. All I could think of was that you were exploring all our research here and fishing to see if you could uncover something that Entropy could leverage into a product. But I never thought neutrinos would come to the top of your list. I didn't see that coming.

"But, it's a good question. I'm sure when quantum mechanics was proven, the people of the day asked the same question. Little did they know that the underlying research of the time would end up as fuel for nuclear power plants to make electricity or power submarines and aircraft carriers. Little did they know their research would allow us to produce medical radioisotopes to kill cancer cells. But there was a big gap in time between when the electron was 'discovered' and when electricity became ubiquitous.

"The answer to your question is 'I don't know.' It's currently hard to imagine a useful purpose for them since neutrinos are so hard to detect. I guess we need to learn more about them before we figure out how to use them.

"But whatever you do, you'll probably need a huge magnetic field and electrolytes. Since trillions of these little guys pass through us every second wherever we are, you could conduct a test anywhere you wanted."

CHAPTER 27

CAPE CANAVERAL, FLORIDA— MARCH 17TH

Phil McPherson had left a text message on Tucker's smartphone to contact Terrie Scruggs in Cape Canaveral. He also provided Tucker with the Entropy charge number against which Tucker could charge all costs associated with this 'investigation,' provided, of course, the charges did not exceed the approved budget. Tucker caught a flight to Orlando, rented a car, drove east on the Bee Line across the 528 Causeway to the city of Cape Canaveral, and met with Terrie Scruggs.

Terrie, dressed in a well-tailored pastel-colored business suit, was a fiftyish woman with a leathery face that looked like she'd spent a few too many weekends at the beach without UV protection. She greeted Tucker as he entered through the door and said, "Mr. Tucker, my name is Terrie. Dr. McPherson told me that you were coming to visit with us. How can I be of assistance to Entropy?"

Smiling with his hand out, he said, "Tucker is my first name, so go ahead and just call me Tucker. It happens all the time—that people think Tucker is my last name. I'm looking for a place where we might be able to employ laid-off NASA professionals to do some testing for us. I don't think it has to be large, say ten thousand square feet or so, with utilities available like power, water, natural gas or propane, and compressed air."

"Unfortunately for us, but fortunately for you," Terrie said, "we maintain seventy-five buildings and warehouses that are not currently in use. The cutback in funding for NASA programs has had a grave impact on our local economy. Also, NASA reassigned many of our funded projects to Marshall Space Flight Center in Huntsville, Alabama."

Tucker empathized and said, "I'm sorry that your community has suffered from the NASA cutbacks, but if you have a list of people, by skill, who have been laid off, we'd like to identify potential candidates to help us with our testing program. This may be a silly question, but are there any facilities available that used magnetic fields?"

Terrie answered, "I have no idea, but, I'll find out for you." She thought for a moment and added, "You know, the University of Florida in Gainesville and Florida State University in Tallahassee are part of the National High Magnetic Field Laboratory, along with Los Alamos National Laboratory in New Mexico. You might want to check with them for technical support. I understand Los Alamos recently produced a magnetic field in excess of 100 tesla."

"Tesla," thought Tucker. He immediately thought of Maya and her Tesla Roadster. "Magnetic fields are

173

measured in tesla? What a coincidence! Or not? Nikola Tesla was a famous physicist who invented many electrical components for George Westinghouse, including those that used permanent magnets."

"Terrie, I'm very impressed with your knowledge about magnetic fields."

"Don't be. My son is studying to be a physicist at the University of Florida in Gainesville. I just parroted to you words that I've heard from him. But I can give you his phone number if you want to speak with him."

"That would be great. Thanks."

Terrie gave Tucker a tour of Cape Canaveral, inside and outside the security zones, and identified potential sites for his new project that met his selection criteria. But Tucker's mind was thinking that, maybe, he should go to the sites that were already producing magnetic fields instead of trying to build a test unit from scratch in Cape Canaveral.

Tucker thanked Mrs. Scruggs for her tour and said he'd be getting back to her. He crawled into his rental car to get out of the hot sun, turned on the ignition and air conditioner, and called Maya.

"Hi, Dr. Li," Tucker said after she picked up, "how's my favorite particle physicist?"

"Tucker, I'm the only particle physicist you know, so, of course, I'm your favorite. How's my favorite man?"

"Whoa, I like the sound of that. I'm seeking professional advice. What kind of relationship does Fermilab have with Los Alamos?"

"Well, we are both Department of Energy labs, but we compete for research funds and investigate entirely different things. Why do you ask?"

"Well, you told me I should look at magnets as it relates to finding something useful for neutrinos. I understand Los Alamos's National High Magnetic Field Laboratory has created the largest magnetic field in the world. Do you think you could put me in contact with someone there?"

Maya said, "As you know, I'm a junior scientist. I don't know very many people and no one at Los Alamos. But I can find out for you who to contact. Let's see here; I'm at my computer, and I'm inside the DOE contact list. Apparently, the Director of the NHMFL is Dr. Harvey Mendelsohn at 505-555-7921. That's the best I can do."

"Thank you, my darling."

"I love the way you talk."

Dr. Mendelsohn answered his phone on the third ring. "Hello, Dr. Mendelsohn. My name is Tucker Cherokee. I understand you run the National High Magnetic Field Laboratory there in Los Alamos. I work with Entropy, and I was wondering if you would consider running an experiment with Entropy taking advantage of the world's largest magnetic field." Tucker waited for a response but was greeted with silence. "Sir," said Tucker, "do you have a long backlog of experiments for the NHMFL?"

Dr. Mendelsohn finally replied with a booming, resonating voice you would expect to hear from a radio announcer, "It would be NHMFL's pleasure to make available our magnetic field to Entropy for your experiment. But first, you will need to submit an application through our Department of Energy Office of Science grant program. You'll need to submit your test program and your scientific justification for why you believe your test program has merit. You'll have to include your project approach, capabilities of your research team, provide a statement of project objectives, a project execution plan, a commercialization plan, a risk management plan, and a technology readiness level assessment. After you submit your grant application, we'll score your application against other submittals, compare the request against the fiscal year budget and see if you make the cut.

"If I may speak frankly, Mr. Cherokee, your chances of success will be significantly improved if a university leads the application you submit."

Tucker asked, "What kind of a timeline are we talking about to receive approval?"

"I'd guess the process shouldn't take more than two years to get the approval you're looking for," said Harvey Mendelsohn.

Tucker responded, "Ah, we really don't have two years to commit to the research we're proposing. Do you have any thoughts on how to expedite the request?"

"No," said Harvey, "not if you want to use Los Alamos's magnetic field. If you want to use a magnetic field of less flux, you may want to contact Florida State University or the University of Florida."

"Thank you for your time, Dr. Mendelsohn," said a frustrated Tucker Cherokee.

Tucker got on the phone and called the number Terrie Scruggs had given him for her son studying at the University of Florida but got his voice mail. He decided to text the number to see whether he could get a response. Fifteen minutes later, Tucker got a text reply from Tommy stating that he was in class and would contact Tucker later that night.

Tommy Scruggs was an underweight youth with too much nervous energy, as if he was on speed or some other recreational drug. He was wired and slept an average of only four hours a night because he couldn't stop his mind from thinking when it was time to sleep.

But he was just wired that way, not a substance abuser. He enjoyed physics but had no idea what he wanted to do when he graduated from college. He didn't see a future in the space industry because employment was too unpredictable.

His mother had told him to expect a call from Tucker, which was exciting because it was his first contact ever that could lead to a real job in the private sector after he graduated. Entropy's web page looked fascinating, so Tommy called Tucker as soon as he got out of class.

"Hello, Mom told me to expect contact from you. What can I do for you?"

"We would like to conduct an experiment in the presence of a magnetic field."

Tommy asked, "How large a magnetic field? Does it need to pulse or vary? What is the duration of exposure? Do you have a test plan I can review?"

"Yes, I've developed a test plan, but I'd like you to review it only from a magnetic field standpoint. What I want to do is insert various metals, electrolytes, and other chemicals into a magnetic field and determine if neutrinos can react in some way and record any reaction. We'd like to see if neutrinos react differently to different elements."

Tommy said, "Say what? Neutrinos? You're kidding, right? Good luck with that!"

"Tell you what, Tommy, you review the test plan for me, and Entropy will pay for your next semester's tuition."

"Cool."

"You decide the magnetic field parameters, and we'll provide you the chemical testing protocols. Deal?"

Tommy said, "Deal."

After speaking with Tommy, Tucker called Phil and asked, "Since you are a chemist by education, would you like to review the mixture of electrolytes and other chemicals I've included in our test program?"

Phil said, "That would be fun. All I seem to do anymore is administrative bullshit. I'd love to do a little lab chemistry work. I'm getting excited just thinking about it. I haven't done any real work in years.

"By the way," Phil continued, "have you prepared a budget request yet?"

Tucker said, "You mean, that administrative bullshit?"

Gainesville, Florida

Tommy Scruggs worked two solid days on about six hours of sleep to review and comment on the test plan for Entropy. He wanted to impress Tucker Cherokee. This test plan could end up being the foundation for his master's thesis and lead to a postgraduate job. The basis for his contribution to the test plan was to take an MRI machine used in the medical industry that uses superconductive rare earth metals to create a magnetic field. Then he designed it vertically instead of its usual horizontal position to maximize the time the chemicals were in the magnetic field and spray chemicals and electrolytes into the top portion of the MRI machine. Anodes and cathodes would be attached to see whether it created a charge. The anodes would be attached to a volt ohm meter and recorder. Concentration and mixtures of feed material would continuously be varied but recorded. Variations of chemical feed could be random. The test would be self-sustaining. It could take months or years before anything registered.

Probably nothing ever would.

Once something stimulated the neutrinos to create a charge, Entropy could replicate the experience with different feed concentrations and see how the reactions differed. The detailed test plan edited by Tommy was 175 pages long. Tommy saved the modified test plan as a PDF, attached the plan to an e-mail, and forwarded the plan to Tucker for his consideration.

Three hours later, Tommy was asked to call in on a teleconference with Tucker and Dr. Phil McPherson of Entropy. Tucker said, "Thank you for your comments on the test plan. Dr. McPherson and I think it has merit. We have a customer that manufactures MRI machines. We're going to see if they can rent or lease one to us and ship it down to Cape Canaveral. We'll design and build a frame to mount it vertically. Phil, here, will develop the testing parameters for the quantity, variations, methodologies, and protocols for the introduction of chemicals."

Tommy Scruggs' mother, Terrie, found the perfect location to perform the Entropy tests. She also identified highly qualified former NASA lab technicians to run the tests once they finalized the test program and procedures. Former NASA structural engineers were contracted to design and have fabricated the MRI machine support tower. Entropy shipped an MRI manufacturer's in-house test unit from Newark, New Jersey, to Cape Canaveral, Florida.

While Entropy installed the test facility, Dr. Phil McPherson developed the test parameters. Thousands of combinations of chemicals could be introduced to see whether neutrinos were somehow stimulated as they passed through the magnetic field created by the MRI. There were an infinite number of combinations when varying quantity and exposure time for each of the combinations of chemicals were taken into consideration.

Fifty stainless steel chemical feed tanks were set up around the MRI machine. A programmable logic controller was programmed to change feed quantities against an algorithm prepared by Phil. The system was designed to run twenty-four hours a day, seven days a week, 365 days a year.

All systems and subsystems were checked out and readied for operation. The first test started on August 21st. Every hour of every day, the lab tested twelve combinations and recorded the results. By August 22nd, 288 tests had been conducted and documented, but no electrical charge or reaction of any kind had been observed. By August 27th, the experiment had completed 2,016 tests—still nothing.

On August 30th, however, during the $2,865^{th}$ combination of chemicals, there was a massive explosion in the test facility—the entire test unit caught fire. The sprinkler system activated, and the electronics were fried and subsequently soaked. The odor of burning insulation and electronics was overwhelming. The City of Cape Canaveral Fire Department put out the fire and submitted a report that attributed the fire to an electrical component failure. Scattered around the test facility were pieces of the MRI machine.

Tucker was devastated and dreaded the call he had to make to Phil McPherson.

Phil said, "Shut the program down. There is no way I can justify securing another MRI machine. Our insurance will cover some of the cost, but not all. There is no sense throwing good money after bad.

"But, Tucker, just out of curiosity, what was the chemical combination being fed into the MRI when the explosion occurred?"

Tucker said, "The records show fluoroantimonic acid, lithium diethylamide, and sodium acetate."

"Somehow, my friend, we need to replicate the test and rule out that the last combination of chemicals did not cause the electrical accident. Contact Tommy Scruggs at the University of Florida. See if he has any ideas as to where we can produce a magnetic field for one short test."

Tucker got on the phone and discussed their options with Tommy Scruggs. Tucker and Phil were determined to find out whether something other than just an equipment failure caused the explosion.

Gainesville, Florida

Tommy Scruggs used a University of Florida chemical laboratory and brought in a series of neodymium permanent rare earth magnets and arranged them to maximize the magnetic field. He bought the chemicals Tucker wanted to be tested over the Internet and had them shipped to his apartment. He used three small metering pumps that were available in the lab for such experiments. Though the magnetic field Tommy created was much weaker than the one produced by the MRI machine at Cape Canaveral, it was the best he could improvise. Tommy had absolutely no hope that this experiment would accomplish anything, but he'd promised Tucker and Phil that he'd do it. After all, they were paying for his next semester's tuition. Tommy turned on the three metering pumps simultaneously.

That was the last thing Tommy ever did.

A high voltage electrical discharge arced into Tommy, paralyzing him instantly. His eyes protruded from his skull as electricity flowed through his fingers to the ground. The University of Florida laboratory basement circuit breaker tripped, and the lights went out. It lasted only twenty seconds. Smoke escaped through his ears, his heart stopped, and his brain was fried.

A university security guard investigated the event. He gagged from the smell of burning flesh before the guard focused the beam from his flashlight on him.

Tommy Scruggs was dead.

CHAPTER 28

CAPE CANAVERAL, FLORIDA— SEPTEMBER 3RD

Tucker was surprised that he had not yet heard from Tommy even though neither of them had high expectations from the experiment that Tommy was conducting for Entropy at the University of Florida. Tucker got impatient and called Tommy's cell phone—no answer.

Tucker texted Tommy in case Tommy was in class—no response. Tucker spent the next hour populating his final report on the accident in Cape Canaveral. He knew his career at Entropy was probably over. His peers at the company had told him that the research project to harness neutrinos was a fool's errand.

Concerned that he had still not heard from Tommy, Tucker called Tommy's mother, Terrie Scruggs, to see whether she had heard from Tommy. The phone went directly to voicemail. A man's voice on the answering machine stated, "Hello, this is the Scruggs residence. If you are calling to express sympathy, please leave a message. If you want to send flowers, the funeral for Tommy Scruggs will be conducted at Titusville Funeral Home on September 6th at 2:00 p.m."

Tucker was shocked. "What the hell happened?" Tucker got on the Internet, opened the Bing search engine, and typed in "Tommy Scruggs + death." An article showed up in the *Gainesville Times,* which included the following:

"Gainesville Police Department's Sergeant Cecile Jones reported that University of Florida Security Officer William Bethune responded to a campus power failure. In doing so, Bethune discovered the body of a student in the basement laboratory of Clinton Hall. Thomas Stevens Scruggs, Titusville, Florida, was a physics student performing laboratory tests. Though the coroner has not completed an autopsy, Officer Bethune stated that it appears as if he had been electrocuted."

Tucker was sad at the loss of the young physicist. He could not image how Tommy's mother, Terrie, must be dealing with her loss. Tucker thought about what he should do for Terrie—attend the funeral, send flowers?

"Electrocuted," Tucker thought. "If he was conducting the experiment Tucker had discussed with Tommy, then the likelihood of electrocution was close to zero. The research required no high voltage components. Tommy didn't have to use equipment that utilized more than 120 volts. Even the chemical feed pumps were low voltage systems. How could he get electrocuted?

"Two accidents in less than a week. Something is not right here." Tucker pulled out his cell phone and called the University of Florida campus police and asked whether he could speak with William Bethune.

"Are you a reporter?" asked the switchboard operator.

"No. The student, Tommy Scruggs, was running a test for me. I want to discuss with Officer Bethune a detail about Mr. Scruggs' electrocution."

"Bethune here," answered his phone after the operator transferred the call.

"Officer Bethune, my name is Tucker Cherokee of Entropy. Tommy Scruggs may have been conducting a test on our behalf."

Before Tucker could continue, Bethune said, "Yes, I know who you are. I had planned to get in touch with you. Scruggs' notes indicated he was running a test and your name and number were on his notes. I have a few questions for you."

"OK," said Tucker, "fire away."

"What was the test he was running and why was he using University of Florida property to conduct these tests for you?"

"I'll try to answer the second part of your question first. The University of Florida is a participant of the US Department of Energy National High Magnetic Field Laboratory Program. Mr. Scruggs was a physics student trying to work in advance toward a master's degree in physics. He was beginning to work on his master's thesis. Hence, I assume the basis for his use of University of Florida property. However, he was in no way directed by me on behalf of Entropy to use UF-Gainesville property.

"Now, to answer the first part of the question, he was introducing chemicals in the presence of a magnetic field to determine if there would be any reaction. If so, could that reaction be because of some stimulus of subatomic particles called neutrinos."

"Well," said Officer Bethune, "there obviously was some reaction. Tommy Scruggs was videotaping the experiment. When he pushed the start button for the pumps, he was immediately electrocuted—the videotaped electrocution is ugly. Before you ask, I will not release this video or his notes to you until I get a release from the immediate family and the university."

"That's understandable. Is there anything else you would like to ask me as part of your investigation? We want to cooperate with the University of Florida in any way possible. And we'd like to get a copy of your report if allowed."

"Thank you. I'll be back in touch with you if I have any questions." With that, Officer Bethune hung up.

Tucker wondered whether the combination of chemicals in the presence of a magnetic field caused Tommy's electrocution or was it something else. He thought, "Was it just a coincidence that the accidents in Cape Canaveral and Gainesville both happened during experiments that fed the same chemicals into a magnetic field? That seemed to be unlikely." Tucker was more determined than ever to find out whether they were "exciting" neutrinos.

Tucker used his smartphone to call Phil. "You may have heard by now that Tommy Scruggs is dead."

Phil said, "No! How horrible. He was so young! What happened?" Tucker explained the background of Tommy's electrocution. Phil said, "We wanted the Scruggs test to confirm that the introduction of the prescribed chemical combination into the magnetic field was not the cause of the Cape Canaveral accident. Instead, the Scruggs test reinforced the possibility that the test itself caused the accident, maybe by stimulating neutrinos!"

"It sounds to me," added Tucker, "that we need to perform a third test to replicate the Cape Canaveral and

Gainesville tests to see if it happens again. This time in a safe environment. If it happens a third time, then we have to figure out how to control the reaction."

"Good idea. But this time, make damn sure that we conduct this test remotely and safely. In fact, I want to review the plan before you implement it."

Phil asked, "What can we do for the Scruggs family?"

"I'll talk to Tommy's mother and make a recommendation. We need to do something meaningful."

Cape Canaveral, Florida

Tucker's thoughts went directly to his favorite subject, Maya Li. He punched the speed dial number on his phone. She answered on the second ring, and said, "Hello, this is Dr. Maya Li, how can I help you?" The cold and all-business response was code for "I'm tied up and can't speak freely."

Tucker said, "Hello, this is Tucker Cherokee of Entropy, and we want to discuss a potential project for Fermilab. Please return this call at your earliest possible convenience." This was code for "we need to talk." They hung up.

Twenty minutes later, Maya called and said, "I hope the project will include some 'body storming.'"

"You can count on that. It'll be the very first item in the statement of work. On a more serious note, I need to tell you that the physics research student with whom we contracted was electrocuted last night. He was working on our neutrino project."

Maya said, "I'm so sorry, Tucker."

"All he was doing was spraying chemicals into a magnetic field. How could that electrocute him? It doesn't make sense to me. The accident we had earlier in Cape Canaveral occurred while introducing the same chemicals.

"I think we're doing something here to excite neutrinos."

Tucker's voice cracked as he continued, "We need to safely replicate the test that Tommy conducted. We still have the Cape Canaveral facility we can use, but the accident destroyed the MRI unit. Do you have any ideas?"

"Have you disposed of the destroyed MRI unit yet?"

"No, it's waiting for a metal recycler to pick it up."

Maya said, "Well, cancel the pick-up. We can reuse the magnets. It is unlikely that the explosion hurt the rare-earth magnets. The magnetic field will be less than it was when the MRI was intact, but we can rearrange and reposition the magnets to be suitable for our purpose."

Tucker asked, "Do you have any vacation time you can use to come down to Cape Canaveral for a couple of days?"

"Let me think," quipped Maya playfully. "Would I rather be on the beach with you in Florida or be alone in cold Batavia, Illinois? Gee, that's a difficult decision to make."

"I'll pay for the flight to Orlando, the beachfront hotel room in Cocoa Beach, and fine dining at restaurants of your choice."

"You sure are a sweet talker."

Cape Canaveral, Florida

Maya walked around the scrap heap that was once an MRI machine with a steel ball bearing. The ball bearing was used to identify all magnetic metals in the scrap. If she had used a flat piece of metal, she could not have physically removed it from the neodymium magnet.

The welders and acetylene torch tradesman cut out the pieces Maya identified. When she had enough to produce an adequate magnetic field, the construction team assembled the scrap neodymium pieces in a circular frame that was built to hold the different fragments. The metal parts were distributed as evenly as they could to create a uniform magnetic field.

Tucker procured a closed-circuit TV system so that they could view the test remotely. Tucker selected three of the original fifty stainless steel tanks with functional metering pumps that were still usable after the Cape Canaveral explosion. Electricians wired the pumps for remote start-up behind a newly constructed cinder block wall and added high-tech instruments to measure explosive overpressure and electrical energy.

Tucker filled the three tanks with the specific chemicals used by Tommy Scruggs and asked the safety inspector for approval to start the experiment.

"OK," said Tucker, "we're approved to start. Clear the area." Maya, Tucker, and two operators occupied a separate, remote room to witness the test through the closed-circuit TV. Tucker turned on the video recorder and started the pumps.

189

Two seconds after Tucker turned on the pumps, the team viewed a bright light—a blinding light. The closed-circuit TV system recorded the event—another explosion. The pumps stopped running, the sizzling sound of electricity and the foul odor of smoldering wiring insulation permeated the air. Minutes later, one of the operators ran out from behind the cinder block wall with a fire extinguisher and suppressed the rest of the flames.

"Three for three," Tucker said. "Three times we introduced the same chemicals and three times there is a reaction. Do we have any more metering pumps so we can run the test changing the parameters?"

One of the former NASA lab scientists said, "Yes, we have fifteen more metering pumps that passed our tests." Within two hours, the team had reset the test facility for additional experiments. The team of scientists ran the test again with only two of the three chemicals—nothing happened.

The team experimented with different combinations of the three compounds at various feed rates. They mixed the same chemicals without the magnetic field to make sure they were not just getting a chemical reaction—nothing happened.

They experimented with using fewer scrap pieces of magnets to lower the magnetic field strength without event. They worked for another ten hours until they could sustain a manageable electric current. The chemical feed system was running at five percent of the original feed concentration of chemicals. The magnetic field was estimated to be only fifteen percent as large as when the MRI was used. After producing electricity continuously for about thirty minutes, they shut the system down.

They started another test to make sure the results were identical to the earlier test. They produced electricity again. At 2:30 a.m. on September 6th, Tucker and Maya claimed project success. "OK everybody, take tomorrow or rather the rest of today off. Meet me here at 0900 on September 7th. Look good. We're all going to be on TV."

Cocoa Beach, Florida

The sliding glass door to the private balcony was open on their seventh-floor oceanfront room. The sound of the ocean was calming, and a breeze was blowing gently through the drapes pushing them out into the room. Maya and Tucker slept soundly in their hotel room until around 8:45 a.m. Tucker awoke first, a little disoriented, and finally remembered that Maya was lying next to him. For several minutes, he just observed her beauty. He thought the most perfect woman in the world was asleep with her head on his chest and her left hand excitedly close to his manhood resting on his thigh. "It doesn't get any better than this," he thought. He didn't want to move. He didn't want to disturb her. But, damn it, nature was calling. He slipped to the side being careful not to wake her, used the restroom, washed up, and wandered onto the balcony to see the view of the sun shining in and the waves crashing on the beach.

Their hotel room was not on the top floor. Tucker felt the presence of another person. He looked up to a smiling woman in her sixties looking down on him from her eighth-floor balcony. He realized that he was completely naked and rushed back in the hotel room.

Maya said, "Are you OK? You look a little distraught?"

He said, "How could there be anything wrong? I'm in a beautiful setting with a beautiful woman."

"I'm hungry."

"They have room service here, what would you like?"

"Not for food, silly!"

Cape Canaveral, Florida

Tucker wanted a video recording of their discovery so he could show it to the world. He knew this was an important discovery, but he wasn't quite sure how important. He wanted to capture the discovery on video to enhance its marketability for commercialization. Tucker contacted a local video production company and asked them to bring their equipment to the test facility in Cape Canaveral.

He asked Phil to fly down and participate in the promotional production. Tucker and Maya wrote a script, the lab technicians painted the cinder block walls, improved the appearance of the lab to be more photogenic, made legible placards, and hung a big Entropy sign on the wall. The team of scientists made sure the experiment worked the same as it did at 2:00 a.m. the previous morning. Tucker, Maya, and Phil were the only people in the video production with a speaking role.

Maya discussed the theory that neutrinos were somehow stimulated and that the stimulation resulted in the discharge of electricity. She further discussed the use of the rare-earth metal neodymium to produce a magnetic field.

Phil explained the concept and reasons for the introduction of electrolytes and other chemicals without specifically mentioning the chemicals used.

Then Tucker closed by discussing the commercial application of the discovery and associated technology. He explained what it might mean to the world. Tucker signed off with his and Phil's name and contact information.

The production company edited and added background music to the video and released the video to Florida-based TV stations and, later, through YouTube. Phil, Maya, and Tucker each kept a copy of the video.

The three of them were sitting around the dinner table in *The Mouse Trap* later that night. Phil did not look as happy or as excited as Tucker and Maya. Finally, Tucker asked Phil, "So why the strain on your face? You should be celebrating. This is a significant discovery and will ultimately result in your personal fame and fortune."

"I don't understand what's going on. The discovery is exciting, I just am not exactly sure what we discovered. It works. It does what we say it does. We make electricity without using any fuel—no oil, no gasoline, no diesel, no natural gas, no wind, no batteries, and no solar. And the cost of the introduced chemicals at the quantity and rate is an insignificant cost."

Tucker asked, "So, what's the problem?"

"Why does it work? Maya, do you know for sure that somehow we've stimulated neutrinos?"

Maya said, "No, I don't know that for sure. We could be doing something else here, but if we're not stimulating subatomic particles, then what is happening here?" She thought for a moment and added, "Physicists have always calculated that the sun produces many more neutrinos than we've been able to detect. Or maybe there is a new subatomic particle that we're stimulating into electrons."

Tucker said, "Phil, it works, that's all that counts."

CHAPTER 29

Maya Li was making good progress on her trip. It was 10:00 p.m., but she was still thinking about driving through Lexington, Kentucky, and on to Elkins, West Virginia. Her plan was to call Tucker when she got to Rupp Arena to assess Tucker's status. She crossed the Ohio River into Louisville, Kentucky, and decided she needed to get a cup of coffee, and get rid of some used coffee. She stopped at a Starbucks, used the ladies room, bought a grande cappuccino, and returned to her Honda .

Maya put her coffee in the cup holder, cracked her driver's-side window to help keep her awake, drove out of the parking lot, and started cruising toward the interstate.

Metal pressed up against the back of her neck. A woman's voice in the back seat said, "Pull over into the parking lot of the school on your right."

Maya did as told. She looked into the rearview mirror and saw that the lady wore a mask.

"Pull behind that school."

Maya followed the instructions.

"Stop, but keep your hands on the wheel." Again, Maya did as told.

"Have you ever endured torture, Dr. Li," asked the woman?

Maya said, "Does listening to my mother's psychoanalysis of me count?"

"That's mental torture. I'm talking about the kind of physical torture that creates excruciating pain—the kind where you get to the point that you ask to be killed rather than endure another second."

"You've made your point. What do you want?"

"The formula and all the trade secrets to produce electricity without fuel."

"I take it that you will not believe me if I tell you they never gave me the chemical formula. I know the strength of the magnetic field, but the chemicals and electrolytes that make the discovery work were kept secret from me by Entropy."

"You were part of the discovery team. Surely you were given the details of the process."

"Yes," said Maya, "I do have some process information I can share with you. It may be enough to replicate the specific chemicals. It is right here."

Maya slipped her left hand into the door side pocket, and the woman thought Maya was reaching to provide a document. Instead, Maya turned around and shot the woman three times with her .38 Lady Derringer. The woman, Gang Chung's handler, had gotten off one shot from her Smith & Wesson.

Louisville, Kentucky

The handler for Gang Chung was motionless—more likely than not, three shots to the head from a .38 special caused that kind of response. The bullet from the silenced pistol that shot Maya had hit her in the neck but, fortunately, missed the carotid artery. It hurt more than anything she has ever experienced, but, luckily for her, the three shots from her derringer were loud enough to be heard in the neighborhood. Someone called 9-1-1.

A Louisville police cruiser pulled up behind the Honda. The officer called in for backup, had the plates run, pulled his weapon, took the safety off, put his finger on the trigger, and gingerly approached the Honda. Before the officer got much closer, he called in and reported his observation about blood splatter on the back and side windows of the CRV. He had his gun in his right hand and his LED flashlight in the other.

A second cruiser pulled up. Out jumped a stout-looking female officer, gun pulled, safety off and with both hands on the weapon grip. She approached the passenger's side while the first office approached the driver's side. On the ready, the male officer shined his flashlights into the Honda.

Maya blinked. The handler didn't. Maya was bleeding out and getting weak. She didn't move. The female officer opened the passenger's-side door while the male officer kept his gun ready to shoot if there was any cause. The female officer gently slid the Derringer out of Maya's right hand. She said to the male officer, "Call an ambulance for this one. I'll call the coroner for the other one."

CHAPTER 30

EXETER, NEW HAMPSHIRE— OCTOBER 7TH

The commute between Exeter and Boston was brutal, but Steven Sanders, the Chief Executive Officer of Entropy, wanted to get away from the congestion in Boston on weekends. He also wanted to give his children an excellent education and felt that Exeter provided that for his family. And unlike Boston, there was very little crime in Exeter.

Steven Sanders was well respected by his employees and peers. He was a visionary with an uncanny skill to identify potential technologies, processes, and materials that had an enormous potential upside. He was also very smart about protecting intellectual property or patentable discoveries from industrial thieves.

He was relaxing in his reading room watching a west coast college football game. His wife and son retired to bed an hour or so ago. "Stop-it" their Jack

Russell Terrier, stared at his master pleadingly and whined.

"OK, Stop-it, let me get my shoes on, and I'll take you out for a walk." Sanders grabbed a light jacket, jammed his feet into his worn-out house shoes, found the leash, and picked the flashlight off its hook. Steven de-armed the home security system and shuffled out the back door. Stop-it immediately started barking, but that wasn't unusual—Stop-it was a barker.

Gang Chung ended Stop-it's barking with a shot from his silenced Type 64 revolver. A second later, the barrel of the ugly handgun was inches away from the forehead of Steven Sanders. "Not one sound. Turn around."

Sanders' anger about the loss of his dog overwhelmed him and clouded his typically impeccable judgment; he did not turn around. Chung's roundhouse punch with brass knuckles severely wounded the side of the CEO's head.

Sanders was unconscious when Chung rolled him over onto his stomach to attach plastic ties around both wrists behind his back. The ruthless killer duct-taped Sanders' mouth so that he couldn't make sounds when he awoke in torturous pain.

Several minutes later, Sanders started to stir. He regained consciousness and found the barrel of the silencer up against his mouth and an icepick pressed up against the flesh under his left eye. He understood his situation immediately, as if someone had put smelling salts under his nose. Gang Chung asked, "Would you be so kind as to invite me into your home?" Sanders nodded, rolled over onto his side, got to his knees and eventually stood, the intimidating icepick never far from inflicting unimaginable pain and damage. He walked, his head hurting like hell, through the unlocked back door of his home into the mud room.

Chung ordered, "Stop" as he closed the back door and listened intently. He heard sounds of people talking but quickly realized that the conversation was emanating from the TV. To Sanders' relief, Gang Chung moved the icepick away from his eye.

The duct tape muffled Sanders' scream when the icepick was driven through his right foot and into the hardwood floor. For the second time in just minutes, he passed out.

Stephen Sanders awoke in the kind of pain that drives people temporarily insane only to hear Gang Chung say, "I'm going to rip the duct tape off your mouth. But if you still feel compelled to scream for help or say anything other than answer my direct questions, I'll shoot your fucking kneecap off. Is that understood?" Sanders nodded. Gang Chung pulled the ice pick out of his foot and waited a minute before he ripped the duct tape off Sanders' mouth.

"I want the formula for how Entropy generates electricity without fuel—the neutrino-electricity formula. You have a copy of the formula, either in a safe, on your PC, on a disk, or on a thumb drive. Don't tell me you don't have it. That answer won't fly. You saw what I did to McPherson, so you know in your heart that I will leave here with the formula."

Sanders answered, "Yes, I have the formula. It is in a safe in my reading room."

Gang Chung said, "You disappoint me, Mr. CEO. You are weak and soft. I was hoping to torture you a little bit before you caved in."

Sanders said nothing.

Gang Chung shook his head and smirked as he said, "Please, my weak man, escort me into your reading room." With the silencer pressed up against the small of his back and the icepick held in a fighting position in Chung's powerful right hand, Sanders limped into the reading room, sat down in his office chair in front of the monitor for his personal computer, and began to weep in silence. In front of him, lying on the desk by the monitor was Stop-it, dead with his tongue hanging out.

Gang Chung said, "Your dead dog should be a reminder to you that I am capable of treachery. Remember that as the evening proceeds. I suspect you have other family members in this house besides your dog."

Gang Chung remembered that he had to cut the ties around Sanders' wrists before Sanders could type on the keyboard or operate the safe combination.

"Open the safe first."

Sanders pulled the bottom left-hand drawer of his desk out only to feel the tip of the icepick against his temple. "Be careful, my friend, I didn't give you permission to open that drawer."

"OK," said Sanders, "you push the button."

"Let me guess: this button alerts local police."

"No."

"Why should I believe you?"

"Because you threatened my family."

"What does pushing the button do?"

"It provides access to the safe."

Gang Chung inspected the button carefully and looked into the eyes of Stephen Sanders. "You know I'll torture you if this is a trick, right?"

Sanders did not respond.

Gang pushed the button.

Sanders's desk moved. It pivoted clockwise thirty degrees revealing a small door in the floor.

Sanders asked, "You want to open it yourself?"

Gang Chung opened the door to view a combination lock. He asked, "OK, what's the safe combination?"

"13-39-47."

Gang Chung placed his hand on the dial. The electrical shock shook him to his core. He couldn't seem to let go. He felt like his testicles were being roasted. Chung finally let go, moved in the direction of Sanders, and jammed the icepick into the fat of Stephen Sanders' side.

Sanders seemed to be unaffected by the attack. Witnessing Chung's pain was worth whatever he was about to endure.

Sanders asked, "Would you like for me to open the safe?"

"You asshole. Yes."

Sanders pushed the button again, which disarmed the shock feature and dialed in the combination. He opened the safe door and pulled out a loaded, safety-off, HK45.

Sanders swung the gun around, but before he could use it, Chung chopped his wrist and removed the gun from his hand in one smooth motion. Chung was ready for the ruse and anticipated the direction of Sanders's rotation.

"Thank you. I can always use another gun." Chung chuckled, "Who knows where I might leave this murder weapon. Now, stand back." Chung forced Sanders's wrists together again behind his back and secured them with plastic ties.

Gang Chung emptied the safe contents and placed them on the desk next to Stop-It. He grabbed Sanders's open briefcase and dumped the cash, gold, and silver coins; what looked to him like bonds; five thumb drives; and two unmarked CDs into it. He left the remaining personal stuff like birth certificates, vehicle titles, and jewelry on the desk. Then he looked around the room and grabbed Sanders' laptop, cell phone, and iPad to add to his collection in the briefcase.

He then slapped Sanders hard across the face, forcing him to fall to the floor, and kicked him mercilessly in the solar plexus. The CEO of Entropy was pretty sure he had just taken his last breath—he couldn't seem to make his lungs work, couldn't inhale, and felt dizzyingly paralyzed.

But just then he was jerked up off the floor by the belt around his trousers and summarily deposited back into his office chair.

The force of the motion somehow triggered a return of his natural ability to breathe, cooling Sanders' burning lungs.

"This is your last opportunity to live. And if I decide to kill you because you've been such a jerk, I'll search the premises for your wife and son. What's his name? Jason? You know, I'm a little partial toward young boys.

"If there is anything on your personal computer, you better hand it over right now. I'll remove the ties around your wrists, and you better deliver."

Sanders rubbed his wrists, patted the bleeding side of his stomach, and flexed his bloody fingers like he was a concert pianist before he started typing in his username and password. As Gang Chung looked over Sanders' shoulder, Sanders opened a file folder entitled "McPherson." Then he opened a folder entitled "research." He said with all the hate and contempt he felt, "Hand me one of the thumb drives you stole from me so I can save what you want on it."

He inserted the portable drive into the computer's USB port and started to save the "research" folder onto the device. Sanders finished transferring the file and was about to remove the thumb drive, but Gang Chung said, "Stop. Show me exactly where in that folder the formula is."

Sanders' pain overwhelmed him but1 he reluctantly responded, "When you open the folder entitled 'chemistry,' you'll see a subfolder entitled 'process parameters.' You see that here?" Chung nodded affirmatively. "When you open that folder, you'll see an excel spreadsheet with chemical names on the left and rate of feed on the top. Do you understand?"

Gang Chung placed his large catcher's mitt sized hands over Sanders's mouth, jammed the ice pick into the back of his neck, pushed him off the office chair, and put a slug into his kneecap.

Chung sat down. He removed the thumb drive, stuck it in the breast pocket of his jacket, zipped it tight so he wouldn't lose it, picked up the briefcase, and slipped out the back door.

He walked slowly and deliberately from shadow to shadow and reached his car parked only a block away without encountering a soul.

Police and ambulance sirens pierced the silent night.

Chung smiled. He didn't understand why but, he was happy to know that Sanders lived.

CHAPTER 31

VIENNA, AUSTRIA—OCTOBER 7TH

Sitting in his lush mahogany-paneled office, the president of the Organization of Petroleum Exporting Nations, Mohamed El-bahar, received via the intercom on his desk notification that the Saudi Foreign Minister was on the line.

"This must be serious," El-bahar thought, as he had never previously received a call from the infamous foreign minister who represented OPEC in the First Consortium of Nations. Usually he interfaced with the Saudi Minister of Petroleum and Mineral Resources. A call from the Saudi Prince was indeed disconcerting. "Yes, your Excellency, to what do I owe the honor of this call?"

"I hope you are in good health and that you are enjoying fall in Vienna on this beautiful day." The prince did not wait for an answer, "I would like to suggest that you call a special closed session of the OPEC Intelligence Committee. I would like to make a personal presentation to the committee members."

El-bahar responded, "Yes, of course. What should I tell the members is the subject of your presentation and when would you like the special meeting to convene?"

"The subject is a potential new threat to OPEC and the impact this menace could have on the Consortium and OPEC's world influence." He paused for effect. "Today, by webinar from Riyadh."

Startled, El-bahar said, "Well, uh, I'm unsure all committee members can make it on such short notice, but I'll do my best to make it happen."

"Don't make me have to call each member myself." And with that, the Prince hung up the phone.

"He is the son of a dog," El-bahar said to himself. The reputation of the Saud family preceded his exposure to them, and the conduct of the foreign minister just reinforced their apparently well-deserved bad reputation. El-bahar had enough on his plate as it was without any new threats to OPEC. The drop in demand for oil coupled with an increase in oil production in North America due to new fracking technologies, along with the surprising strength of the US dollar, had weakened OPEC. El-bahar feared that he might lose his position. After all, OPEC's power and influence had eroded under his watch.

El-bahar picked up the phone to call the first member of the Intelligence Committee on his list, the Venezuelan Minister of Energy.

CHAPTER 32

PITTSBURGH, PENNSYLVANIA—
OCTOBER 7TH

"The next quarterly report damn well better show some growth if we expect institutional shareholders to hang in there with us," said the Chairman of the Board of Charleston Energy Holdings. "CEH stock will drop appreciably if we don't meet the forecasts we projected. The earnings you are presenting on this slide for this quarter are way off the mark. What's the problem here?" The chairman's pomposity didn't impress the company's Chief Financial Officer.

Unfazed, the CFO asked, "Do you want me to feed you some bullshit, or do you want the facts?"

"One thing I know about you accounting types is that you can modify facts with assumptions, which impacts financial results."

The CEH Chief Executive Officer stepped in and artfully suggested that they continue the presentation.

The intensity in the room was palpable. All three of them, along with the Chief Operating Officer, Charles Washington, had a lot at stake.

Charles said, "I can feel the love between you two. It's embarrassing!"

"OK, OK," said the chairman.

"As you know," continued the CFO, "our holdings in the mining, transportation, and sale of bituminous coal generate eighty-two percent of our revenue and eighty-seven percent of our earnings. The past administration openly and flagrantly took an anti-coal position. The Environmental Protection Agency has been encouraged to promulgate rules and regulations to prevent the construction of new coal-fired power plants. Also, new EPA clean air rules require utilities to add expensive off-gas treatment technologies to currently operating plants to remove what they call contaminants down to unnecessary and ridiculously low levels. All this at a time when natural gas is cheap, driving utilities to convert their base load generation away from coal. Add to our problems the breakdown we're facing with collective bargaining negotiations on pensions and health care, and you wonder why our earnings are not up?"

"Well," Charles said, "you dressed that up pretty. Tell us what you really think."

"Bullshit," said the chairman. "Our competitors in the coal industry have been performing well compared to CEH. They must have figured out that we don't share the same planet with the Chinese. Our competitors are shipping coal to China at an exponentially increasing rate. We agreed last year and included in the annual report that we would make up any loss from dwindling domestic demand for coal with sales to the People's Republic of China. Why has that not happened?"

The CFO started to speak, but Charles interrupted him and said, "Mr. Chairman, whereas it does seem like China plays by a separate set of rules in that it is OK for them to 'warm the globe,' we have been unable, or should I say unwilling, to reach terms with them. What they want is unethical. I don't want to have to bring you cookies in prison just to meet our financial projections."

The Chairman responded, "We discussed this before. Just make it happen."

"Sir, with all due respect," said the CEO, "you're addressing a minor problem compared to another potential problem. There is an 800-pound gorilla out there that could bankrupt us if what I hear is even remotely accurate. Or," he paused for effect, "it could be the best thing that ever happened to Charleston Energy Holdings."

Dead silence. Fear, apprehension, and anxiety gripped the room.

"The head of our IT department sent me a YouTube video that has gone viral. It shows the direct conversion of electricity without a fuel source. It could be an elaborate hoax like 'cold fusion' or cars fueled by water. But if it is not a hoax, it will have a much greater impact on our business than this administration, EPA, natural gas prices, or the Chinese. There will be no need for coal."

Charles asked, "How could it be the best thing that ever happened to us?"

The CEO said, "It could be OUR technology."

The chairman said, "Well, I suggest we find the guys that produced this YouTube video. Charles, do you think you can make use of your linebacker experience and tackle the inventor?"

Charles said, "Does a bear shit in the woods? Actually, sir, I already met with the Chief Scientist of Entropy, LLC, and the founder of the discovery.

"As you know, I have been preaching for a long time that diversification is a key to the success of any company. CEH doesn't need to be in the coal business; it needs to be in the energy business. We need to be able to provide energy sources to power users, period.

"This new technology that produces electricity without fuel is world changing and needs to belong to CEH. To make that happen, I contacted the inventors and made a proposal to them I thought they couldn't refuse—not a threatening proposal, but one that was financially attractive. I figured that if CEH was quick enough with the first offer, then maybe CEH could have exclusive rights to the discovery.

"The man I met was murdered for the details of the discovery the very same night I met with him. Apparently, others understand the significance of the discovery. To make matters worse, someone planted my DNA at the murder scene."

The Charleston Energy Holdings Chairman, CEO, and CFO were left with their mouths agape.

"Fortunately, I've been cleared by law enforcement. However, I'm more committed to securing a license for the technology than ever."

CHAPTER 33

RIYADH, SAUDI ARABIA— OCTOBER 8ᵀᴴ

Members of the OPEC Intelligence Committee represented the countries of Venezuela, Nigeria, Iraq, United Arab Emirates, Kuwait, Qatar, Algeria, and Angola. Noticeably absent on the call were representatives from Iran and Libya. Mohamed El-bahar spoke first and said, "I'd like to thank the Saudi Foreign Minister, Prince Saud, for hosting this virtual meeting of the Intelligence Committee. I would also like to thank all of you for attending this webinar on such short notice. The representatives of Iran and Libya had previous commitments and, unfortunately, could not attend." Of course, the Foreign Minister knew better. Iran did not participate because Iran refused to respond to a call by Saudi Arabia. Iran did not jump when Saudi Arabia ordered Iran to do so.

The Saudi Prince thought, "Libya has issues of its own and probably did not attend for internal reasons. It wasn't that long ago when the Libyans under Kaddafi tried to assassinate the Saudi King."

El-bahar said, "With that introduction, I hereby turn this meeting over to our host, Prince Saud."

There was no applause from the attendees. "Thank you, President Mohamed El-bahar for encouraging the esteemed members of the Intelligence Committee to attend this meeting," said Prince Saud. "A discovery has been introduced by the enemy of Islam, the United States. This discovery produces electricity without the need for fuel."

The prince raised his voice and loudly stated, "*Let me repeat myself: this discovery uses a technology that creates electricity without fuel.*"

The members of the OPEC Intelligence Committee responded with incredulity and were somewhat in shock.

"Whereas Western nations do not predominately use oil to produce electricity, oil use does represent approximately twenty-five percent of electricity generated in the US annually, consuming five million barrels of oil per day. We, in OPEC, project a decrease in the demand for oil of three million barrels per day within five years. This is a significant reduction in demand that will have a deleterious effect on our revenues and world influence. The impact is magnified if the technology somehow becomes useful in generating on-board electricity for electric cars. Watch this published YouTube video about the technology."

The attending members of the intelligence committee viewed the YouTube video with astonishment. The anxiety expressed by the OPEC members on the webcast was uncontained.

"I'm not one to just let this happen," continued the Prince. "We need to do something to stop the impact of this discovery from happening through the Consortium.

With the approval of this committee, I hereby request that OPEC supports the Consortium's action."

The ranking member from Kuwait asked, "Dear Prince, exactly what initiative do you think the Consortium can take to stop this assault on OPEC's influence on the world stage?"

Prince Saud ignored the question and said, "I'm asking for carte blanche authority vested by OPEC members to do whatever it takes to mitigate the impact of the discovery by the great Satan, the United States. A majority of OPEC members via a roll-call vote that authorizes Saudi Arabia to address this issue would be enough for us to take control of the situation."

All attendees of the OPEC Intelligence Committee voted for the motion and authorized Saudi Arabia to "handle" the situation.

Of course, the prince was just covering his rear end because he'd already "handled" the situation days ago when he hired "Aaron" to do his dirty work.

CHAPTER 34

WEST VIRGINIA—OCTOBER 8ᵀᴴ

The drive through Oakland, Maryland, along Route 219 into West Virginia to Silver Lake in the Lincoln Town Car after midnight was uneventful. Jenny had fallen asleep. Stiletto Man was tired of her whining—silence was much better. The driver said, "I'm not sure, but we might have been followed in Oakland. Two different county police were behind us at one time or another. Maybe it is just a coincidence."

Stiletto Man considered for a moment what the driver had said, pulled out his phone, and called Brock. "Have you been listening to the police band?"

Brock said, "Yes, nothing of interest. We're in the middle of nowhere, just crossed the Cheat River. We'll be in Elkins in an hour or so. Where do you want to rendezvous?"

"The rendezvous point is the United Methodist Center on Kerens Avenue. Hold back until we get closer, but survey the place to make sure there are no surprises for us. We're probably an hour behind you," said Stiletto Man.

Stiletto Man hung up, called Art Monahan, and asked, "Target still in place?"

"Yes," Art lied. Art was too afraid to hear the answer to ask anything about the well-being of his family. The phone was disconnected.

Quantico, Virginia

From a control room 150 miles away, a twenty-three-year-old FBI agent was operating a General Atomics Gray Eagle drone, which was about two thousand feet the ridges of Backbone Mountain and locked onto the old Lincoln Town Car. The drone was equipped with a laser, video, and thermal detection devices employed to lock-on, track, and closely monitor the vehicle. The drone was unarmed without heat-seeking missiles or cannons—its function was purely surveillance. The FBI Sikorsky UH-60 Blackhawk helicopters provided the firepower that the US Government planned to exert with its 105 mm M119 howitzer and 300 rounds of ammunition.

"Sir," said the young Quantico-based FBI agent to the Agent-in-Charge in Fort Belvoir, "the Lincoln Town Car is approaching Thomas, West Virginia, which is only a few miles from Davis. If the vehicle drives in the direction of Davis, do you want me to alert the team on the ground and get the Blackhawks in the air?"

"No, I'm pretty sure he'll turn toward Elkins and not pass through Davis," said the Agent-in-Charge. "But do inform me if I'm wrong."

"Monahan," said the Agent-in-Charge, "call your blackmailer and tell him the target has moved to a location two blocks west of the United Methodist Center. This detail may convince the asshole that you are indeed tracking the target and that he needs to keep his hostages alive to keep you engaged."

The FBI Agent-in-Charge then contacted the Blackhawk pilot, "What's your fuel status? We'll need to get you airborne in less than thirty minutes."

Elkins, West Virginia

Brock was listening to the police band and simultaneously surfing the news websites. He had heard about the attack in Davis, West Virginia, at a coal mine. He had heard that terrorists destroyed two Blackhawks using RPGs, and most disturbingly, had killed Tucker Cherokee in the assault. It was disturbing because if Tucker Cherokee was in Davis, then he wasn't in Elkins. If he was not in Elkins, then Zytlle was fed bullshit by the NGA guy. Brock knew Aaron would go ballistic when he found out that he'd been dicked around with.

Brock said to Graf. "I'm not sure it's safe to be around Aaron when he discovers Tucker Cherokee is dead, that his intelligence was bad, and that the mission is blown. I'd say he'll take his wrath out on us after he's finished with the hostages."

"Bolting might not be a good idea either," said Graf. "He might come after us. We're already here in Elkins. Let's observe from a safe distance and see if Aaron shows up." The two mercenaries got back into their Buick and staked out the Methodist Center from a quarter mile away. They continued to listen to the radio news, incredulously.

Elkins, West Virginia

Aaron was about three miles away from the Elkins United Methodist Center when his satellite phone rang. He still had seventeen hours left. Why was the Prince calling him? "Yes, your Excellency."

"Congratulations my dear man, you did a great job. The announcement by the President's White House Press Secretary stated that not only did you terminate Tucker Cherokee, but you ensured no one else could recreate the discovery that was such a threat to Saudi Arabia, the Consortium, and our OPEC nation brethren."

Aaron Zytlle had no idea what the Prince was talking about. He cautiously said, "Thank you."

The Prince said, "I'll reward your account in Belize. The deposit will be untraceable. I must say, it was a bright touch by you to make it look like a domestic environmentalist extremist group committed the attack. It was a pleasure doing business with you. Please, under no circumstances are you to contact me again." The Prince hung up leaving Aaron, the Stiletto Man, totally confused.

Aaron said to his driver, "Pull over before we get to the rendezvous point and turn the radio on. Find a news station." It took less than a minute to find a news station that was reporting the tragedy. The report described in detail the Davis Coal Mine attack, the downing of two Blackhawk helicopters, the number of Hostage Rescue Team and Critical Incident Response team fatalities, the death of co-inventor Tucker Cherokee, and the potential explanation for the attack by an environmental extremist group.

Dana Monahan was in the back seat of the Lincoln Town Car and also heard the news. She knew immediately that she and her daughter were no longer needed as hostages. Dana started to cry but decided she needed to concentrate, think more, and cry less. She had to save her daughter somehow.

Aaron called Brock. He picked up reluctantly, expecting to incur the wrath of Aaron. Instead, the Stiletto Man said, "Aaron here. It appears that we have been paid for completing our mission. We need to celebrate. This is the easiest money we ever made. Watch for our Lincoln Town Car as we drive by the United Methodist Center, our original point of rendezvous. We should be driving by there in a couple of minutes. Don't stop for any reason. Just follow us."

Aaron thought, "I need to disappear off the face of the earth for the rest of my life. When the Prince discovers that I did not accomplish the mission for which OPEC and the Consortium contracted me and that someone else completed the task, I will be hunted down, tortured, and murdered. I need to leave no trace of myself. Only the driver, the hostages, Brock, and Graf know what I look like. No one knows my real identity. I must eliminate all five of them."

Aaron said to Brock, "I anticipated mission success. I previously made reservations at the Cheat River Cabins Resort. We have a three-bedroom cabin reserved under a fake name. I'll have my driver pay cash when we check in. I have requested that the cabin has a fully stocked bar. We'll settle financially while we are at the cabin and then we will be free to separate and go our ways. You can leave anytime you like. We will never see each other again. I am retiring. We made enough money on this mission for all of us to also retire, especially since we get to split the shares of our three mercenary friends killed in that Grant County log home screw-up."

Brock was reluctant to go—Zyttle's reputation preceded him. However, if Brock didn't go, he was unsure how Aaron would react. Would Aaron stiff them out of Brock and Graf's fee if they didn't go? If he didn't get paid by Aaron, what could Brock do about it? Brock and Graf decided that they'd follow Aaron in the Lincoln Town Car, but they would be very careful and vigilant—they did not trust Aaron Zyttle, the Stiletto Man.

Tucker County, West Virginia

Ram cocked his head, his ears picked up, and then he buried his snout into his paws. Tucker was talking incessantly aloud to Ram as if the warrior understood every word Tucker said.

"We need a win-win solution, here, Ram, if we're going to survive. There are winners and losers. We won life's lottery, Ram, by discovering this technology that makes electricity without fuel. The Russians were losers when we created this technology, which makes all their oil and natural gas less valuable. Russia tried to turn the tables and make me the loser by killing me and burying the knowledge of the discovery somewhere under the Siberian tundra.

"If Russia felt threatened, can you imagine how Saudi Arabia and the other OPEC countries must feel?" Ram ignored the question.

"I bet the People's Republic of China would want this technology. You know, Ram, China is the world's most populated country with over 1.35 billion people. Though a suppressive communist regime controls China, it adopted capitalism to bolster its economic prowess and international influence. Its rate of economic growth has been breathtaking over the past decade or two. Unfortunately, an equally breathtaking demand for electricity accompanied the growth. China built coal-fired power plants to produce electricity with no concern for its environmental consequences.

"The air quality in Beijing and Shanghai became abominable. The Chinese people had little opportunity to express their displeasure, but the politburo recognized that continued pollution of the environment would encourage civil unrest. Do you know Ram that China became the largest carbon dioxide emitter in the world? Allegedly, CO_2 was responsible for the threat of human-made global warming. China was not a signatory of the Kyoto or Copenhagen agreements to reduce CO_2 emissions. However, the United Nations and China trading partners were putting an enormous amount of pressure on China to cut back the production of global warming gasses, which are byproducts from the production of electricity. China was building non-CO_2 emitting nuclear power plants at a fast pace, but nuclear power stations took much longer to construct and could not keep up with the electrical demand.

"So, I bet Beijing was excited about the new American discovery of electricity without the need for a fuel source. This discovery could change their energy strategy and further boost their economy. In the long term, they would no longer have to import coal, build more land-flooding hydro plants, or add expensive and nonproductive off-gas cleaning equipment to existing coal-fired power plants. The air would be cleaner, and the European Union, Japan, and the United Nations could get off their back." Ram put his paws over his ears.

"Obviously, US energy companies, especially coal mining companies, are losers if our discovery becomes ubiquitous. So, Ram, thanks for your ear, because I now have a plan for everyone to profit from the Entropy discovery."

It took Tucker only fifty minutes to drive from Thomas, West Virginia, to Elkins, West Virginia, including the extra time it took to find the Methodist Center. Tucker parked the Silverado about 150 yards away from the alleged rendezvous point. He decided to take advantage of the opportunity and walk Ram a few yards while he had a chance.

Tucker and Ram saw the Lincoln Town Car and a Buick following the Town Car drive by the United Methodist Center. He recognized the Buick as one of the vehicles that followed him through Grant County a few days ago. Earlier, Tucker had overheard the FBI Hostage Rescue team discuss a Lincoln Town Car and the hostages taken because of Tucker's deadly discovery. Tucker decided to follow the two vehicles out of town.

Elkins, West Virginia

All three of the vehicles were followed by the General Atomics drone, two thousand feet overhead. The FBI agent operating the drone from Quantico said, "The night vision capabilities of the drone will come in handy if they are leaving the street lights in Elkins. The heat signatures still identify four passengers in the Town Car."

The FBI Agent-in-Charge spoke into his headset to the Hostage Rescue Team and said, "We have to assume that the perpetrator has heard about the Davis Coal Mine attack and the death of Tucker Cherokee. He, therefore, knows Art Monahan lied to him about Mr. Cherokee being at the Elkins United Methodist Center. His mission failed. He will likely dispose of the hostages soon, so time is of the essence. Is the Blackhawk idling? How much time after I say 'go' before you actually lift off?"

"Yes, sir," said the pilot. "The Blackhawk is idling, and we'll be airborne within five seconds of your order to 'go.'"

"Do you have visual on your tablet on the drone feed?"

"Yes, sir. We have a visual of the subject Lincoln Town Car."

"Ok, we have visual on the car. Lift and covertly follow it. Stay two miles behind the vehicle and out of audio range."

"Yes, sir."

Elkins, West Virginia

No one saw Tank and Powers shadowing Tucker. Between the two of them, they had two sniper rifles, four handguns, two hand grenades, two night vision goggles, and powerful binoculars. Tank was using the binoculars and said, "What the hell is Tucker doing following these guys? These are probably the same people hired to assassinate him. For such a smart guy, his elevator doesn't go to the top floor sometimes."

Powers said, "He might understand particle physics and stuff like that, but he sure wouldn't make it in our business. He's not playing with a full deck. For example, Tucker should have figured out that there was a GPS tracker in Ram's collar."

The caravan proceeded from Elkins to the Cheat River Cabins Resort—the Lincoln Town Car, the Buick, the Silverado, a drone, the *White Knight* contingent in Powers' Durango, and the Blackhawk.

CHAPTER 35

CHEAT RIVER CABINS—OCTOBER 8TH

The owners of Cheat River Cabins Resort maintained their log cabins in a clean and beautiful state. The cabins sat on twenty acres of land, including roughly two acres of open space leading up to the entrance. The spacious three-bedroom 3,100-square-foot "cabin" had a spectacular A-frame great room with a sixteen-foot solid pine pitched ceiling and two 60-inch ceiling fans. The twelve-foot-wide stone fireplace which was preloaded with kindling and split hardwood reflected off the equally beautiful and recently polished solid pine floors.

The back of the cabin had a sliding glass door that allowed the occupants to walk out onto a redwood deck that overlooked a heavily wooded area and a roaring Cheat River only twenty yards away. The owners of the Cheat River Cabins Resort provided special services for Charleston corporate renters that occasionally used the cabins for retreats and board meetings. One of the services they offered was a stocked bar located in the great room with preselected wine, beer, and liquor. Aaron checked the bar to see whether the owners had stocked it as he requested. There were two fifths of Glen Livet Scotch Whiskey, two bottles of Dom Perignon Champagne, a case of Beck's Beer, and a quart of Wild Turkey "101" in the bar.

Aaron's driver escorted the hostages into the spacious and well-kept master bedroom with a king-size bed and a master bathroom. Neither Jenny nor Dana Monahan had been able to change clothing or take a bath since their abduction. It was Stiletto Man's intent to enjoy his time with the hostages for a couple of days before he killed them. He wanted the girl and her mother to be clean and wear clean clothes when he played with them, so he told his driver to learn the correct sizes and then sent him back out late at night to find a place for a change of clothing for the hostages.

With Brock and Graf present to oversee the hostages, Stiletto Man ordered Dana to fix a meal for six with whatever was available in the fully stocked kitchen. Graf had his 9mm P200 H&K out of his shoulder holster and supervised Dana's dinner preparation while Aaron and Brock talked in the great room. As Aaron poured himself a drink of Scotch on the rocks, he told Brock, "Our sponsor attributed the successful attack on Tucker Cherokee at the Davis Coal Mine to us! They paid us. I checked the account from the Town Car. We are wealthier than we were yesterday. Congratulations."

Graf said, "When are you going to transfer funds into my account?"

"Soon, my friend."

"What is your plan," Brock continued, "for when our customer discovers that someone else killed Tucker Cherokee?"

Aaron said, "I expect to be in hiding permanently. He doesn't know my real name. He doesn't know your name either. I have protected both you and Graf."

Brock asked, "What is your plan for the hostages?"

"Not your problem," Aaron responded curtly. "Would you like a celebration drink?"

Afraid to reject Aaron and incur his wrath, Brock said, "Yes, please."

Randolph County, West Virginia

Tucker followed the caravan from Elkins to the Cheat River Cabins Resort at a safe distance. He pretended to drive on when the Town Car and Buick turned left into the resort entrance. About a half mile later, Tucker turned the Silverado around and returned just short of the entrance. The cabin was roughly a quarter of a mile down a private road from the entrance. Tucker did not have binoculars with him—an oversight. He didn't want to wander down the private road—he would be too vulnerable. So, he decided to take his flashlight and Ram into the dense forest surrounding the south side of the Cheat River Cabin Resort complex.

Randolph County, West Virginia

Tank and Powers were even farther back from the caravan than Tucker. Their focus, their first priority, was Tucker, not the hostages or the hostage takers. However, Tank and Powers agreed that given the opportunity, they would protect the hostages and eliminate the assassins.

They were still following the GPS signal in Ram's collar. "I see that Ram has left the road and is now in the forest," Powers said to Tank.

"I might kill Tucker myself when this is all over after we've saved him," Tank said. They saw the Lincoln Town Car drive past in the opposite direction. Tank said to Powers, "Tell you what, I'll take a sniper rifle, night vision binoculars, and the GPS monitor and wander into the woods. You follow that Town Car and improvise depending on what happens. Keep your earpiece open so that we can communicate."

"This isn't my first mission, son," said Powers. Tank jumped out of the Durango on the north side of the Cheat River Cabins Resort complex and into the forest. Powers followed the Town Car back in the direction of Elkins. The Town Car pulled into a Walmart. The driver parked, locked the Town Car, and walked into the store. About fifteen minutes later, he walked out of Walmart with a bag, opened the Town Car door, and started to shut the driver's-side door when Powers hit him with the butt of his Glock 20.

The driver slumped over onto the steering wheel. Powers removed his Beretta and checked for other weapons. Powers then handcuffed the driver's hands behind his back before he regained consciousness. Powers checked the Walmart bag for the articles purchased by the driver.

Powers opened communications with Tank. "It is confirmed that the hostages are still safe and in the cabin. It is also confirmed that they won't be leaving there alive. The only things in the bag are a pair of little girls' pajamas and a woman's nightgown—no travel clothes or food. There is a pack of cigarettes in the bag."

"Is there a way," asked Tank, "to disguise yourself to look like the driver from a distance? The Town Car is our best chance to get close to the cabin, and maybe, inside."

Powers said, "I don't look much like this guy, and we're not the same physical size. He's bigger than I am, but I'll figure something out. Before we finalize a plan, though, I need to have a little chat with the guy. He might be able to provide some information that's useful input for our plan. Over and out."

Powers pushed the driver over to the passenger's side and duct taped him to the seat. Powers would normally find a secure location for the interrogation but, in the interest of time, he got into the driver's seat, started up the Town Car, and drove around the back of the Walmart to a loading dock where he would have limited privacy.

CHAPTER 36

ELKINS, WEST VIRGINIA—
OCTOBER 8ᵀᴴ

The Blackhawk helicopter pilot spoke into his headset to the Agent-in-Charge, "Looks like we have some civilian volunteers engaged here, sir. The drone, still following the Town Car, presented us with an interesting video. Any ideas as to who the 'good guy' is?"

"We have not heard from the *White Knight*s since the Mount Storm debacle. My guess is they have somehow picked up on the hostage situation and decided to be heroes. Damn these guys, they're going to complicate our rescue options. Stand down until we figure out a revised course of action."

Cheat River Cabins, West Virginia

Tucker and Ram moved slowly through the forest on the south side of the Cheat River Cabin Resort campus. Dead branches and dry leaves covered the dense forest ground, which made much too much noise with each step Tucker made, so he had to move slowly. As he got closer to the cabin, he had to move even slower. He wished his dad taught him the art of stealth. Ram, for some reason, didn't seem to make any noise.

Tucker reached a position 200 yards away from the cabin. He couldn't see shit yet, but he did identify which set of windows into which he was going to peer.

At the same time, Tank was making progress toward the cabin on the north side of the Cheat River Cabin Resort complex. He was probably seventy-five yards away from the cabin and 300 yards away from Tucker, yet he could hear Tucker banging around in the woods. Tank was hoping that no one in the cabin would step outside and hear Tucker rummaging through the forest. Tank himself intended to move around to the back of the cabin where he was sure he could get the best view inside the cabin; he expected floor-to-ceiling windows in the back.

Inside Cheat River Cabins, West Virginia

Brock asked Aaron, Stiletto Man, "Has it occurred to you that the weasel Monahan lied to you about the whereabouts of Tucker Cherokee?"

Aaron grinned, "Of course, that's why I'm going to follow through with my threat to his family. Watta shem!"

"Did it also occur to you that the Elkins United Methodist Church was a setup and trap for us by law enforcement?'

"Yes, that is why we just drove on by and didn't meet and shake hands on the property, we were just another set of vehicles driving through. Did you notice anything unusual?"

Brock said, "Only that there were no cars in the parking lot as if law enforcement cleared all civilians from the Center. And I thought a Silverado was following us, but it drove past the turnoff to this resort campus. It didn't come back. My point is that maybe we need to get out of here."

"My dear friend, if the US Government knows we're here, there will be nowhere to hide. Where could we go where they couldn't follow us? That bell has been rung and can't be un-rung. Either they have us, or they don't. I'm going to stay here and enjoy myself on the premise that they don't have us. After my driver returns, you're free to leave."

Cheat River Cabins, West Virginia

Tank worked himself to where he could peer into the back of the cabin. As he had hoped, the whole back of the cabin was practically all windows. With his high-powered digital camera-capable binoculars, he could view and record everything he saw. He observed two men talking and drinking in the cabin's great room. He saw a woman and a little girl preparing food in the kitchen under the guard of a man with a gun in his right hand.

"Powers," said Tank, "I have the hostages in view and they appear to be all right."

"Great," said Powers. "The driver here confirmed that the hostages were all right but that he was sure they would be abused and killed. He said that the guy they refer to as 'Aaron' is a sociopath and will enjoy killing the hostages. The guy also said he was worried about whether Aaron was going to kill him because the driver knew what he looked like. He said he thought the hostages had about twelve unpleasant hours to live."

Tank said, "I could take out all of them with my sniper rifle. But after my first shot, the other two or three would move and shield themselves with the hostages. If you can drive up in the Town Car and start to open the front door, you could take one of them out while I got the second one. That only leaves one bad guy remaining with whom we need to contend.

"Before we do anything," asked Powers, "where is Tucker and what is the FBI Hostage Rescue Team doing?"

Tank said, "I've lost contact with the Agent-in-Charge. They must have changed frequencies after Mount Storm. Tucker, on the other hand, is about 150 yards away and sounds like a herd of buffalo."

Tucker and Ram were only twenty-five yards south of the cabin, on the side where the stone chimney rose. There were no windows on that side of the cabin, so he felt safe as he was out of the line-of-sight of the cabin occupants. Tucker extemporaneously developed a plan to rescue the hostages using the rarely used offensive fighting skills taught to him by his father. He took a few steps in the direction of the cabin when a hand grabbed him around his mouth from behind. It was a large and powerful hand and Tucker could not budge it off his face. Another huge hand simultaneously grabbed his wrist when Tucker reached for his revolver. Tucker knew he was experiencing his last moment in life and wondered why Ram wasn't attacking the perpetrator.

Tank said, "Be quiet, and I will slowly lift my hand off your mouth."

Tucker whispered, "How the hell did you get here?"

"Not now, stay put. Don't move another inch. Powers is about to drive up in the Town Car. I don't want you to think it isn't him and do something stupid. Ram, 'stay' with Tucker. I'm going back behind the cabin with my sniper rifle. Don't get in the way." With that, Tank left.

Elkins, West Virginia

Powers had duct taped the driver's mouth and put him in the trunk of the Town Car. He started to open the driver's-side door when four police vehicles with lights flashing and sirens blaring drove into the Walmart parking lot and headed right toward him. Powers casually put both hands on the top of his head—he knew the drill. One of the police cruisers, a West Virginia state trooper, shined a spotlight directly on Powers. The trooper's voice over a megaphone instructed, "Lie down, spread your arms and legs and keep your hands visible at all times." Powers followed the order. Eight officers evacuated the four cruisers and surrounded Powers with weapons drawn. One of them patted Powers down and pulled out two handguns and a knife.

"State your name," demanded the lead officer.

"Powers, no first name."

"OK, Mr. Powers, you can get up and put your hands down. The Feds asked us to verify your identity. The FBI also advised us that you are an accomplished and dangerous man and not to try to approach you without adequate backup. I apologize for the extreme show of force, but we believed it to be necessary."

Powers asked, "Who gave you this information? I need to move as soon as possible because some wicked men expect to see this Town Car return. If it doesn't, a woman and child are at serious risk." Before the officer could answer the questions, Powers heard it—a Blackhawk helicopter. He looked in the direction of the sound, then looked at the officer and said into his microphone, "Did you get all that, Tank? Help is on the way."

Cheat River Cabins, West Virginia

The Blackhawk landed on the front lawn of the Cheat River Cabins Resort complex. Six well-armed FBI Hostage Rescue agents quickly jumped out of the helicopter and split up—two to the front door and two each on the sides of the cabin. Aaron got off the first shots from his G23 Glock. He hit one of the Hostage Rescue agents in the chest as he was rounding one side of the cabin. Fortunately, the agent was wearing his Kevlar vest. Aaron Zytlle had four 13-round magazines. He was spraying lead everywhere he saw movement. Brock was covering the back of the cabin from where he expected some of the FBI agents to ultimately approach.

Graf ran out of the kitchen where he guarded the hostages looking for guidance from Brock.

Instead, Graf's head exploded as if it were one of Gallagher's watermelons. The shot came from Tank's sniper rifle on the river side of the cabin.

Dana grabbed Jenny and headed for the rear deck sliding glass door. With her daughter in her arms, she raced onto the deck that overlooked the Cheat River. To her surprise, there were no stairs down to ground level. Dana decided that for them to escape, they were going to have to jump off the deck and drop ten feet onto river rocks. She didn't want to go back inside the cabin for fear of the gunfire, so she started to jump with Jenny in her arms.

She hesitated when she suddenly saw a man standing below yelling up to her over the cacophony of weapons discharging. She couldn't hear what he was saying, but she recognized him from the photo that Stiletto Man had continually referenced. It was the guy Stiletto Man was after. So, Dana took Jenny by her hands and held her over the deck until the man was directly under her. Dana let go of Jenny who dropped directly onto Tucker. He caught Jenny, fell backward, and hit his head on river rocks but used his body to absorb the fall for Jenny. She was unhurt but screamed hysterically for her mother. Dana didn't hesitate and jumped, barely missed landing on Tucker, fell hard, and twisted her ankle.

Right after Dana jumped, Aaron emerged onto the balcony. He was also trying to escape out the back of the cabin.

Brock was dead, Graf was dead, and the driver was AWOL. Aaron knew he was going to die if he didn't try to escape into the woods. Stiletto Man jumped, landed hard, but rolled to one side without injuring himself.

He rolled right into Ram.

When Aaron Zytlle raised his weapon and aimed it at Dana, Tucker said, "Bad-bad."

It was messy.

PART THREE

RETRIBUTION

CHAPTER 37

CHEAT RIVER CABINS—OCTOBER 8TH

Their faces were black with paint and their eyes black with hate. In the pitch-black night, each had a finger in contact with the trigger on their assault rifle.

Yet, there was hope under the early morning moonless and starless sky—none had yet fired their weapon.

Slowly, very slowly, with palms out, and arms spread wide apart, Tucker raised his hands over his bleeding head. He said, loud enough to hear over the roaring Cheat River, "Good, good. Stay."

At the odd reaction, one of the FBI Hostage Rescuers actually showed the whites of his teeth with something that resembled a smile, but he still demanded that Tucker lay face-down on the ground. He roughly patted Tucker down and removed a loaded handgun.

The FBI agents' kid gloves came off.

A Deadly Discovery

While the barrels of three M4s closed in on him, the lead agent cuffed Tucker's hands behind his back, lifted him roughly up onto his feet, took a digital photo of him, read Tucker his rights, arrested him, and escorted him at gunpoint into the Blackhawk where he was restrained in leg irons and cuffed to the helicopter frame. One of the agents stood guard over him while the rest of the team completed their mission.

It could have been worse. A lot worse. He'd never know how close he and Ram had come to death. Tucker never mentioned his innocence or who he was to the FBI. He suspected that he was safer as a prisoner than if he was running around free.

Two other members of the FBI Hostage Rescue Team offered aid and comfort to Dana and Jenny, attended to their minor injuries—suffered because of their jump off the deck— and wrapped them in warm blankets. Jenny had her arms around her mom in a death grip, her face in the crook of her mother's neck, and sobbed. Dana couldn't walk on her twisted ankle, so two of the rescuers literally carried Dana—with Jenny attached to her—to the helicopter.

The Hostage Rescue Team stealthily conducted a thorough room-by-room search of the cabin without disturbing forensic evidence, opened closets, inspected bathrooms, and explored potential hiding places for additional kidnappers or their victims. The remains of the dead kidnappers, Brock and Graf, were left undisturbed during the search of the cabin. An all-clear was eventually given.

The by-the-book leader of the Hostage Rescue Team, Bull Brown, contacted the Quantico-based FBI Agent-in-Charge, Samuel Davis, and said, "The hostages are rescued and unharmed. The crime scene is secured.

We captured and disarmed one of the hostage-takers. Three perps need body bags. One is spread out over a wide area. Tell the crime lab to bring a shovel. What are my orders, sir?"

"According to the infrared camera on the drone, there are two heat sources about 150 yards from you to the east along the river. Check it out, but do not engage until you verify who they are. I repeat, do not engage unless threatened."

The FBI Hostage Rescue Team spread out, crossed to the other side of the river, donned their night vision goggles, and searched the adjacent forest. Ten minutes into their search, the Agent-in-Charge instructed the team to stand down and return to the cabin to deal with a more pressing issue.

As Tank scratched Ram behind his ears, he heard the sounds of incoming police sirens and ambulances from the City of Elkins approach the cabin. Tank sighed with relief—relief that **he** didn't have to fill out all the incident-related paperwork.

Quantico, Virginia

The Blackhawk landed in Quantico at 0213. The FBI Hostage Rescue Team never let their guard down and stared menacingly at their prisoner—Tucker was clearly under constant adult supervision. When the blades finally slowed to rest, the helicopter door opened, rescuers lowered stairs and assisted Dana and Jenny out of their ride into a cool, dark, and blustery early morning.

Dana screamed.

A joyful and tearful Art Monahan waited on the helipad. The three of them group hugged, cried, and laughed and cried some more. They couldn't let go of each other.

No one disturbed them, but every one of the young, intense, rock-hard members of the Hostage Rescue Team wore genuine and heartfelt smiles. This is why they do what they do. This was their reward for a job well done.

A short, slight, black man wearing a headset and speaking into a microphone as he walked with purpose, approached the big Hostage Rescue Team Leader, Bull Brown, and got right into his face. Words were spoken between them, the team leader listened intently, glanced over in Tucker's direction, and nodded his head in acknowledgment of his new orders.

Bull pulled the keys from his jacket, reentered the Blackhawk, approached Tucker, and removed the handcuffs from the frame. He then removed the handcuffs from behind his back, and finally, the leg irons.

"Mr. Cherokee, we thought you were dead." The small man added, "I'm, Samuel Davis, the Agent-in-Charge responsible for the mission to protect you and to recover the hostages. We were shocked and pleasantly surprised to view the digital photo taken of you during your arrest. We're all very relieved to see you with the hostages. You'll have to explain to us later how you managed to survive the attack at the Davis Coal Mine. But we apologize for your treatment by the FBI at the Cheat River Cabins."

"That's perfectly all right. At least they didn't shoot. I think they were tempted. Your men were just doing their job, and they were professional," said

Tucker. "Congratulations, by the way, for the safe rescue of Dana and Jenny. Good job."

The Agent-in-Charge hung his head and looked away as he said, "We lost a lot of good men and women. No offense, but at this moment, recovering the hostages and finding you safe and sound is overshadowed by yesterday's tragedy."

There was an awkward moment of silence before he said, "I'm sorry, Mr. Cherokee, but we have to inconvenience you further and ask you to stay here in Quantico. I am under strict orders to hold you here. We have many questions for you, and I'm afraid, time is of the essence. Apparently, things have elevated to the highest levels of the government, and they want all the facts before they make any tactical decisions as to how to respond to the act of terrorism in West Virginia.

"Listen, it looks like you need medical attention for your head wound and you must be tired and hungry. Since we're not giving you a choice and forcing you to stay here, we'll extend to you the FBI's version of hospitality. Let's see if we can scrounge something up for you to eat."

Tucker nodded his head and smiled.

"I'll call a medic and ask him to meet us in the mess hall. By the way, there's a locker room adjacent to the mess hall where you can wash up."

Nothing prepared Tucker for the surprise he encountered in the men's locker room. He was shocked. Was that really him? Tucker stared at his reflection from a full-length mirror. He looked like something out of a horror movie with blood congealed on his forehead—more blood matted in his hair on the right side, dirt on the left side of his face, mud all over his jeans and shirt, his hair stuck straight up, and there were bruises on his neck.

He dabbed his face with wet paper towels, brushed some of the dirt off his shirt, finger combed his hair, thoroughly washed his hands, and wandered back out into the mess hall. The medic was waiting for him to clean and apply antiseptics to his wound.

There was no beer in the mess hall. He wanted to drink beer to flush out the Tc-99 from his system as Doc Garfunkel had recommended. But there was no beer. Though Tucker was starved, the food at 0230 was less than desirable. He ate half of a dry, tasteless, cold ham and cheese sandwich just to kill the hunger pangs.

While he ate, he wondered what had happened to Ram. A big German shepherd with blood all over his snout would frighten just about anyone who encountered him. Somebody might be tempted to shoot him thinking him to be rabid. But Tank was also near the cabin, so Tucker figured they were together somewhere and that he needed to quit worrying about Ram.

He wondered about Powers and where he ended up. Last he'd heard, Powers had been chasing down the guy that blew up the Blackhawks in Davis.

Then he started wondering how he was going to reach Maya. He was supposed to meet her in Lexington, Kentucky.

He also remembered that he'd left JJ's truck on the side of the road at the Cheat River Cabins Resort entrance. He worried about JJ's condition. He sighed and thought, "There are a lot of loose ends out there that I've got to make right when I get back on my feet. I've got a lot of work to do."

Sleep deprivation combined with a decrease in adrenaline flow caught up with him. He was crashing, hitting the wall. Tucker grabbed a paper cup and walked over to a coffee thermos. Before he got to pour himself a cup though, an unfamiliar young FBI agent stopped him, showed him his badge, and asked Tucker to follow him.

He recalled Tanks advice, "Trust no one."

Wary, he followed the unknown FBI agent into a small conference room or training center on the basis that, surely, he was safe in Quantico. After Tucker had passed through the doorway, the agent pointed to a spider phone on a table in the center of an otherwise empty room. The agent said, "The call is for you." He left and closed the door behind him.

Apprehensively, Tucker answered the phone, "Hello."

"Oh, Tucker," said Maya, "I'm so glad you are safe, but I won't be able to meet you at Rupp Arena in Lexington."

Tucker said, "Maya! It's you! Are you OK? Where are you? You sound troubled. I was trying to figure out how to reach you and tell you the same. I've been 'apprehended' so to speak and sequestered here in Quantico. What happened to you that you can't make our rendezvous?"

"I'm in a hospital in Louisville, Kentucky. I was shot through the neck, but it was a clean shot and missed everything important. It hurts really bad, though. I'm under guard here by a new pair of US Marshals. I understand the guys in Chicago are pretty pissed at me, but they are still up there in case another assassin shows up. The doctors here said I might be out in a couple of days."

"Maya," said Tucker trying to maintain his composure, "I am so sorry. You could have died. When will this nightmare ever end? Do you know who tried to kill you? How did you survive?"

Maya said nonchalantly, "They tell me the woman who tried to kill me was Chinese. Tucker, she wanted to know how the discovery worked. I killed her, Tucker. I had no choice."

Tucker was speechless at first but finally said, "You are one amazing woman. The more I know about you, the more you impress me."

"Me? I understand you killed three mercenaries that were after you in West Virginia! How did you do that? Who do you work for? Who trained you?"

Tucker answered, "Hold on, Maya. I didn't kill anybody. We got a lot of catching up to do."

Maya said, "Tucker, I didn't get to tell you because you hung up the phone too fast the last time, but, I love you too."

Tucker said, "Those are the best words I have ever heard in my life."

Maya said, "I have to hang up; there's a nurse here with an ugly looking needle. How can I reach you the next time I need to speak with you?"

"I lost the disposable phone I was carrying somewhere along the way, but I'll get another one. Whatever method you used to track me down here in Quantico, do it again."

"I had a little help from the marshals, but, yes, my love, I'll call you when I can!" Tucker listened to the dial tone and stared at the phone like it was its fault that had Maya abruptly signed off and wasn't speaking to him anymore. Her nurse must have forced an end to their conversation.

He stood up, stretched his weary body, slowly walked to the door, and opened it—two new serious-looking men were waiting for him.

Quantico, Virginia

The two Secret Service agents escorted Tucker to a secure conference room three levels belowground. The agents used palm prints and retinal scan biometrics to pass through three consecutive doors. Finally, he was escorted into a large conference room where a half a dozen seventy-two-inch flat-screen TVs hung on the wall. Ten people whose faces he recognized but whose names and titles he couldn't remember stared back at him. None of them looked like they were happy to be there. Nor did they look like they had gotten much more sleep than Tucker—sleep deprivation apparently was contagious.

No one attempted to introduce themselves to Tucker. He guessed they thought he should already know who they were. So, he introduced himself. Half of them said, "We know." The other half said nothing. Against the wall were several thermoses of coffee and fine china mugs with FBI logos on them. Tucker filled one of the mugs with coffee and sat down.

The FBI Agent-in-Charge, Samuel Davis, and the Director of the FBI, Michael Vincent, walked in together. The Director nodded deferentially to the famous people at the table and said, "On behalf of the President of the United States, I'd like to thank you for coming to Quantico on such short notice and at such an ungodly hour. President King will be on the monitor in the center here in just a few moments. On another monitor, the Secretary of State will attend from his bedside. As you may know, he suffered a mild heart attack today, uh, excuse me, yesterday."

The center monitor activated, and President Jefferson King sat behind the desk in the Oval Office in uncharacteristically casual clothing. President King asked, "Michael, is everyone in attendance?"

"Yes, Mr. President, in attendance are the Secretary of Defense, as well as National Security Advisor Smith, Director Watts of the CIA, Director Becker of the NSA, Director Bowman of the NGA, and the Attorney General. Secretary of State Askeland just joined us by video feed from his bedside."

The president asked, "Walter, how are you feeling?"

"I'm fine Mr. President," he laughed. "I hope this call doesn't exacerbate my weak heart."

The president said, "We can't promise you that, Walter. Maybe you better sign off."

"No, I don't want to hear about it first on the news."

"OK, then, you have been warned," the President said lightheartedly. "Is Tucker Cherokee in the room there with you, Michael?"

"Yes, Mr. President," said, the FBI Director.

"Well, stand up, Mr. Cherokee. I want to get a good look at you."

Tucker stood and walked closer to the video camera.

"Well, aren't you a mess. I can see you've been through a lot. But you sure are a lot of trouble to keep alive, Mr. Cherokee. Or should I say you are a lot of trouble to keep dead."

"Excuse me, Mr. President?" said Tucker incredulously.

"Don't take this wrong, but when we announced your death along with the loss of the details of the discovery, the world calmed down a bit. We might want to keep you dead, the discovery hidden, and find a more beneficial time to introduce it to the world. I think we should put you under witness protection and allow you to remain dead as far as the world is concerned. In the meantime, we have assigned a Secret Service security detail to protect you.

"We called you here and convened this meeting to determine if that course of action is in the best interest of the United States. We understand that the murder of your co-discoverer, Dr. Phil McPherson, and the attempted murders of both you and Dr. Maya Li are all a result of the threat other nations feel from your discovery. At least a dozen countries were co-conspirators in the attempt to assassinate you. In my opinion, that means that more than a dozen nations have declared war on the United States. We'll take care of these international indiscretions in our own way in due time.

"I also understand from a joint conference call late yesterday with Director Watts and Director Bowman that there are even more nations, allegedly allies, potentially out there either trying to steal the details of the discovery or eliminate the discovery from existence.

"Mr. Cherokee, to your knowledge, who else knows the particulars of the MEG discovery, the formulas, as it were, and how to make electricity without fuel? And what does 'MEG' mean or designate?"

Tucker was extremely nervous and took his time to pick his words carefully. "Entropy is vigilant about keeping trade secrets, secret."

Tucker continued, "Dr. McPherson always followed protocol on all discoveries and saved the details of Project MEG onto two disks. The first disk was supposed to be placed into an Entropy safe at our headquarters in Boston. Phil always backed up the disk and put the backup in a safe deposit box in a major bank. Only he knew which box and which bank. So, to answer your question, I think only the CEO of Entropy has a soft copy of the details of the discovery. There are no hard copies that I am aware of. Though I know how to re-create the discovery in my head. No hard or soft copies of the details of the technology exist with Maya Li or with me. Though Dr. Li determined the magnetic field requirements for the discovery, she was not privy to the chemicals used or, as you say, the formula. To my knowledge, no one else knows how to make it work.

"As to why we named the technology MEG, Entropy gives every project a name. My late friend Phil McPherson assigned the project the name 'Magnetic Electric Generator.' Hence, is was given the acronym, 'MEG.'"

"Mr. Cherokee," asked the President, "are you aware that the Entropy CEO, Sanders, is in the hospital recovering from an attack from a Chinese assassin—the same assassin that killed McPherson?"

"No, I was not aware."

"Fortunately, your CEO is an intelligent guy and gave the assassin the formula," the President paused for effect, "the formula for a pharmaceutical discovery for treating Restless Leg Syndrome. Also, I might add, the woman who was shot and killed by your associate, Dr. Maya Li, was a black operative from China. Am I right about that, Director Watts?"

Watts said, "Yes."

"Eventually," President Jefferson King continued, "China will learn they still don't have the details of the discovery and they'll be back. Better to make them think it doesn't exist. Same fallout as it relates to the oil and natural gas-rich nations like Russia and Saudi Arabia.

"Your CEO swears that McPherson had not yet put the disk in the Entropy safe before his murder. That means you are the only person in the world that knows how to replicate the discovery. You see my point here? You need to stay dead."

"Sir," Tucker said, "would it be acceptable if I could have a word with you privately. I have a plan I'd like to share with you, and only you."

CHAPTER 38

WASHINGTON, DC—OCTOBER 9TH

The President of the United States was alone as he paced back and forth in the Oval Office and contemplated the ramifications of Tucker's suggested plan. He had to admit, it would take some brass ones. He sat down on the plush office chair, engaged the voice-activated function on the phone, hesitated, and thoughtfully disengaged. POTUS stood up, paced around the room again, dragged his fingers across his scalp, continued to assess the risks associated with the plan, and balanced them against the potential benefit to all.

Washington, DC

Before President King considered Tucker's plan, he wanted to make damn sure that the Entropy discovery, the formula, as POTUS referred to it, actually existed. POTUS reached out to Tucker when Tucker was in an FBI safe house in Manassas, Virginia, just before he was placed formally into witness protection. POTUS said,

"Mr. Cherokee, as you are the only person who knows how to re-create Project MEG, I need you to formally document all aspects, including trade secrets, in the event we need the 'formula' for national security reasons."

"Mr. President, I have some good news for you. I believe I now know where one of the disks that Dr. Phil McPherson created is. No soft or hard copy of the invention, its formula, or the information to make the technology work was ever found—until now. We may no longer have to depend on what is in my head to make the discovery work."

With raised eyebrows, the president said, "Continue."

"The FBI sent people to my apartment in Alexandria to clean out all my possessions and bring them to me here in the safe house. I was going through my back mail, including bills, and found a letter from Phil. In the letter was a key that looks like one you would expect a safe deposit box key to look like. The number 112 is on it. In the envelope was a note that said, 'Trust the Sun at the Cape.' I conclude that the disk we are searching for is somewhere around Cape Canaveral in a SunTrust Bank safe deposit box. As I am sequestered here in the safe house and protected by Secret Service, I am unable to personally check it out."

TWO DAYS LATER—A half-dozen FBI agents in an armored tactical vehicle guarded the bank as three US Marshals and two Secret Service agents escorted Tucker Cherokee into the SunTrust Bank in Titusville, Florida. This was the third bank near Cape Canaveral that they had investigated. The lead US Marshals handed the bank manager a subpoena, which required the bank to allow the government to check the key in the possession of Tucker Cherokee on the bank's safe deposit box number 112. The nervous and intimidated bank manager escorted Tucker and two of the marshals into the bank vault and tested the key.

BINGO!

In the safe deposit box was a disk and a letter to Tucker. The letter to Tucker explained that Phil McPherson was concerned that the unintended consequences of their discovery were scary and that they must stay vigilant. He was concerned about the safety of all people involved with the discovery. Tucker wondered why Phil hadn't taken his own advice and stay vigilant. Maybe he'd still be alive today. Failure turned out to be a product of Phil's own success.

The note advised Tucker to keep an extra copy of the trade secrets in a place no one will look.

Tucker turned the disk over to the lead US Marshals, who promptly, under heavy guard, delivered the disk—now valued at more than three trillion dollars—to the President of the United States.

CHAPTER 39

CHINATOWN, NEW YORK CITY— OCTOBER 11ᵀᴴ

On the second floor of a restaurant owned by a Bahama holding company closely held by a People's Republic of China shell corporation, Gang Chung placed the suitcase on a Formica-top kitchen table.

For the fourth time today, he pulled out his throw-away cell phone and tried to reach his handler. She was supposed to have arrived at this rendezvous point long before he had. He needed her because she was much better with all this electronic stuff than he was.

He got impatient. Chung clicked the suitcase locks open to inspect all the goodies stolen from Entropy's CEO. He pulled out Sanders' cell phone first to see whether his email features were activated.

They were, but he had pass-coded access to them. "Damn, I wish my handler was here."

Gang Chung was pleased with himself when he discovered that he could hear Sanders' phone messages.

The first three messages were mundane and useless. The fourth message panicked him. "Mr. Sanders, this is John from GeoPos, Inc. We're a little concerned that you haven't responded to our notifications and warnings. Tracker number 16-B is in New York City, yet tracker number 01-A remains in Exeter, New Hampshire. Please, call......"

Chung flipped his knife out and slit the lining of the briefcase and found nothing. He cut the leather cover in the top lid of the briefcase and discovered nothing. He pulled out the laptop from the leather briefcase and inspected it carefully, opened the battery case, and found a GPS transmitter.

"Fucking Sanders."

Gang Chung quickly transferred the contents of Sanders's briefcase into his travel bag. He threw the transmitter into the toilet and ran out the door to distance himself from his current location and into the hallway where he was greeted by four Critical Incident Response Team officers fully outfitted in full FBI tactical gear and with automatic weapons pointed at Gang Chung's head.

His instinct was to fight. He didn't immediately surrender. Chung looked around for an escape route and then aggressively flinched as if he would run. The movement invited a few jacketed 9mm rounds.

Chinatown, New York City, NY

He woke up abruptly to bright hot light, shook his head violently back and forth to get away from the nasty smell of ammonia placed under his nose, and tried to reach down to feel whatever it was that caused his pain. But he couldn't move his hand—it was handcuffed to the bed frame. He squinted to see where he was but couldn't see anything except for the equivalent of a scorching sun.

Gang Chung struggled to separate his parched and swollen lip and asked in Mandarin Chinese, "Where am I? Is anyone out there? I need water."

He was answered in his dialect, "Yes. There is someone out here, and no you cannot have any water."

Chung's memory of his predicament in the hallway of the PRC safe house started to return. "What is it you want?"

"You know what I want."

Gang Chung stated in English, "I have diplomatic immunity."

The man laughed a Bella Lugosi laugh for a good fifteen seconds before he said, "No, Mr. Gang, you don't. At least, not here as a guest in Guantanamo. You are, at this moment, under arrest under *Title 18, US Code, Chapter 113B, Terrorism*. You should thank us. We did not kill you in China Town. Only because we were under orders to take you alive. Do you know why, Mr. Gang? Because the President of the United States, Jefferson King, wants to find out who hired you to steal the technology for making electricity without fuel.

"Guess what? It's our job to provide the answer."

The unseen interviewer let that sink in.

"I need some water if you want me to talk."

The agent said, "Oh, you'll talk. Sooner or later."

It was only then that Gang Chung noticed that he had an IV in his arm. "What's in the IV?"

"Currently, it's filled with antibiotics and Fentanyl. You took six jacketed 9mm rounds in your legs. We're trying to save them, but nothing is guaranteed. When we think you are stable, we'll add some sodium pentothal. So, you see, you'll tell us what we want. If the truth drug doesn't work, we'll use other means."

"Please, cut the lights. I can't see."

The agent said, "Good idea. I have something to show you, anyway."

The agent dialed back the power and placed something in Gang Chung's handcuffed right hand. Chung looked at the printout of a digital photo of his obviously dead handler.

The agent said, "You're all alone, Mr. Gang, so how is this going to go? The easy way, or the more painful way? Do you want us to save your legs or do you want to suffer and still eventually tell us what we want to know?'

Chung said, "Give me some water, and I'll tell you what you want to know."

The interrogation went almost too smoothly.

The CIA operative walked out of the interrogation room in East Orange, New Jersey, not Guantanamo as alleged and called McClean, Virginia, to report the results of the interview.

CHAPTER 40

WASHINGTON, DC—OCTOBER 11TH

The long black Lincoln limousine was bulletproof and hardened, much like a military mine-resistant ambush-protected Humvee used in Afghanistan. But this limousine was traveling around DuPont Circle on its way to the White House. The ambassador from the People's Republic of China didn't appreciate the tone of the request by Secretary of State Askeland to attend a meeting with the president. It wasn't presented to the ambassador as if it were an invitation—it came across more like an order.

Even when he had arrived at the White House gate and was escorted to a small waiting room by two Secret Service agents, he was forced to endure the indignity of waiting another fifteen minutes. While still in the waiting room with only his security guard, the lights dimmed, a wide-screen panel dropped from the ceiling, and the ambassador was subjected to a video of the confessions of Gang Chung.

At the end of the short video, an unsmiling President King entered the room with a solemn Secretary of State and three Secret Service agents.

POTUS said, "Mr. Ambassador, please relay to your General Secretary and President that I interpreted their unlawful actions against US civilians as an act of war on the United States of America, and I take the People's Republic of China's declaration of war very seriously."

The Chinese ambassador vehemently responded, "Mr. President, this is an atrocity. The American CIA must have tortured and drugged this alleged man to falsely accuse our government of criminal activity. We deny any culpability for engaging in industrial espionage and the People's Republic of China would never consider violence against US citizens."

The ambassador stormed out of the room while accusing the United States of mistreatment and torture of citizens from the People's Republic of China.

It escalated from there.

POTUS instructed the Chairman of the Joint Chiefs of Staff to prepare the Pacific Fleet for war and move to DEFCON THREE. He held a press conference and announced his intent to convene an open joint session of Congress to ask for their approval to declare war against the PRC. He announced that he intended to address the General Assembly of the United Nations and present to them the United States' case for retaliation against China.

POTUS was bluffing, playing high-stakes poker. He knew full-well that Congress would debate the issue for weeks before they denied the president his request. He was betting that China, however, didn't know for sure whether Congress would approve the war.

President King thought the bluff might work because China depended on US trade for a significant fraction of its economic survival. The United States, in turn, depended on the PRC to buy US Treasury notes to sustain its increasing national debt. The United States was in debt to China for more than three trillion dollars.

Antiwar protests became violent in both the United States and in Europe. Chinese civilians flooded the Internet with fake news and false accusations against President King. Fear of nuclear war and the environmental consequence of a nuclear winter populated the twenty-four-hour news media.

The Pacific Fleet conducted war games in the China Sea. The PRC retaliated by demanding that the United States pay down its debt, knowing that there was no way the United States could do it.

President King issued executive orders to stop trade immediately and indefinitely with China and Hong Kong.

War was imminent, and the Pentagon ordered a DEFCON TWO state of readiness. Protests in front of the White House and Capitol Hill forced the National Guard to maintain order. The President and key members of the cabinet took up residence in Camp David.

The PRC's naval fleet took positions near US antimissile defense systems. American B-52s were circling over the South China Sea 24/7. Satellite images relayed to the Pentagon showed that the PRC was ready to retaliate if the United States made the first strike.

The President of Taiwan begged President King to back down.

Congress debated the merits of war around the clock on C-SPAN. There was very little support for war.

It was time.

Beijing, People's Republic of China

Speaking before a late-evening meeting of the Politburo, the Minister of National Defense presented the likely scenario when war with America started. The minister painted a colorful picture—it made little difference who struck first.

The President of the People's Republic of China asked, "Can we win a military war with the US?"

"No one can win. There will only be losers. Both sides will lose millions of people, spend trillions in currency, and contaminate large areas of land which will be rendered unusable for decades. Beijing, Shanghai, and Hong Kong will receive the same fate as Honolulu, Los Angeles, San Francisco, San Diego, and Seattle. In the end, both we and the US will be weakened. The Russian, Japanese, and North Korean vultures will be able to pick our collective carcasses.

"The People's Liberation Army is strong; we have the largest army in the world. We will fight with honor, but we do not have technical parity with America. The US has a limited number of Aegis Ballistic Missile Defense Systems, and we'll eventually manage to break through, however…" The Minister of National Defense reacted with anger after he was interrupted by the Minister of Industry and Information Technology, who stood up, bowed in apology to the minister, and asked whether he could approach the General Secretary of the Communist Party and President of the PRC.

The IT Minister's severe break in protocol, whispered in the ear of the President of the PRC, informed the President that the minister had just received electronic correspondence from the President of the United States, Jefferson King, which included a video attachment.

The President of the PRC instructed, "Put it up on the screen. Let the entire Politburo see what the Americans have to say."

On the prerecorded video, POTUS sat in his Oval Office chair, looked fresh and dignified, and spoke.

"Mr. General Secretary and President, Mr. Premier, ministers, and Congressmen, the US is prepared for war with the People's Republic of China. If we do not avoid war, tens of millions of your people will die. And hundreds of million will suffer."

POTUS waited five seconds before he continued.

"The US has both air and naval superiority over the People's Liberation Army."

Another five seconds.

"You have a responsibility to avoid the ugliest war in world history. As do I."

Five seconds.

"I took an oath of office to protect citizens of the United States from foreign aggression. I do not want even one nuclear weapon to land on US soil. But if one does, thousands of nuclear warheads will turn most of China to an uninhabitable wasteland. Collectively, we have a responsibility to prevent this tragedy. The conflict between us started because you chose to steal US industrial secrets. You were willing to kill US citizens for knowledge about a US discovery."

A long pause.

"To avoid war, the US will give you that technology."

All members of the Politburo were smiling, internally celebrating, until the video continued.

"Under our nonnegotiable conditions:

"One: China can use the technology, the discovery, for internal purposes only, and it shall not be repackaged and exported."

The Politburo audience still smiled.

"Two: The US shall not be required to repay our three trillion-dollar debt. Our calculation is that the war and its recovery would cost you more than ten trillion dollars.

"Not to mention that you get to live."

No one in Beijing was smiling.

"And Three: You agree to help us with our disposition matrix."

Washington, DC

The deal negotiated by POTUS allowed the People's Republic of China to install MEG units to meet their ever-growing demand for power generation. China's aggressive implementation of the technology permitted a sizable increase in electrical generation without further degradation in air quality.

The White House Chief of Staff arranged the conference call between POTUS and six others. President King knew that the US Government had no legal rights to have offered to China the discovery details owned by Entropy. He also knew that the US couldn't deliver the technology to China without Entropy trade secrets, not all of which were on the Titusville disk.

On the conference call were the White House Chief Counsel; the Speaker of the House; the Senate Majority Leader; the Secretary of Treasury; Entropy's CEO, Stephen Sanders; and Tucker Cherokee.

Jefferson King spoke first, "Tucker, my young friend, your plan worked. However, I must say, it reached a point where I was scared to death that we'd actually go to war. Or that I'd be assassinated by an antiwar protestor.

"I hope life under witness protection is not too difficult."

Tucker said, "No sir, if it is not a permanent situation the target on my back should go away."

POTUS continued, "And Stephen, are you recovering well from your injuries?"

"Rehab is underway, but I'll never fully recover and will always walk with a limp."

"I have to say," said POTUS, "that was ingenious of you to give Gang Chung false information on a laptop with a GPS tracker inserted in the battery case. I don't know how you did that under the torturous circumstances."

"Thank you, sir."

"OK, all," President King stated. "Here's my suggested offer to Entropy for the right to license the MEG technology to the People's Republic of China. I propose that the US Government pays Entropy a license fee of one-tenth of one percent of the three trillion dollar forgiven debt to be paid annually over five years. I also propose that the same fee is offered separately to Tucker Cherokee for his role in the discovery and for his proposed solution for avoiding war with China."

CHAPTER 41

MONTE-CARLO, MONACO—
NOVEMBER 30TH

Though he'd lost a sizable amount of money at the roulette wheel this evening, he was still euphoric. The penthouse suite in Hotel Metropole Monte-Carlo was adorned with gold hardware, brand new Persian rugs, and lovely young women. He provided the girls with all the cocaine they needed or wanted. When they were high on cocaine, they were willing to do whatever he asked of them. The suite had an extra-large canopied bed with a soft down feather mattress on which the four of them could fit comfortably.

He thought, "Life is good."

He liked different cultures—each had a different perspective on sexual pleasures. The perky fifteen-year-old French girl was totally uninhibited. There were no boundaries, no limitations to her willingness to experiment—as long as he kept the cocaine stockpile open.

The nineteen-year-old Nigerian girl was shy and inexperienced, but her almost desperate need to please him made up for it. This was her first exposure to life outside Lagos and her first exposure to cocaine. She was very tight and used muscles he thought most females didn't know they had.

The sixteen-year-old Chinese girl prided herself as an expert at fellatio; she did most of the preparatory work for the games that followed.

When the games ended, the sixty-nine-year-old Saudi Foreign Minister fell asleep. The French and Nigerian girls went into an adjacent room to snort some additional cocaine. The Chinese girl said she'd be right in after she used the restroom.

In the bathroom, she pulled out the "KA-BAR 4-⅜" Skinner knife that she'd hidden in the toilet bowl. She returned to the bedroom to find the Saudi Prince, and head of the intelligence arm of the First Consortium of Nations, still asleep, his disgusting body fully exposed. She considered castrating him for her own pleasure, but those weren't her instructions. She only slit his throat from ear to ear as she whispered "Ebn el matnakash."

One less person was on the disposition matrix.

CHAPTER 42

ARLINGTON, VIRGINIA—
NOVEMBER 30ᵀᴴ

Lt. Col. Ray LaSalle had no idea that the sun shined brightly outside on a calm and cloudless sixty-eight-degree day. He put in another long hard day in a windowless room at the Pentagon. On this day, he and his team had developed a conceptual contingency strategy in the event that the cartels were successful at assassinating the newly elected pro-American, anti-drug-cartel President of Colombia. LaSalle's team had assessed four different scenarios and developed an interdiction response strategy for each.

He'd finished writing the report's executive summary, saved the file, and started to shut down his computer when he was distracted. He saw movement out of the corner of his eye; visitors stood in his office doorway. Never in his career had the Chairman of the Joint Chiefs of Staff, much less the Secretary of Defense, stood in his doorway.

He thought, "This can't be good." Lt. Col. LaSalle jerked up, stood at attention, and saluted the four-star Chairman.

"At ease, Colonel," said the Chairman. "The Secretary and I wanted to see where you do all your good work."

LaSalle answered, "It's a team effort, sir."

"Understood. We also want to talk with you about General Woodhead. You reported to Chris, correct?"

"Yes, sir."

"Did you know him outside of work, on a personal basis?"

"No, sir, we never fraternized outside of the office."

Ray LaSalle looked into the expressive eyes of the Chairman of the Joint Chiefs and then into the unreadable eyes of the Secretary of Defense. Ray added, "You said, 'did I know him' instead of 'do I know him,' sir."

"Yes, that is correct. Woodhead was found dead floating in the Chesapeake Bay over the weekend. I understand it was not a beautiful sight. Do you know anyone who might have wanted to murder General Woodhead? Do you know if he was engaged in any activity that might be considered inappropriate?"

"No, sir, I did not know General Woodhead that well. I just provided the scenario assessments which he asked me to draft."

SecDef asked Lt. Col. LaSalle, "What role did you play in providing him with the scenario assessment and potential mitigation strategies when the issue of the Entropy discovery, MEG, came up."

"I gave him a full analysis on the military consequences of the discovery and offered suggestions for a plan of action."

"Please hand me a complete copy of that study, the one you provided to Woodhead," said the chairman.

The Secretary of Defense and the chairman waited.

"You mean now, sir?" They nodded their heads.

LaSalle was already on his computer. It took him a couple of minutes, but he pulled up a file, printed out two copies and handed each a copy of the study. "Top Secret" was watermarked across each page.

The two highest-ranking people in the Pentagon remained standing while they simultaneously scanned the documents. They flipped pages and occasionally looked at each other, nodded, and returned to their reading. When they both finished their reading, the chairman addressed Ray and said, "Thank you, colonel. This information is enlightening and should bring us closure."

LaSalle saluted again. On his way out the door, the Chairman of the Joint Chiefs of Staff said to LaSalle, "Colonel, you have a new assignment. You will ascend to Woodhead's position and be promoted to Full Colonel."

LaSalle beamed.

As the Secretary of Defense and the Chairman of the Joint Chiefs of Staff walked down the corridor, SecDef said, "Well, I think that clinches it; we found our mole: General Woodhead."

"Yes," the Chairman said. "Though we'll wait until NCIS submits a final report, I think the fact that Woodhead redacted the most important parts of LaSalle's assessment implies culpability. He failed to mention Russia's possible actions as discussed in LaSalle's original assessment. That pretty much confirms our suspicions."

"He had means and motive," said SecDef. "His forty-foot sailboat was no doubt motive. Thus far, the Russians eliminated anything that leads directly back to them. We'll have to pull that thread a bit more to confirm that they're the source of Woodhead's funds. Maybe we should give LaSalle another assignment. What would he recommend to us that our response be if we confirm our suspicion that Russia had a spy in the Pentagon?"

CHAPTER 43

MOSCOW TO SOCHI, RUSSIA— DECEMBER 5TH

Patches of brown appeared on the predominantly snow-covered landscape as the four thousand horsepower diesel locomotive manufactured at the Kolomensky Zavod plant pulled a six-car train south. The first and sixth rail cars contained armed security to protect the elite passengers. The second rail car contained a fully functional high-end kitchen, while the third car contained access to the formal dining room, complete with a fully stocked bar. The fifth car was a sleeping car. This train ran on time, an otherwise unusual event in Russia.

The members of the Intellectual Property Monitoring Ministry occupied the fourth uniquely designed mahogany-paneled private rail car used to conduct business on the train ride down to Sochi.

It was always good to get out of Moscow—especially during the Russian winters—to meet on the Black Sea in a resort Dacha in Sochi. The air was always fresher, the sun shined more often, and the pleasant mood of the people contrasted the generally depressing atmosphere in the Kremlin.

The "hard man" always knew that he was emotionally void. He knew that he should feel melancholy about the death of his cousin, Alex, but, instead, his feeling of elation over the successful assassination of Tucker Cherokee overwhelmed all other emotions. So, Petrov was forced to act sad as he lectured his subordinates, "Mother Russia will sell her natural gas and oil to Western European nations and neighboring former Soviet Bloc countries at a high premium this winter when they are desperate and have no other viable options. We will use the windfall to rebuild the military, which will take a shitload of money," announced Petrov.

Through Gazprom, Russia was one of the largest exporters of oil and natural gas in the world, and Petrov intended to keep it that way. "Russia will use its natural resources aggressively." He was proud that he was the Russian president during a period when Russia's Gross Domestic Product doubled.

"The day will come when jokes about empty shelves in Russian grocery stores will end. As the Russian economy grows, so will its military and geopolitical influence. The Russian economy is highly dependent on its energy exports. Therefore, Russia's power and influence are reliant on the export of natural gas and oil."

Petrov thought, "Thanks to Alex and the nonexistent Christian God, the new American technology is no longer a threat to Mother Russia."

The eight high-ranking members of the Russian hierarchy were imbibing some refreshments on their trip south. It was an unusually pleasant event up until the point when Vladimir Petrov said, "Let's conduct a little business on the ride down. Serge, what can you tell me is the status of the new technology under development by the South Koreans that represents a breakthrough in the lithium ion electric car battery business? I understand we are close to securing the trade secrets that allow a midsized vehicle to get 600 kilometers on a charge."

"I'm pleased to announce that we have successfully stolen their trade secrets," said Serge Novak, "and we should be able to manufacture an equivalent battery in Russia to compete with the South Koreans. I believe we can manufacture the battery in Vladivostok for sixty-five percent of the cost they can manufacture the battery in Seoul." Everyone lifted their glasses to celebrate their success.

A serious-looking man resembling Joseph Stalin entered the executive car, nodded in Petrov's direction, and gestured with the ubiquitous "you have a telephone call" sign with his right hand. Petrov's personal security officer wouldn't have entered unless it was crucial.

The President of Russia stepped from the fourth rail car into the dining room rail car.

The call was from the General Secretary and President of the People's Republic of China. He stated, "Vladimir, you need to end your theft of intellectual property starting right now. I strongly advise you to disband the Intellectual Property Monitoring Ministry and abide by international laws on patent protection."

The President of Russia asked, "Are you threatening me, Mr. President?" He laughed and asked, "Is this what they call the 'pot calling the kettle black'? What if I say 'No'? What are you going to do about it?"

"Actually, yes, I am threatening you. You are not immune to tragedy, tragedy similar to what your cousin created on US soil. You have less than two minutes to get off that train."

The "hard man" continued to walk through the dining car into the kitchen, the second rail car and said, "Why warn me if you were serious? You wouldn't do that."

"Ninety seconds."

Petrov passed through the kitchen with his chief security detail in tow and into the armed first car behind the locomotive.

He turned to his security detail and stated, "Separate, now."

The coupling between the first rail car and the second rail car opened. But the separation between the locomotive-pulled car and the uncoupled rail cars was virtually nonexistent.

The bright light preceded the heat and flames by only a fraction of a second. The force of the explosion ripped the roof and both sides of the fourth rail car—the executive rail car—as if the car was made of cardboard. None of the Intellectual Property Monitoring Ministry member passengers ever knew what hit them. They were all literally blown apart a quarter of a second after the initiation of the explosion. Debris and body parts spread over a square kilometer.

Enemies were removed from the disposition matrix.

Chechnya activists took credit for the act of terrorism. The mission was well organized and extremely well executed. No one was ever held accountable for one of the most successful terrorist acts committed on Russian soil in history. The passengers in the first rail car were injured, some seriously, but all survived.

The "hard man" would learn that Russia would soon lose trillions of dollars in revenue when the launch of the discovery would drive the price of oil and natural gas into the cellar. The Russian bear's dream of reconstructing the Soviet Union and regaining superpower status would be in hibernation indefinitely.

The "hard man" was already planning his revenge.

CHAPTER 44

DAVIS, WEST VIRGINIA—FIFTEEN MONTHS LATER

The demand for personal protection services and electronic physical security systems increased exponentially for *White Knight Personal Security, LLC,* services. The increase in demand far exceeded Tank's wildest expectations. After the conclusion of the Entropy contract to protect Tucker Cherokee, news organizations discovered Tank's role. He had a couple of radio and television interviews, which caused his phone to ring off the hook in his small Warrenton, Virginia, office.

White Knight's business with the federal government also increased as they were awarded contracts by the Department of Justice, the State Department, the Executive Branch, and the Department of Homeland Security.

The consulting side of the business also grew— people wanted *White Knight's* advice to select arms, entry-control systems, perimeter-intrusion detection systems, and surveillance systems.

The demand for *White Knight* services outgrew its organizational ability to hire qualified employees. Tank needed to expand from a mere fifteen qualified personal security experts to 250 qualified personal security experts needed around the world without affecting quality and the company's reputation. The growth required a lot of time and energy.

Tank needed to staff up. He, Jolene, and Powers were forced to continuously interview potential candidates to support the demand. *White Knight's* growing customer base grew to include corporate executives, entertainers, well-known sports figures, and wealthy civilians who needed personal protection or private investigators.

White Knight Personal Security, LLC, was required to move its headquarters to an offshore location near their biggest and most important customer. They needed to maintain a United States presence, an office where *White Knight* could provide a help desk and travel logistics for North American customers.

They needed a desk jockey, someone they could trust to maintain secrecy and protect all client information. Tank decided to hire a disabled person. The person they hired would undergo weeks of training by Tank, Jolene, and Powers. The person they selected was wheelchair-bound most of the time but could stand and walk ten or fifteen feet on his own with a walker. He had been through a lot. Shrapnel had torn through his legs. He had third-degree burns on the entire right side of his body. He'd gone through five skin grafts and three leg and back operations over a seven-month period.

But months after his tragic accident, Jimmy Jordon (JJ) was ready to run the newly established Davis, West Virginia, office of *White Knight Personal Security, LLC.*

CHAPTER 45

LEAVENWORTH PENITENTIARY, KANSAS—TWO YEARS LATER

To get him to talk, the CIA interrogator had exaggerated the damage that they had inflicted to Gang Chung's legs when they shot him in Chinatown. During his trial, Chung regained most of his leg strength and continued his self-taught physical therapy all through lockup.

Gang Chung was found guilty of murder on three counts, including the capital murder in the first degree of Dr. Phil McPherson. He was incarcerated in Leavenworth Penitentiary and placed on death row in solitary confinement.

Over the months that he awaited his final punishment, he grew to anticipate his one hour a week outside in the courtyard. The fresh air was delicious and invigorating, even in bad weather. Four well-armed guards would shackle his hands and feet and place a restraint mask over his face before escorting him to the courtyard.

A Deadly Discovery

In general, there are three categories of inmates in Leavenworth: whites, blacks, and Hispanics. The Asian prison population was small. A Chinese inmate had to take care of himself—he had no protectors. Because Gang Chung was a death row inmate, his exposure to the general prison population was inherently limited. The courtyard hour, however, was the only time Chung was at risk of attack from others, men who were as bad as he was.

He was escorted in shackles into the well-guarded outdoor courtyard. Gang Chung was thirty-one years old and in good physical condition. He was five feet eleven inches tall and weighed 210 pounds—not a small guy. To be selected for black operations by his government, he had to go through significant hand-to-hand combat and martial arts training.

It was inevitable that he would eventually be tested by the prison big dogs. His first encounter in the courtyard was with a wiry 130-pound Hispanic inmate. It was a requirement of the El Salvadorian contingent that to rise in the prison gang organization, an inmate had to prove his toughness. The small El Salvadorian had a shiv made from a piece of PVC pipe that he'd filed into a sharp weapon. The rumor within the Hispanic community was that this big Chinese guy was not an American Chinese man, but a Communist Chinese man who murdered only weak unarmed people. A false rumor was started that he was an easy target because he was a lone wolf.

Gang Chung, if nothing else, was always alert and aware of his surroundings. He saw the little El Salvadorian coming. With the side of his hand, he chopped the throat of the little guy, collapsing his windpipe. A fraction of a second later, Gang Chung, even with leg irons, stomped on the El Salvadorian's right leg just above the knee, causing the leg to fold in the wrong direction. In one continuous motion, he smoothly removed the shiv from the little guy's hand before he hit the ground.

Sirens blasted and guards in the courtyard quickly limited the fight so that it didn't expand to include others.

Gang Chung won that battle, but, unfortunately, now had all the Hispanic gang bangers' attention. There was no way he could win the war.

The guards were slower, much slower, the next time he shuffled around in the courtyard. After another confrontation with Gang Chung, two Mexican tough guys and one Panamanian were taken to the prison medical emergency ward.

Two body bags were required to move Gang Chung.

One for his body.

A second for his head.

CHAPTER 46

PITTSBURGH, PENNSYLVANIA—
THREE YEARS LATER

"You can make a difference," stated the deep voice of the actor Sam Elliott. The screen showed a polar bear with mud smeared on its fur stranded on a small block of ice. The roar of the bear sounded pathetic, as if it were crying. In the next scene, glaciers cleaved.

"Together, we can reverse the climate change caused by the burning of fossil fuels." Black soot rose from tall power plant smokestacks. In the next scene, coal miners were carried from a mine in body bags with family members sobbing in the background.

Sam Elliott continued, "You can help save the planet and save thousands of dollars while doing so." In the latest scene, a beautiful family vacationed on a tropical beach. Children laughed against the backdrop of waves crashing. In the next scene, the camera zoomed in on the distinguished and handsome face of Charles

Washington, the Chairman of the Board and Chief Executive Officer of Charleston Energy Holdings, LLC.

Charles looked directly into the camera and said, "Replace your greenhouse-gas-polluting heating and cooling system with the EPA-recommended 'Green Renewable Energy Generator' or GREG. You have nothing to lose, and we all have so much to gain. Thank you." The final scene showed happy-looking penguins playing in Antarctica.

Charles flipped the video off and turned the conference room lights on. He asked, "So, what do you think of our advertising campaign?"

"GREG?" answered Stephen Sanders. "Where in the hell did that come from?"

"Our New York advertising agency recommended that we call the devices something more memorable than MEG. I had to agree with them."

Sanders stood, wielded his cane, and limped around to the end of the table where Charles sat and said, "The technology stands on its own merits. We don't need to pull on people's guilt-strings and fear of global warming to make it attractive to buyers. So why the 'save the planet' approach?

"Besides, the whole concept of man-made climate change is a little overblown. The earth is at greater risk of a nuclear winter if crazies get and use nuclear weapons. Millions of square miles of land would be contaminated and unusable. That seems to be a much greater environmental disaster than a one or two degree increase in global temperatures over a century. Charles, you just don't need to play the global warming card."

"The real winners of the discovery are the children of the next generation. They've had a portion of the national debt reduced equal to roughly ten thousand dollars per every man, woman, and child in America. The entire world's next generation will have access to plentiful and cheap energy, be rewarded with improved air quality, and be shown hope that science will continue to evolve and improve the quality of life for all."

"Stephen," asked Charles, "have you heard from Tucker and Maya since they have been in the witness protection program? Do you know where they are? Is it possible for me to consult with them? I'd really like to pick their brains."

"I have spoken to Tucker a few times. I have no idea where he is hiding. Each time I call, my encrypted satellite phone gives me disinformation. Once it showed that he was in Montana; another time it revealed that he was in Quebec. I can tell you that he and Maya are working on an improvement in the design that will have a profound impact on your business.

"Charles, you won't need to advertise. But I do agree we need to rename MEG units. Refer to them as McPherson-Scruggs Generators."

CHAPTER 47

WANAKA, NEW ZEALAND—FIVE YEARS LATER

POTUS had persuaded the Prime Minister of New Zealand to allow the US Justice Department to relocate Tucker and Maya to Wanaka under the US Marshals Witness Protection Program.

Maya Li Cherokee sat in their great room and looked out their thirty-foot floor-to-ceiling picture window at a spectacular view of Lake Wanaka and snow-capped Mount Aspiring. She'd designed their 17,500 square-foot glass home on a fifty-acre lot outside the ski-resort town of Wanaka, located in the center of New Zealand's South Island.

The deal President Jefferson King had struck with the People's Republic of China had rewarded Entropy, Tucker, and Maya handsomely to the point where the Cherokees found themselves at such financial height that they could be on the Forbes' list of the *Top 100 Wealthiest People in the World*. In POTUS' opinion, every man, woman, and child in the United Sates would be grateful to Tucker and Maya for reducing the next generation's debt and for making electricity inexpensive. That is, if the American people knew that Tucker and Maya existed. The US Treasury agreed that a fraction of one percent of the national debt owed to China that was awarded to Tucker and Maya for their role to make the deal possible was a small price to pay for the United States to keep the other ninety-nine-plus percent.

Tucker had financed the estate construction and subcontracted the compound's physical security design and supply to *White Knight Personal Security, LLC.* Tank and Powers had installed an intrusion-detection system around the perimeter of their fenced property. A guard shack was also staffed with *White Knights* twenty-four seven at the compound's single-point entrance-way. Tank had designed the security system to include strategically located closed-circuit TV cameras with zoom, pan, and tilt features to remotely monitor and record activity by *White Knights* from a hardened control room. As part of the overall security contract, Tank had insisted that Powers conduct a training program to teach Tucker and Maya hand-to-hand combat and how to handle all weapons in the Cherokee compound's armory.

Tank and Jolene lived closer to town but were currently in the basement control room verifying that all the electronic security systems were working properly. They ran *White Knight's* growing business from Wanaka and were currently planning a trip to Tokyo to negotiate a contract to help guard the Prime Minister of Japan and his entourage during the next World Trade Organization meeting in Washington, DC.

Though no one had attempted to hurt either Tucker or Maya in five years, they still needed the sense of comfort provided at the estate and chose to stay in

285

Wanaka even after witness protection was deemed to be no longer necessary.

Maya was multitasking as she monitored world news on cable TV: she brushed Ram, who still provided their final line of defense, and contemplated her next charitable contribution. Maya checked Ram's collar for the umpteenth time to make sure that a miniature thumb drive, which contained the extra copy of the discovery secrets was still in place. As Chairman of the McPherson-Scruggs Endowment, she enjoyed prioritizing the use of funds for philanthropic causes. Though the locals didn't know Maya's real name, she was revered in the town of Wanaka.

The cold weather in Wanaka was not an issue. Though glass houses are not energy efficient, Tucker and Maya maintained their home in tropical warmth. The heated indoor pool, sauna, indoor tennis and racquetball courts, hot tubs, and gym required a lot of electricity to keep the temperature comfortable and enjoyable. The greenhouse gas-free McPherson-Scruggs generator ran efficiently and continuously with little required maintenance in the basement room they called 'The Scruggs Electrical Room.'

Tucker sat in his office's extra-wide La-Z-Boy while on a conference phone call with Stephen Sanders and Charles Washington discussing the merits of various manufacturing techniques for the McPherson-Scruggs generators.

"Charles," stated Tucker, "I'm proud to announce that my brilliant wife and I have finalized the next generation design for use with automobiles. Electric cars will not require recharging stations, there will be no limit to their range, and the additional weight and cost should be minimal."

Tucker spent most of his time managing Wanaka Entrepreneurial University, where he conducted Internet-based classes to teach students how to market their inventions. People of every stripe, all over the world, would present their patentable idea to Tucker electronically. He would assess marketability and recommend paths forward. The truly exceptional ideas would be considered for Wanaka Entrepreneurial University venture capital.

That was their life until baby Cherokee was born. Her perpetual smile; wide aqua-colored eyes with long, thick eyelashes; and long, curly auburn hair changed their lives forever. By age three, she could list the elements on the periodic table. She was a child prodigy who exhibited unusual, almost mystic, skills. There was no doubt that three-year-old Star Li Cherokee would have a role to play in future scientific discoveries. There is nothing more intimidating than a capricious child of brilliant parents.

We don't know what we don't know.

The End

Ed Day's

COLD TO THE

BONE

(Available in the Summer of 2017)

DESCRIPTION OF THE NOVEL

We, the people of planet Earth, were unprepared. We had no defense against the confluence of events that transpired. We were vulnerable to natural phenomena and a psychopath who took advantage of our vulnerabilities. A year of conspiracy and evil damned near killed us all. Literally millions of people would freeze to death unless Tucker and Maya find a solution to the mystery in time.

Made in the USA
Middletown, DE
06 March 2023

26305258R00169